JOURNAL OF THE LATE AMELIA EARHART

FRANK OKOLO

Disclaimer:

This is a work of fiction. Any resemblance to actual persons, living or dead, is purely coincidental, except for historical figures used fictitiously.

ISBN 979-8-9999840-4-3

www.bitterleafpress.com

Cover design by Milan Jovanovic (Chameleonstudio74)

To my brother Emmanuel Adinweruka "Chuks" Okolo. A fervent scribe in his own right. Forever remembered, forever loved.

PART I

1

L ae, Papua New Guinea, July 2, 1937, 10:30 a.m.

AMELIA

AHEAD OF US LIES THREE THOUSAND FEET of usable runway. Then a twenty-five-foot drop to the waters of the Pacific below. Beyond that 2,556 miles of ocean to our next destination, Howland.

I stand on the brakes and firewall the throttles. The mighty Wasps roar and thunder, the Electra bucks and shudders. I hold on, make sure I have full manifold pressure and output, then let her roll. The Electra trundles forward, not in her usual sprightly manner but more like an arthritic old maid. The weight is much—no doubt there. Shall we be able to lift off before the runway end? During the first few moments of the takeoff roll in the Electra, you have a limited view of the runway—until the tail comes up, giving you forward vision. Before then, you sort of dance on the rudders and use a combination of the side windows and acute peripheral vision to stay aligned with the runway. At this weight, it takes forever for the tail to come up. I weave a bit, using aggressive rudder inputs to stay on the runway. I relax back pressure and nudge the wheel forward to encourage the tail to rise. Forty knots. The airspeed is alive, yet the tail remains firmly on the ground. I'll be riding a Texan bronco soon if I don't see the runway in front of me. She takes her time, the old hag. Fifty knots. The twin-boom tail comes up at last and we race down the runway on an even keel. I feel in charge once again.

The bumps and ruts on the grass are routine, no worse than expected, perhaps even smoother than, say, a New Jersey airstrip or one in California. But the runway edge— and the green bay waters—rush up to meet us.

"Can we make it?" Fred yells above the engine din.

"Yes." I hope we will. The runway surface is uneven and our bodies dance on the seats.

"Damn it. Not enough speed. We don't have the speed."

Panic in his voice. I just hope he doesn't grab the wheel and throttles and do something stupid.

"We'll make it," I yell just as urgently. "Calm, Fred."

Eighty knots.

Eighty-five knots. Runway end approaching fast.

"Jesus, lady. You'll kill us!"

Ninety knots!

Suddenly no more runway. I haul back on the control wheel just as the frothy green waters of the bay reach for us and the Electra staggers into the air.

A hurried peek at the airspeed indicator. 95 knots.

We would be airborne normally and climbing away—I can feel the lift on the wings—but the aircraft is sluggish due to the weight.

"Gear up!" I yell at Fred as I hold the Electra down, skimming the waters at 30 feet.

Fred promptly cranks up the gear lever. We didn't so much take off as lumber airborne and point down toward the water.

As the gear embeds inside the fuselage, the airspeed improves. A split-second panel scan shows 100 knots on the airspeed indicator, and feedback from the controls tells me the trustworthy Electra is flying, albeit barely. We are heavy, scaling above the max takeoff weight, and the short runway did not help. I could have sworn the stall horn was on the cusp of blaring once or twice during the liftoff, but it didn't. I could feel it.

I couldn't just climb away, not with the stall warning horn doing its pre-bleat jingle on and off. Pulling back on the yoke would just put us faster in the drink. Less than thirty feet between us and frothing ocean. I soldier on, converting energy to speed. It's a trade-off, skimming the ocean surface to gain forward speed. The ocean is relatively flat with occasional whitecaps. Behind us, I imagine the airplane's propeller wash is throwing spray, leaving a wake.

The speed inches up to about 110 knots. I can risk a shallow climb away from the ocean surface. The airplane struggles upward at a miserly 200 feet per mile.We soon pass five hundred feet even with our anemic rate of climb.

Only then do I glance at my navigator. He pushes his rumpled brown hair back from his forehead, flicking the cowlick in place. He does this twice, his face white and strained. The Lae villagers and our hosts, who came to watch the takeoff, would wonder what on earth is going on. To them, we must seem to hug the ocean surface, unable to climb.

It takes an eternity to climb to three thousand feet. I maintain this altitude for some time until we have burned enough fuel to permit a higher climb. Speed is now 140 knots steady. I engage the Sperry gyro-pilot (I believe the more common term for this now is "autopilot") and set the throttles and prop and mixture levers. I pick up the microphone and make my first call to Lae to give a flight update. The radio operator responds dutifully and, with the crackle of static, I cannot tell from his voice if he saw the dicey takeoff or not. Then I lean back and ponder again that close call at liftoff.

"There's that." No conviction in my voice.

"That takeoff," Fred says on cue. "That isn't my idea of a safe takeoff."

"Nor mine. We got off the ground. Each minute we're airborne we're getting lighter. Ought to be okay from now on."

He nods absently, first gazing at the green waters below, then running another callused hand through his hair. At this rate, Fred will coif his hair and apply rollers by the time we begin the

descent into Howland.

"Hadn't we better get the maps out and figure out where we are, sailor?"

"Sure. But if I may say so, that was a takeoff I never want to be in again. You understand that?"

I nod. "Not the safest takeoff. I agree."

"We need to maintain heading, Amy. The compass is off five degrees."

I glance at the heading indicator. "She's slaved to the Sperry autopilot." A bit annoyed, I make a slight correction. "Look at those maps again, Fred. We got work to do, haven't we?"

"Work to do," he sings. "Work to do. Couldn't agree more."

He picks up the maps and arranges them so he can follow the flight's progress. I don't envy him. Later in the flight, he must leave the copilot's seat and crawl over the four big fuel tanks anchored to the cabin floor to the navigator's desk in the rear, just opposite the entry door. For now, he's content to remain in the cockpit. His is a daunting task where there's nothing to see on the map except thousands of miles of nothingness, an infinity of the blue ocean. A few specks on the map represent some of our important checkpoints. The rest are lines of longitude and latitude, our positions in theoretical space. We pass our first checkpoint, Finschhafen, about twenty-eight minutes after departing Lae. Through scattered clouds, we can just make out the little island to the left. I begin my climb to five thousand feet. The next checkpoint is Kundrian, 119 miles from Finschhafen, and by Fred's calculations, we should pass it thirty-eight minutes after Kundrian. Between these two islands, we are straddling the Bismarck Sea to our left and the Solomon Sea to our right. I pore over Fred's navigation log. After Kundrian, Fulleborn is seventy-five miles away, Buka Town 283 miles after that, then the Nukumanu Islands at 337 miles from Buka. At Nukumanu, we shall be about eight hundred miles from our departure point of Lae. From the Nukumanu Atoll, things will get lonely and more difficult. We'll be flying for six hours in a relatively straight line through some of the remotest parts of the planet, with nothing to see or to guide us other than the science of celestial navigation. Until we sight the Kingsmill Islands in the Republic of Kiribati—1,192 miles from Nukumanu—we won't be able to relax. Conceivably, we could even miss the island, and in that case, if we cannot get guidance from the United States Coast Guard cutter *Itasca*, we would have to continue seeing nothing again until we inevitably run out of fuel. That part of the trip—Nukumanu to the Kingsmill Islands—I am not looking forward to it.

The airplane still feels heavy, but it's settling down. The twin Pratts purr soothingly. My faithful Wasp engines—oh, how I love them! They have served me so well, with so few complaints, since my Vega days. We pass Kundrian three minutes later than estimated because of headwinds. Fred corrects the rest of the Estimated Time of Arrival for the following checkpoints. We make our radio calls on schedule, but nobody answers us. They are probably hearing us, though, which I deduce from the carrier wave humming in the Western Electric receiver on board. It is frustrating.

We pass the Nukumanu Islands three and a half hours out, and I make the usual radio call. We are about eight hundred miles into the 2,556-mile journey. The radio reception has not been the best since Lae. But hooray! Over Nukumanu we have a clear, crisp radiotelephony reception. The USS Ontario. Bless them. We hear them and they hear us—great! — I pass on our estimates for the next checkpoint. They also have a visual sighting on us, which is good. I relax a bit. Something nags at me, and I feel a vague discomfort I have not known since this round-the-world-at-the-equator flight began one month ago to the day. Fred is having problems with celestial navigation. He couldn't set his chronometers in Lae because of radio issues, and the work the excellent KLM Dutch technicians in Bandung performed on our instruments has gotten us this far. But if the chronometer is off by a few minutes—plus or minus—they degrade the accuracy of celestial navigation. Still, we have his dead-reckoning navigation which we have relied on much of the trip.

It's a long haul to our next visual checkpoint, the Kingsmill Islands. As the last island in the Nukumanu Atoll recedes in the distance, a sense of foreboding descends over me. I steal a glance at Fred, who sits in the copilot's seat between taking sightings in his rear cubicle. His face has a grim set to it, and he is peering out the window at the ocean whitecaps barely visible below. The same thought is in our minds: this is the moment of truth. This leg is the most hazardous of our trip. We are traversing one of the most hostile and remote oceans on earth. There is not a single stretch of coastline or another atoll for the next seven hours and fifteen minutes. Even the sky feels remote, stretching into infinity, its blue-black horizon casting a hazy pall as the engines pull us—enthusiastically now—into the unforgiving abyss that is the Southern Pacific Ocean. Here, we are relying on a heading and a prayer. If we sight the Kingsmill Islands after seven hours, the next major task would be to find Howland our destination. Howland will be three hours and five minutes after Kingsmill, again over stark ocean devoid of any discernible landmark. Howland is only a flat sliver of land, just over one mile long and a quarter of a mile wide. Once we get to the vicinity—or our reasonable charted estimate of the vicinity—the USCGC *Itasca* will stand by to the lee of Howland Island to receive our radio transmissions. They'll get a bearing on us and guide us to the island. Fred has taken readings on the sunline with his sextant, and I don't see any visible stars he could use for reference—but then, what do I know about celestial navigation? It's still a chancy call, as the island is so small it may not even be visible. It may resemble one of the many scattered clouds that dot the Southern and Central Pacific at various times during a full day.

Are we lost? Are we even on course to Howland?

 MELIA

I FISH OUT MY FLASK OF CHOCOLATE MILK and offer it to my navigator, knowing he would refuse.

"Thanks, no thanks, Amy." He calls me that when he wants to. We've spent so much time together in this cramped cockpit, I'm not annoyed about it anymore. "I prefer my ale," he says.

I sip my chocolate milk. Who's he kidding?

"I thought you had coffee?"

"Could be ale, could be coffee. It could be anything in that mug of mine, you know. Sailor's standard quaff."

"Yeah. I know."

"You think you do."

"Been a while since you heaved anchor, Fred."

"Stays in you though," he says.

"After many years as pilot and navigator?"

"I tell you. Once an old sea salt, you remain an old sea salt."

He drinks from his mug, pouring from a flask he's used since Brazil. Just one cup. He needs more. I could tell he's sleepy, and I want to suggest it to him to catch some sleep. I defer that, knowing he would take offense easily, especially if he had a few tots the night before and barely got two hours of shut-eye.

Fred crawls over the fuel tanks to the rear again, to tinker with his sighting equipment. This part will tax his navigational skills to the utmost. Since leaving Miami on June 1, 1937, my navigator's dead reckoning, and celestial navigation have been uncannily accurate. He's the one who charted and trained Pan American's Clipper navigators on this same Pacific route. This is his territory: he surveyed flights from Honolulu to the Philippines, Midway Island, Guam. His navigation skills are beyond reproach, surpassing even my expectations. From conception right through planning and then actual inception, I had always recognized—as had Fred (and before him Captain Harry Manning)—that this leg from Lae to Howland (or Howland Island to Lae, had we left Honolulu during our first attempt in March 1937), would be the longest and most difficult part of the journey.

Anyway, when the Sperry gyro-pilot flies the airplane—which is over 98 percent of the time—I reach into the recess behind my seat and bring out my journal and pencils to scribble a few words. Then I follow Fred's progress with the charting, and I drink more milk chocolate. Our hosts back in Lae packed some sandwiches for us, but hunger is never one of my priorities on these long-distance flights. Fred eats a sandwich and drinks some coffee from his thermos. After Nukumanu, I climb to eleven thousand feet to get above the clouds and allow Fred to take sightings. I am worried about the poor radio reception and Fred's issue with the chronometer. He's at his desk in the aft cabin concentrating hard, peering into the sextant through the viewing port, and trying to take readings. When he's plotting our course, the little protrusion above his right eyelid throbs with independent life. It's not a nervous tic—it just seems to pulse and breathe. I've never asked him where that protrusion came from. It's like swelling from a head-butt in a bar fight that never went away. Sometimes when he is not quickly forthcoming with a course correction or validation, I get this strange urge to take that protrusion by my thumb and index finger and twist counterclockwise.Once Fred finishes his sightings, I descend again to eight thousand feet because of concerns about hypoxia.

Speaking of counterclockwise, we should cross the 180th meridian on this leg, which means we will need to switch our clocks back twenty-four hours. Even though we took off from Lae on July 2, it is still July 1 at our intended destination of Howland. By the time we land in Howland, it really will be July 2—though in Lae it will already be July 3. Do you ever wonder why Australia and New Zealand and Papua New Guinea celebrate the New Year twelve hours before we do in America? Well, now you know.

I make our reports every half hour, on Greenwich civil time, as agreed. The *USS Ontario* is on station to receive our transmissions. The *Itasca* too is on station two miles west of Howland to give us directions to the island with the radio finding equipment onboard and smoke signals. But so far I have received no transmissions from either ship. Fred suggests a heading ten degrees farther right to compensate for drift. After the Kingsmill Group of islands, he will see if we need adjustments.

The lack of communication with the ground ships worries me. I'm suspecting—as is Fred—that our problems may have something to do with the RDF loop antenna. As I've said before, in the frenzy of those weight-reducing measures we took in Lae, we abbreviated the length of the wire coil. I think we did so because—though it rolls out automatically in flight to accommodate the wavelength and range of the transmitting station—Fred must manually wind the long wire in again after each use. It is distracting and tedious work. From Miami, we found it to be unwieldy and mysterious, and frankly, not much use; Fred's excellent navigation skills kept us perfectly on target.

Out of 29,000 miles, we have so far accomplished 22,000 miles of our journey. Only 7,000 miles remain. After we land in Howland, we shall have less than 4000 miles to go. Three-quarters of the way there, and we haven't needed to use the radio direction finder at all. Once we land in Howland, we will only have 1,880 miles to Honolulu, and then about 2,032 from Honolulu to the mainland. We'd been hoping to be home by July 4, our country's birthday, but now that is looking doubtful, as we will need sleep and rest in Howland and again in Honolulu. We might get there on July 5, if no further mechanical issues dog the Electra.

Anyway, I am getting ahead of myself. The radio direction finder is a new and marvelous thing—if one knows how to use it. It's a Bendix receiver incorporating a loop antenna with a tunable loading coil. Joe Gurr at the Lockheed factory back in California showed how it works, and he explained some of its intricacies. I promptly forgot much of what he told me. Seeing Fred struggling to wind up the dangling wire against a 160-knot slipstream when we use it occasionally around Brazil and Africa reminded me of a DC-2 copilot at gear-up time. Together, we discarded much of the excess wire (as we thought it) in Lae, and our over-weight takeoff showed that our conservative stance regarding our all-up weight was in order. On the whole, we have been averse to accumulating any unneeded extras on our flight; the only temptation I succumbed to was an exquisite Javanese bone-handled sheath knife I bought back in Bandung. I intend to give it as a gift to my favorite geographer, George Loft. There are also the postmarked letters and commemorative stamps in the baggage compartment in the nosecone, which will become collectors' items when eventually we land in California. These were authentic US Post Office commemorative stamps, printed solely for this west-to-east round-the-world trip. They destroyed the plates after the printing. It's a philatelist's delight and would fetch a lot on the collector's market a few years from now.

I now wish I had paid more attention to Gurr's lecture. The receiver box itself is under the copilot's seat. Six hours of being suspended between two throbbing engines is a long time. Fred orders a further five degrees heading change to the right, to compensate for drift.

Seven hours is a long time in a noisy cockpit. And you're just about halfway to your destination.

Each second, our two faithful Pratt & Whitney Wasps pulling us inexorably further into the ocean void. We have passed the GO/NO GO point. Some airmen call it the point of no return. This means, if we were to have an emergency that mandated landing at the nearest airport, it would be better to continue to Howland than to turn back to Nuku-manu or the Solomon Islands. It's comforting to deceive yourself. Fred and I both know, flying in this unforgiving, pitch-black void, that if an engine caught fire and we couldn't extinguish it, we would have to descend and ditch in the swells as best we could. If we're able to extinguish the fire, we could continue on one engine—albeit a little slower —until we land at Howland or run out of fuel, whichever came first.

Eight hours since Lae. Time becomes you, Meeley. My nickname by many friends, my husband included. We are suspended above the firmament—no, ocean—in the pitch blackness of night, with only the soft glow of the instrument panel telling us we are right-side-up and moving in the universe. We have fought mostly head-winds from Lae as we calculated, even though our indicated airspeed hovers at 150 knots on the dial. Since leaving Miami one month ago, and before then on our first attempt westward through Honolulu—and even during my solo North Atlantic flight—I have formed a mystical union with my beloved Wasp engines. It was different on the Vega, with her one engine. Hearing the two engines droning at the same power setting hour after hour after hour lulls you into a semi-hypnotic state. I can hear every stroke of the cylinders—smooth-bored though they are—the quiet hiss of exploding gas, the burr and swoosh of oil smoothing the innards. Sonorous music, yes.

It's also businesslike, comforting, mesmerizing. Every ten minutes, the sound changes ever so slightly—you only notice because your ears are so attuned to it. The Wasps seem to adjust themselves, pausing, then resuming the drone on a lower or higher note. But sing they do, and I admire them for their forthrightness, for doing their job without complaint. So long as I feed her avgas and enough oil cools her innards, she will run, it seems, interminably. Someone once said Pratt & Whitney engines are so reliable they can almost walk on water. Here, suspended at the witching hour over the Southern Pacific, I believe that. The

Wasps are the reason we are not down there in the drink, drowning our lungs in seawater.

Time becomes you, Meeley. Yes, I said that before. That's what it feels like, this endless droning into the night, the repetitive déjà vu. We don't even get a glimpse of the Kingsmill Islands. No lights, no beacon, no sign of human settlement. The settlements Tabukiniberu or Rungata, which I have penciled on the map and which are part of the Kingsmill Group, are nowhere in sight. For seven hours and thirteen minutes, we have held more or less the same heading, give or take some adjustments from Fred. That's a long time flying in the wrong direction, if wrong we were, moving over a seemingly limitless ocean at 170 miles an hour. From Fred's calculations after each checkpoint, we have been bucking strong headwinds. Our groundspeed hovers between 132 -139 knots for hours, even though our airspeed indicator reads 160 knots now that the airplane is lighter. We may be over Kingsmill—or a hundred miles from it. The thought is unsettling. Fred's navigation has been stellar up to this point, and I have to rely on it, and I calm my doubts when he tells me we are just passing Kingsmill. That means about five hundred miles to go to Howland. Just over three hours left on this—the longest flight I will have made in the Electra. Once we land in Howland, I intend to give Fred an enormous hug and a kiss. For being the best navigator in the world. I don't think GP, my nickname for my husband, would mind. No, he'd hail me enthusiastically and say, "You both deserve it, my dear." No, Fred deserves it. If we reach Howland, we are virtually home. From Howland to Honolulu is only three-quarters of the distance from Lae to Howland Island, and you can't miss the Hawaiian Islands if you're blindfolded and told to fly only a compass heading for the ocean crossing. Then Honolulu to California will be hard for me to get worked up about, having flown between Honolulu and the mainland more than once.

It is around here that we pass the 180th meridian and adjust our clocks backward. The meridian passes between the Kingsmill Islands and the Phoenix Islands of Kiribati. It feels strange flying without having contact with anybody; we've gone nearly eight hours now since the Nukumanu Atoll. I make my half-hourly transmissions and get no reply. I can only assume they transmitted from the low buzz carrier wave after I've finished. I'm just not hearing the *Itasca*. Their transmissions seem on the threshold of a static breakthrough. The voice just doesn't come through. I've not received any transmissions from Ontario, either.

I make a call at 4:57 a.m. on Kilohertz 3,015, stating our position and weather. Streaks of orange, red, and grey presage the coming of dawn. Below us: overcast clouds. I repeat the message. No answer from the *Itasca* or *Ontario*.

We must be within three hundred miles of Howland. Fred isn't getting a bearing from the *Itasca* when they transmit using our direction finder. Even if we can't hear them, the carrier wave from their transmission ought to point us in their general direction. But when we get radio contact with them, they'll be able to give us vectors to Howland based on the direction of our transmissions. The *Itasca* has the equipment to do just that.

We review the charts once again, Fred and I, preparatory to a letdown. I rarely take coffee, preferring my usual milk chocolate, but this time I accept a cup of strong joe from Fred's thermos. I need to be fully alert during the last stages of the flight. I leave Fred on the copilot seat and the Electra on Sperry gyro-pilot for a bathroom break. I crawl down the narrow space between the cabin roof and the conjoined extra fuel tanks, my second time doing that on this flight. In the compact space behind Fred's navigator's desk, I do some stretching exercises and visit the bathroom. Fred is minding the store in front. Don't forget he is also a licensed pilot.

Back in the cockpit, I feel alert and refreshed. Fred calculates that we are two hundred miles (about one hour and fifteen minutes) from Howland. As the fuel decreases during the flight, the airplane gets lighter and the speed increases for the same throttle setting. In effect, this means I have to bring back the throttles a bit every hour. This saves fuel and increases our range while also preventing the speed from moving close to redline.

We have less than three hours of fuel remaining.

I make another call at 6:14 a.m. "This is KHAQQ calling Itasca. KHAQQ calling. We estimate two hundred miles from you. Request you use Romeo Delta Foxtrot to give us a bearing to your station, KHAQQ over."

I hold the cupcake-like microphone in my hand and whistle into it with the transmit switch depressed. When you transmit, the radio operator on the ground or a ship can gauge the direction of the transmitter. If the station has the equipment, he can use that to plot a bearing to his position. He could also give you bearings to another location using this information.

I wait a while. No answer. This bothers me. I could understand it when we were six hundred or five hundred miles away. But not 190 miles. Nor is the radio I'm using the VHF one, which is limited to line of sight. I'm using the long-range HF radio, which can transmit over impressive distances. If they cannot hear me, then something is wrong —or I'm transmitting on the wrong frequency. Fred is watching me, knows exactly what I'm thinking. He scribbles another frequency and hands it to me. I try again on the new frequency of 6,210 kilocycles. No reply.

Fred has some frequencies for the Pan Am stations in this region. He had them written on a little black notebook. But he couldn't find it. Maybe he left it in Lae. Not that they would have helped. Every ten minutes I spend three minutes whistling into the microphone, hoping the *Itasca* could hear me and provide vectors.

At 6:45 a.m., I make another voice call to *Itasca* requesting bearings to Howland Island. No answer. We have descended to nine thousand feet and have a wide range of views. But it is time to descend, to arrive at Howland in good altitude for landing. I run through my pre-descent checks and at a distance of eighty miles begin a 500 feet per minute rate of descent toward where Fred's chart shows Howland should be. I feel the same growing excitement I always do when approaching a destination after long hours suspended in the sky.

I am uneasy. I cannot explain it.

3

MELIA

I LEVEL OFF AT TWO THOUSAND FEET AND pull back the power until the Electra is coasting at 120 knots, as we arrive where Fred's calculations show Howland Island to be. There is nothing beneath us, ahead of us, or around us. Just inexhaustible green ocean. The time is 7:23 a.m. We both peer out the windshield, trying to spot an island from among the low-scattered clouds dotting the sky. Some clouds resemble islands, and I fight the impulse to dive toward each one of them to confirm if it's our destination.

"I'll descend to one thousand feet," I tell Fred.

"Sounds good," he says.

He presses his face to the side window, alternating between looking through the windshield and the side one. I descend to one thousand feet and after nearly five minutes of maintaining heading with no sight of our island; it is clear we have either passed it or have yet to reach it. Since we are almost ten minutes past our estimate for Howland, Fred reckons we should turn back on the reciprocal heading and search again. We must have missed it somehow on the first run.

The second run past the charted area produces nothing. I let the Sperry autopilot fly the airplane and I look out the window for the island. Scattered stringy clouds complicate the search. The clouds are just short of being labeled "broken layers." They cast ominous shadows on the water and confuse us. We make two more passes, and it becomes clear we do not have Howland in view. I get on the radio once more.

"We must be on you but cannot see you. Gas is running low. I have been unable to reach you by radio. We are flying at one thousand feet."

No reply.

I pull back yet further on the power until the Electra mushes along at 110 knots. I check the fuel burn rate and note that our current power setting will stretch our fuel another two hours to dry tanks.

We start a grid pattern, five miles by ten, searching, searching for the elusive island. Or even the *Itasca*. Since we cannot hear them, if we sight the ship, I intend to fly low and slow alongside and have them point with hand gestures toward Howland Island. At one point, Fred spots what looks like smoke from a ship's boiler, and we leave our grid and head there. It shrivels into another mirage, a harmless cloud deck.

Fred looks at me, and I look at him. He's wearing the same dark-brown shirt he wore in Bandung when the Electra had instrument problems; we had spare time, and our hosts took pictures of Fred. He wore the same polka-dot black tie, the ridge above his right eyebrow pulsing, the cowlick in his hair like a large inverted comma. Then, as now, his face has the gaunt, haunted look of the seasoned wayfarer. The look says it all. He's ripe, and I am sure he is thinking the same of me: sweaty and scared as I've never been before. My legs want to start their unique St. Vitus dance again, but I cannot allow it. Not this time. Not with Fred as a witness. Not if I can help it.

The radio crackles. "Itasca to KHAQQ. Go ahead on 3,105 or 500 cycles."

A voice! Thank God.

I quickly palm the mike. "KHAQQ calling Itasca. We received your signals but unable to get a minimum. Please take a bearing on us and answer 3,105 with voice."

Fred and I feel like pounding the glare-shield in glee. Finally, we are talking to somebody! But the hope fades just as quickly as it came. For the next twenty minutes, I try to keep trying and receive no further acknowledgment from *Itasca*. All *Itasca* has to do is give us a bearing to Howland. Even if we hear nothing else, just give us a bearing—a heading to fly that will take us to where they are. Even if the rest of the message is inaudible but we receive the bearing, whether 357, 287, 165, whatever bearing they calculate for us, we'll be just fine.

Nothing. No word. Just crackle and static on the radio.

Less than ninety minutes of fuel left.

In the middle of the Central Pacific.

I make another call, trying to keep the desperation off my voice. I tell *Itasca* that we cannot read them. Could they transmit Morse code instead? We'll use the direction finder to locate their ship. Fred nods approvingly. He once told me he'd written articles about the shortcomings of the radio direction finder. Now he can disprove some of his theories.

He puts on his earphones, and sure enough, the Morse keys start coming in. Dit-dit-dah. ... The receiver is under the copilot's seat—Fred's seat—and the dial with the needle that points toward the transmission is curiously idle. Still, I am poised—between flying the airplane (that is, watching Sperry fly the airplane)—as is Fred with his pencil and calculator, to plot us a new heading to the *Itasca*. If we can get to the *Itasca*, then we'll have gotten to Howland.

Ten minutes later, it is all hopeless. We are receiving the Morse signals, but the direction finder cannot pick the direction the transmissions emanate from. I don't want to admit this, but I don't fully understand the RDF and how to use it. I regret not grilling Joe Gurr back in the Lockheed factory in Los Angeles about the workings of this strange instrument. It holds the key to getting us safely back to land.

Not good. Not good at all. Beginning to look hopeless. We have come overhead where we expected to see Howland. Nothing but endless ocean. Not even a ship in sight. We have been patrolling the general area for an hour and a half by now, scouring every square mile of ocean and hoping against improbable hope to spot the island—any island, a ship, skiff, anything. The sun has come out fully; the morning is halfway gone, and we have been airborne over seventeen hours.

"I've got an idea," Fred says, scrambling from his seat to the astrodome behind the cockpit. He grabs his sextant and says to me as he works, "I'll plot a sun-line that runs right through Howland. We'll stay on that line and run it north to south. Howland will be beneath us on that line. It'll just be a matter of seeing it."

"Okay, Fred," I say. "I'm with you. Let's hope it works."

My voice sounds faint, strained, even to me. Dare I hope?

In flying, you never give up. You fight and fly the airplane to the very end.

"It should," Fred says. "If these maps are any good."

So he doubts the authenticity of the maps? A good mariner or navigator should, if your plotted course does not take you remotely near where you're supposed to be.

Soon Fred hands me the plotted course. It runs northwest to southeast, on the 337-degree heading, and its reciprocal 157 degrees. He has drawn a small circle where he calculates Howland Island to be.

"Tell them on the radio where you'll be," Fred says. "What we're doing. That way they'll have an idea where to look."

I call the *Itasca* once more on 3,015 kilocycles. "KHAQQ to Itasca. We are on line 157–337. We will repeat this message. We will repeat this on 6,210 kilocycles. Wait."

"Tell them we are running on line north and south," Fred suggests.

"We are running on line north and south, KHAQQ over." I pray my voice reflects the fresh hope.

I switch over to 6,210 kilocycles, but I have to fly the airplane for a few minutes. The speed has bled off to 110 knots as I try to conserve fuel. I increase power a bit, though I'm afraid to lean the fuel mixture more than I already have, lest an engine flameout ditches us prematurely in the drink.

"I think Howland should be way south of us," Fred says again. "I would suggest we continue south on this heading."

"You think so?"

"Yeah. Best guess under the circumstances. I think we overshot it by a long way. My thinking is southeast. One-five-seven magnetic ought to do it."

My legs shake again. I have an impending sense of gloom and déjà vu all rolled into one.

This can't be happening to me. I'm Amelia Earhart. I am resourceful.

ABOARD THE USCGC *ITASCA, July 2, 1937, off Howland Island.*

CHIEF RADIOMAN LEO BELLARTS FELT like crying. He could hear the Electra's transmissions, but apparently, Amelia Earhart couldn't hear him. How could she? She was transmitting on 3,015 Kilohertz, which *Itasca* couldn't transmit on. He'd just found that out. It frustrated him and his fellow operators. Even her half-hourly transmissions were not on schedule. He suspected that she was on Greenwich civil time and had not yet changed—or else had forgotten to change to the naval time he was on. The *Itasca* was United States government property, and would never make that basic error.

He keyed his mike again, "KHAQQ from Itasca. We read you strength three. Unable to locate you. Unable to give bearings. Howland weather is 2,000 feet scattered clouds, 10-mile visibility, temperature 72 degrees Fahrenheit, winds 240 at 7 knots, barometer 2,994 inches of mercury. Itasca over."

He waited for some minutes. No answer. The silence in the radio room was heavy. The second radio operator shook his head. The two observers in the room looked grim.

A shout as a Navy brass hove into view.

"A'tion!"

"At ease." The officer waved Bellarts and his colleague aside as they scrambled to grab bulkhead, dragging wires and equipment. The officer was Richard Black, USN administrator for the Howland Island airstrip, which was a part of US territory. "You got updates for me?"

Bellarts cleared his throat. "Sir, she's asking us to locate her on 3,015 Kilocycles. Our RDF cannot tune in on that frequency, sir."

"Explain, sailor."

"Aye, sir, aye. The frequency she is using would appear to be Hotel Fox. We can use RDF only on the Very High-Frequency line-of-sight radio used in normal air-to-ground and ground-to-air transmissions. She is using the long-range radio used for oceanic flights. Sir."

The officer blinked several times. "So why are we not in contact with her?"

"Sir, I suspect her radio has a problem. Probably an antenna problem. Cut off or shortened, or it's not unwinding from its receptacle, sir."

The officer pondered this. "She's due overhead Howland in less than an hour."

"Yes, sir."

"The Colorado report anything?" The Fleet Commander had spread out the *USS Colorado* and *Ontario* in the South Pacific to aid the aviators. All those ships had radios. The *Colorado* was a full-dress battleship and even carried her warplanes on board.

"No, sir. Nothing reported. I talked to them ten minutes ago. They'll advise if they have contact."

"I thought Ontario made contact?"

"Aye, sir. A fo'c's'le watch reported the sound of an airplane going overhead. That was at least nine hours ago."

"No definite sighting?"

"Just the airplane sound, sir."

"Can we try reaching her on Morse?"

"We could, sir."

"Do that, then. I'll inform the captain. The barrelman should continue scanning. Let him use light signals. She may see us when she's close."

"Aye, aye, sir."

The ratings shot to their feet again as Black turned to leave. He looked troubled and barely noticed. He was thinking: There's still time. Lots of time.

4

AMELIA

I DON'T KNOW HOW LONG WE FLY SOUTHWARD. I am in a daze. My thinking is not clear; I am confused. This can't be happening. I can't believe I'm lost in the middle of the biggest ocean in the world, no ship or island visible.

And we're running out of fuel.

I want to make water; I want to defecate, all at once. I have felt paralyzing terror before. Every pilot with enough hours behind them has. You go lengthy periods—years, even—when you fly routinely and without concern and no emergencies, and suddenly in a few seconds, you have a period of absolute terror, where the next few seconds or minutes will determine whether you live or die. This moment is creeping in on me; I feel it. The Pratts are performing beautifully as they have for the past eighteen hours—what faithful engines those Wasps—their song steady, not missing a beat, pulling us to our uncertain destination with the revived energy of horses nearing the barn.

We stay locked on a southerly heading. Aimless drifting will get us nowhere. We look out for our destination. If I sight a ship now, I intend to ditch alongside it to quit this adventure gone wrong. Fred has the same idea, for he is looking desperately out the window, using his binoculars, looking for any sign of a habitable island or ship. His seaman's eyes are better attuned to spotting a ship's hull or infrastructure or the telltale smoke puff from a ship's boiler.

"Stay on this line," he says, peering through his binoculars.

"What?"

"This heading. Southeast. Stay on it. We ought to spot something."

"What makes you say that?"

"The Phoenix Islands. There are a few islands south of Howland. Best we maintain heading. Going around in circles will not do us any good."

One hour past our ETA (estimated time of arrival) in Howland. One hour and ten minutes of fruitless searching for both Howland and the *Itasca*. Not looking good.

"How much gas do we have?" Fred asks.

"Less than an hour."

I can't print what he said.

"What?"

"Nothing." He's mumbling to himself. "This isn't mariner's luck."

"Just over an hour's gas if we're lucky," I say, more for my comfort than his.

How do you contemplate dying in one hour? It's an alien

feeling. For most aviators who have folded their wings forever whilst flying, the end, at least, was mercifully instantaneous. Having time to contemplate it happening is not pleasant at all.

The Phoenix Islands? Fred knows this area from his days with Pan American, but the sheer size of the South Pacific is daunting enough. He once told me that navigating the African continent was more challenging than navigating the oceans. Irony.

I cannot lean the fuel mixture further. My leg shakes again. I cannot stop it. Attempting to stop it makes it worse. Fred pretends not to notice. I can smell his fear too. It's contagious.

My eyes glance at the fuel gauges every few minutes. It has become my primary focus instead of the vital instruments that tell me we are right-side-up and have enough airspeed.

"Fred?"

"Yes?"

"Could you—."

"Yeah?"

"Get the Mae West ready. And the raft in the back. Just in case."

He nods. "Sure."

He leans over to retrieve my Mae West from behind my seat and asks if he should put it on me right then. I decline, but I have him place it within reach. In case you're wondering, Mae Wes refers to the personal flotation devices or life jackets for emergency ditching.

It is all a dream. Somehow the engines keep turning, not missing a beat. Somehow the ocean seems like a universe without end. I don't know how long this goes on. We motor on, maintaining a southeasterly bearing. It's getting harder to keep going, to keep from diving the airplane into the drink and just ending it right there. I've climbed to two thousand feet again, hoping against hope to see something familiar. Nothing. The ocean is remorseless. I want to beg, plead, bargain with... God—Satan, even—for a reprieve. I didn't expect to die like this. Fred sneaks a glance at me, and we lock eyes, and that says it all.

I don't want to remind Fred that he was punch drunk on the eve of our flight from Lae and barely had up to an hour's sleep the night before we departed. He was sleepy and uncoordinated through much of the flight, though he seemed to recover and pay attention the last two hours. I think at that point he suspected something amiss. It's an aviator's nightmare: unsure of your position, lost in the middle of a vast ocean, and the airplane engines sucking the last of your fuel.

We droned on. An hour, minutes seem an eternity.

I don't know what is happening. We are both sobbing. I don't know who went first. Does it matter? The tears roll down my face in two huge rivulets. I don't have even the luxury of tasting the salt in the tears. I am too frightened at my approaching death to notice. Neither one of us wants to die. Yet, surely we are about to. The tanks are nudging "E" now. We exhausted the auxiliary tanks in the cabin ages ago; the wing tanks will soon suck air into the breathers. There is no shame anymore. Fred weeps silently into his stained shirt collar. The tears roll down my cheeks, and I wipe them away to see the instrument panel. Which option is better: make a perfect ditching after the Electra runs out of fuel, float in our Mae West, and get into a tiny rubber dinghy to die hours, perhaps days later of dehydration and hunger? Or when the engines sputter and cough into silence, rollover into an uncontrolled dive to the ocean bed? That would be quicker.

Death is death. Whichever—

"LAND! AN ISLAND!"

I almost jump out of the airplane, if that were possible, at Fred's shout.

"What?"

"Right, turn right! Come right about degrees."

He's gesturing desperately. I bank the airplane and coming through about sixty degrees to starboard; I see it. But no. I refuse to see it. Where did it come from? An uncharted island four times the size of Howland? No, no. Not another mirage. Fred and I are hallucinating in our desperation.

"It can't be," I say. "It can't be."

"Who cares?" Fred shouts. "Let's go down. Whatever it is, we just ditch alongside it. There's got to be natives around."

"God, please. Please. Let it not be just another large cloud." My voice breaks with emotion.

"That's no cloud," Fred says. I note the excitement in his voice. "I've seen enough islands in my time at sea to know a sand bar from a cloud base."

It is a mirage. I keep waiting for it to disappear, as the apparition looms closer. I resist the urge to firewall the throttles to get there faster, as that will guzzle the last of our fuel. We've been fooled before, five or six times when we thought we'd sighted an island and that wasn't the case. The Central- and South Pacific is such a remote place, you could cut a swath ten football fields wide and travel a distance equal to the one between New York and California and see nothing but ocean, never sight a single island or boat. How is it possible that just as our fuel tanks are running dry, a coral island appears from nowhere on our flank?

Another thought hits me. Is this for real? Are we already dead, Fred and I? Are we existing in an alternate universe? A separate reality, the second of our nine lives, etc., etc.?

The land-mass is surely there, growing bigger. A paramecium-shaped island, looking from the air to be about four miles long and one mile wide. No time to be philosophical. The island is there. Too many trees, flora, to be an article of imagination. A large, oval-shaped lagoon in the middle and a white sandbar encircling the island. There's a red object southwest of the island and it looks like a huge, beached whale. No time to consider niceties. I could ditch wheels-up on the water next to the sandbar. Or drop the gear and land normally on sandy loam.

"I'll land gear down," I tell Fred.

"Go for it," he says. His voice is impatient, as if the island will disappear if I don't hurry and get us down in time. He reaches over and fastens his seat belt.

You can misjudge glidepath on a straight-in approach over the water. I would have preferred a circuit over the landing area to give me a better perspective, but we don't have that luxury. The engines might just quit during the circuit. I quickly call for flaps and the gear, and Fred obliges me. Props come full-forward, and we're out of eight hundred feet, nosing down for the sandbar. It feels strange hearing the clunking sounds of the gear running out after nineteen hours in the air. It feels strange to be deliberately aiming the airplane into a sandbar in the middle of the widest ocean in the world. The last notch of flaps and power comes up again to hold the airplane. It must be a three-pointer. If I land on the mains, the Electra would nose over as the soft sand took a grip. Better to alight on all three at once, hold the control wheel to my chest, and fight the bucking to a stop. No chance to gauge the swells for hints of wind direction. The dominant idea is just to get down. It's a ship as the red object appears closer. It is to my right, a steamer probably beached and scuttled long ago and now hosting its coral reef.

The Electra is so light from being nearly empty of fuel that she floats and floats, leaving valuable sandbar behind us. I force it down. I almost land tail first. It has to be a full aerodynamic stall as the airplane settles. I wrestle the airplane onto the wet sand. She settles perfectly on the sandy loam. I feel the sudden backward tug as the soft sand grabs the main wheels. I haul back instantly on the control wheel, and we buck through a rough, bronco-like sudden deceleration that has us pressing hard against the seat harness restraints. I refuse to let go, hugging the wheel against my chest, feeling the individual ruts and bumps. There will be bruises, but who cares? The foremost thing is: the Electra mustn't nose over. We stop soon enough, and I feather the props and cut the mixture to idle. The big Wasps splutter, belch smoke, cough, and quit. I switch off the fuel pumps, the gyros, the beacon, nav lights. I cut the radios and the master switch.

Absolute silence

Eerie. Except for the tinny sound of the gyros winding down. The ticking sound of the hot engines as they cool.

The silence of the catacomb. Despite the swish-swash of the ocean currents, and the crash of the water against the natural breakers upwind. Utter silence. Even the sound of the ocean swells seems part of the sudden silence.

It feels that way after nearly twenty hours of the continuous racket from the engines. The clap of the breakers just yards away from the airplane wakes me up to the other-worldly reality of our situation. Did we land, or is that the

River Styx swishing nearby? Fred and I look at each other, amidst the settling sounds of the engine, the smell of varnish, and aviation gasoline on a sultry morning.

Fred shakes his head from side to side and makes the sign of the cross.

I burst into tears.

5

F RED

WE MADE IT! GODDAMN IT, WE MADE IT!

I think I punched the air with my fist and made a noise that sounded like "Wahoo!"

Amelia looks at me. Her lips quiver, she is breathing hard and her eyes are wet. But she is smiling.

"Yes, we did, Fred. We made it."

"Well done, Amy. Mighty good forced landing."

On impulse I lean over and flat-kiss her.

She hesitates, too stunned from recent events and what we just avoided. I don't give a whale's ass, I'm just happy to be alive, and even then, I'm still uncertain if we, in reality, escaped what seemed a certain fate. For this alone, I don't think her husband would have minded. Still smiling, she leans sideways, and I plant another slobbery kiss on her cheek.

"Apologies to George Putnam."

"That's okay," Amelia whispers. "My husband understands."

We scramble out through the top hatch onto the sandy loam of the reef. We check the airplane; me going clockwise; she counterclockwise. I'm unsteady on my feet after nearly twenty hours in the air. The thrumming of the engines still echoes in my ears. The Electra is not too much damaged. The engines are undamaged. On a proper grass or tarma-cadam runway and with minor repairs she could fly again. But not here, never. Not if the two parallel deep ruts made by the main wheels are any sign of the sand type we landed on.

I notice Amelia's left leg shaking. A palsy. It will dimin-ish. The fear of an off-airfield arrival in an uncharted area had preyed on us. Now replaced by relief—joy at being alive, surviving the monumental odds. It's only a matter of time before we're rescued from this island.

We ponder our circumstances. The epic round-the-world attempt just got scuttled. No matter how glad we are to have escaped certain death, the reality of the aborted flight, just when we are three-quarters done, is depressing.

"We made it," Amelia said again. "Thank you, Lord."

"Roger that," I said.

I hear a strange sound, and turn. Amelia is sobbing.

∾

USCGC Itasca

"BRIDGE, RADIO."

"Talk to me, Sparky."

"Sir, she says she's running on line 157–337 north and south. She still cannot see us."

"Thank you. Keep listening. Advise when contact established."

"Aye, aye, sir."

A pause. Then the speakers blasted, "Do ye hear there! Do ye hear there! This is the bridge. All nonessential hands on deck to look for the airplane. Electra 10 Echo model. Do ye copy?"

"Aye, Crow's Nest."

"Aft deck, aye aye, sir."

"Boilers, aye."

"Hatch aye, sir."

"Bridge to Boilers. Fire up oil burners for smoke signature. I repeat, light up for visual smoke. Proceed until further orders. Acknowledge."

"Aye, sir. Donkeyman visual smoke. Aye, aye, sir."

"First mate, all deckhands, all nonessentials to deck watch duty. Aye, aye, sir."

"Ensign McCurdy, fo'c's'le, full alert. Aye, aye, sir."

"Midshipman Renfrow, aft watch, full alert. Aye, aye there."

"Bridge, out."

The captain replaced his bridge mike. He picked up the binoculars once again to scour the blue white-speckled skies. Beside him stood Richard Blackburn, the US administrator of the Howland Island scheme. Their binoculars surveyed the horizon, searching. All officers on the bridge on edge. Not only was Amelia Earhart a close friend of Eleanor Roosevelt and President Roosevelt, but they also had signals on PACFLTINT telex to locate her and guide her to Howland Island and to make sure she departed safely to

Honolulu the next day. A screwup here could be career-destroying.

Within minutes of the captain's order, two heavy plumes of smoke rolled into the sky from the furnaces of the cutter. If Amelia and her navigator were anywhere in the vicinity, there was no way they could miss the sudden and extensive pall of smoke that hung over the inert sky and then billowed southward in a slow arc.

~

FRED

I SCOUT THE AREA. AMELIA SCURRIES about, gathering our belongings from the Electra. I think she wants them on firm ground in case the overnight tide floats the ship out to the mid-ocean. I know for sure we shall not sleep on the bare ground out in the open until we take stock of any dangerous creatures on the island. This South Pacific island reeks of salt, tropical sea breeze, and scrub fauna. So many coconut palms. So many land crabs. I'm just glad to be alive. We couldn't possibly take off again, stuck in this reef marsh.

I am disappointed by this first walk. I'm trying to see how the *Itasca* or any rescuing ship will dock when they arrive. Most times the ocean foams submerge the reefs. The volcano which formed the island left dangerous rocky outcrops beneath the foam. There's already a shipwreck on the island which I saw just before we landed. I haven't had time to get to it yet. It looks like the rescue ship or ships will berth offshore and offload skiffs to evacuate us. The endless crash of the ocean swells echo in my ears, music I got accustomed to decades earlier as a maritime sailor. The memories rush back, but I don't want to dwell on those. Best to get out of here first.

When I stroll back, Amelia has removed her aviator's cap. Her look says we could sleep in the airplane if we don't get rescued before nightfall. Her streaked blond hair spills out, a horrendous mess. The curls sit on her head resembling those military caps officers wear. When she is this way —without her cap—she reminds me of Lucky Lindy. Tall, slim, and more boyish than I care for.

"They should have ships in this area," I say.

"Ships? Merchant ships or navy ships?"

"Naval ships. The US Pacific Fleet has several ships that-a-way." I point eastward. "When I was laying out Clipper routes for Pan Am, I got to know a lot about our presence in these waters."

"So, there's a chance they'll come to get us?"

"An excellent chance." I put on a pensive face, and she waits. "Though, I don't know. The Itasca—"

I let the words hang there. I need not say it. Neither the Electra nor *Itasca* got bearings from each other's transmissions, either with voice or Morse code. The *Itasca* had the Radio Direction Finder.

"Where are we exactly? Do you know, Fred?"

"An island."

"Which?"

"Not sure yet. I must use the sextant. Find out exactly where we are. Perhaps if our radios are still working, get word out on our location."

"The radios should work," she says. "On battery, it should."

As an afterthought, she adds, "The props don't look damaged. They never touched the ground, though sand may have blown into the engines. They should start, though."

"I hope so."

Lengthy silence. The susurration of the waves and the breakers continue the rhythm they have maintained for eons in the background. It's reassuring. And frightening in its impersonal grandeur.

Amelia runs a hand through her pale blond dishevelment. Looks around wildly.

I stare at her. "You okay?"

"I'm good." Yet the wild look persists.

"Do you mind, Fred?" she says.

"I don't see any kings or queens here. A queen, yes. Do your business and mind me not."

"Sorry?"

"You don't need my permission."

"Courtesy," she snaps.

"You're the captain."

I move away while she reenters the airplane. I see a few crabs moving across the sandy reef. They seemed to have climbed off breakers to the right of the reef. This place could be a tropical paradise. For now, it's a tropical terror, because I don't know the first thing about how we shall get out of here unless we're rescued. The air smells clean and vegetation-heavy, cloying a fruity, tropical tang as if smog and the smoke of coal-burning factories have never spewed their detritus onto this part of the world. Though the humidity stifles, the whiff of pristine ocean air and tropical flora provides a refreshing antidote.

When she comes out, she says, "When do you think they'll start looking for us?"

"I imagine they already are."

"Silly question."

She climbs up on the wings, opens the neck fillers to the tanks. She peers inside—not for long because the fumes from the aviation fuel can overpower a person. She does the same for the starboard wing. She's a competent mechanic, I recall.

"Just air in the tanks?"

"Not really," she says. "Too low for me to even use a dipstick. But I would guess about five to eight gallons left, some of it unusable fuel."

"We were running it close."

She nods. "That we did. The gauges read empty. They build in some margin, I guess."

"They do."

I climb back into the Electra to retrieve the sextant and take some sightings. She waits while I plot our position. She knows the basics: that celestial navigators use the sextant to determine the angle between a known star and the horizon. Knowing the angle and the time it's measured, one could calculate one's position.

"Where does that place us?"

"I'm working on it."

She's worried. I can tell. She has a woman's intuition and a pilot's sixth sense to boot. A formidable combination and I bet that intuition is telling her right now this adventure will not end like the others.

How do I just know?

Maybe sailor's sixth sense.

6

N EW YORK CITY

IN HIS OFFICE, WHERE HE'D PRACTICALLY spent the night flitting between radio channels and fielding transatlantic phone calls, George P. Putnam tried to snooze. His secretary interrupted. "Call for you from Mr. Cerf, sir."

He picked the phone with hands that felt like starched paper. "Allo?"

"George, this is Bennett. Hope I didn't wake you too early?"

"That you, Bernie? I'm awake. All I can ask for."

"I heard what happened. Devil's luck is what I say. Amelia is a courageous woman. We all know that. I pray she pulls it off, and we find those two out there somewhere."

"We need all the luck we can wish for Amy and Fred."

"Hey, listen, your wife is among the best pilots around. Everyone knows that. Right up there with Lucky Lindy and

Paul Mantz. If anyone can pull off a landing in the middle of the Pacific, she can."

"Thanks, Bernie. I appreciate that."

"I just want to tell you that Sylvia and I—we still talk, she and I—we're rooting for Amelia and her navigator." Bennett Cerf paused. "They're out there somewhere, alive and well. Our prayers are with them. I hope to God it's only a matter of hours before they're found."

"Yes. Well, I hope we find them quick. Their supplies are limited, and Amelia's a poor swimmer. I pray they're aboard a life raft as we speak."

"I should think so. I pray so."

"Yes."

"She's a resourceful woman, your wife. There's a wonderful chance she and her navigator will pull through."

"I hope so."

"Let me assure you that everyone here at Random is hopeful the Coast Guard will rescue them—and soon. Meanwhile, if there's anything—anything at all—we can do to help the situation, you will let us know, of course?"

"Certainly."

"I mean that George."

"I know that. Thanks for the offer. Best we can do now is pray."

The Random House chairman hesitated. "Have they heard any more transmissions from her airplane?"

"There's a coast guard ship in the vicinity where they should have landed. They could hear Amelia's voice, her transmissions, and they replied. But apparently, she wasn't hearing them. Strange thing."

"Strange."

"Quite."

"Amelia's luck and skill have been extraordinary. We all know that."

"She'll come through, Meeley will. She always has."

"Yes. Cheer up, George. I'll be at the Club later tonight, and I look forward to raising a toast to her safe rescue."

"I'll drink to that."

"You take care now."

"You too."

Putnam hung up. The call cheered him immensely. The diehard competitive world of New York book publishing had discarded vitriol for the moment, rallied around him. He'd remember in future during the cut-throat frenzy of book auctions.

By noon that second day, he had gotten calls from Alfred Knopf and later Arthur Hays Sulzberger of the New York Times. From the west coast, Charlie Chaplin and Paul Mantz called. Mantz should have been Amelia's navigator on this trip, but he had pulled out pleading Hollywood commitments.

∾

USCGC Itasca

ON THE BRIDGE ABOARD THE USCGC *Itasca*, the captain surveyed the horizon with his binoculars. He lingered on the southeast and southwest quadrants, while behind him on the other side of the bridge, the first mate panned the northeast/northwest quadrants with similar binoculars. Nothing. The bridge telephone rang.

The captain lowered his binoculars and picked up the phone. "Bridge"

"Radio, sir."

"This is the captain. Pass your message."

"Some transmissions coming in, sir. Faint. It's readable. It appears to be from KHAQQ."

The captain looked startled. "You sure about that?"

"Aye, sir. Positive."

"They ran out of fuel at least twelve hours ago. How come they're making transmissions, Sparky, you tell me."

"No idea, sir. But they are. We can confirm it is their signature transmit. Sir."

"Nothing, no word from Howland?"

"None, sir."

"The Electra must be at the bottom of the Pacific," the skipper said. "Sparky, please tell me we didn't get transmissions from a source that sank twelve hours ago?"

"I cannot answer that, sir."

"Right. Continue to—"

A metallic female voice broke through the static: "KHAQQ transmitting on 3,015 cycles."

On the bridge, the captain's face turned ashen. He replaced the telephone and hurried down the staircase to the radio room. When he entered the radio room, the radio officer was in his shirtsleeves from the stifling heat. The equipment had to stay cool and even with two overhead fans and a locked standing fan pouring forth a mini cyclone — the room felt muggy.

Officers crowded the radio room, and they shot to their feet on seeing the captain. "At ease." He waved them down as they cleared a space for him.

To the radioman, "Can we tell where she's transmitting from?"

"No, sir. Still trying, sir."

The captain looked at his watch in disbelief. "They can't possibly still be airborne. I—" He listened again as the brief crackle and scratch of static announced another transmission. "KHAQQ unable to read you. We are declaring ... down..." The rest was indecipherable. Sounded like an SOS call, though.

The *Itasca* operator keyed his mic. "KHAQQ, this is Itasca. I read you Strength Two, intermittent. Confirm status, please, and your location."

No reply.

They waited. Four more times the static came, with a carrier wave only showing an ongoing transmission. It was not audible.

An officer present shook his head in disbelief. "Impossible."

The Second Mate nodded. "Ever hear of a ghost ship?"

The captain sighed. "I've heard of ghost ships. Never heard of a ghost plane." He paused, thoughtful. "Is it possible they made these transmissions yesterday and that transmission somehow hung in the air, and we're only now hearing it? Atmospheric propagation, or something of the sort, eh, Carver?"

Carver was the second radio operator. Leo Bellarts, First Radioman, was sleeping in his berth—a well-deserved rest after the night's vigil in the radio room. Carver tried not to smile, and the other ship's crew in the room nodded gamely. "Beyond me, sir. I couldn't say, sir."

"Stay on it," the captain ordered.

Back on the bridge, he picked up the phone. "Do ye hear there! Do ye hear there! Bridge, all hands. We've got transmissions — source appears to be the aircraft we're searching for. We'll start our search again, establish a grid ten nautical, steer southeast one six zero. Got that? Grid south ten nautical. Hard a-starboard, for'ard one-five knots."

The first mate by the engine controls pulled the handle,

and the bell sounded in the engine room deep in the bowels of the ship.

"Engine, aye, sir. For'ard fifteen knots."

"Hard a'starboard, aye, aye, sir," yodelled the coxswain, only feet away from the captain, as he swung the enormous control wheel several full revolutions to the right.

"Starboard one sixty."

"One sixty on the steer, aye, sir."

From amidships came the increased rumbling of the engines. The Tannoy crackled as all stations checked in. The main deck buzzed with activity. Slowly, the *Itasca* swung to starboard.

It was as if they'd sighted an enemy submarine and were waiting for the call, "Batten down main hatches. Stand by for depth charges."

7
———

MELIA

WE SLEPT POORLY THAT NIGHT. SOMETHING
otherworldly about all this. Like we can't believe this is
happening to us. We turn the crowded cabin of the Electra
into a makeshift bedroom. The battened fuel tanks in the
cabin make an adequate bed. Fred's the perfect gentleman,
offering me the uninflated raft and the Mae West as a pillow.
He is restless, exploring the crawl space looking for comfort,
saying the tank fittings dug into his back. I had the raft
bedding and offered him part of it. He refused. The smell of
aviation fuel is overwhelming, so we crack open the entry
door to provide ventilation. I hope fruit bats won't fly in
during the night—or vampire bats, whatever. The cabin
floor slopes a bit, as with most tail-wheel aircraft, but after a
while, I hardly notice.

The surf crashes against the reefs often, throwing a fine

spray on the airplane. If we get rescued today or the next, we could still salvage the Electra. Get her on board the rescue ship somehow, even if we have to dismantle parts of her, as we did in Honolulu after the ground loop during the first around-the-world attempt. Otherwise, I fear eventually, the waves will float her into the sea. A strong riptide could do it. Even now, the sands shift imperceptibly with each fresh wave. We have little time.

That night would be one of the worst I have ever experienced were it not for the sheer joy of merely being alive. We would long since have been sea-bait by now had Fred not spotted this island. Still, I toss and fret during the night and hear the buzz of a few insects that gained leeway into the airplane. I hope they're not mosquitoes.

Daytime does not come soon enough. By the time we get up and leave the airplane, it is 7:20 a.m. Yesterday must have exhausted us. I am disappointed that even though we spent the rest of the day after our landing looking for ships and firing the Very pistol whenever we thought we sighted one, it was to no avail.

We clamber outside. I retrieve some work rags from the baggage bay and spend some time cleaning sand oil and grit from the engines. Fred helps me, but I can tell his mind's not on it. The landing on the beach was messy, but I think the engines will run if fired up.

Fred goes off to smoke. He doesn't dare light up inside the Electra cabin with all those residual fumes from the disconnected auxiliary tanks. I watch him steal outside, shuffle to the edge of the clearing and pull out his pack. It's a delicate ceremony he acts out with ritualistic precision each time. He extracts the pack—Marlboros—his angular, rugged features bent slightly, the famous cowlick falling into place. His delicate hands—Fred should have been a concert pianist instead of a marine navigator—shaking loose the pack, withdrawing the most convenient one. He sticks the cigarette into the side of his mouth in the same fluid motion, flicking his Zippo up and flaming the tip. He clicks off the Zippo and takes a deep drag, almost religious in intensity, inhaling and imbibing the smoke, drinking it in, feeding on it, a satisfied, unholy gleam flashing into his eyes. With a flourish, he removes the cig from his mouth, pouring smoke like a chimney. I can see and feel the subtle transformation as the nicotine floods his system. He is at peace with the world and himself. Nothing else matters but his romance with that glowing fag. Phew! I like to observe that ritual, especially when he's unaware he's being observed. If he knew he was being watched, he'd become self-conscious and ruin the process. I hope he has enough cigarettes to last until we're rescued from this humid place.

I hate the cigarette smell. Awful. Men seem to revel in it. Many ladies smoke, too. They think it gives them an aura of invincibility. I think not.

It is all unreal. Amelia Earhart Putnam is missing. Famous aviatrix believed to have run out of fuel and ditched or crashed in the ocean.

I push those thoughts from my mind. They've dogged me since yesterday. The sailors on the *Itasca* and *Ontario* must all have crick necks from searching for us.

How did we get so lost? It baffles me. Fred is one of the best navigators in the world. He set up this Pacific route for Pan American Airways. He knows this backcountry better than anybody, both as a seagoing mariner and an airplane navigator. What happened, Fred? Would the outcome have been different if the others—Paul Mantz and Harry Manning—had been on board? Would Harry, a navigator, have given me a fresh course to Howland Island?

Why couldn't they hear us? The *Itasca*, I mean. They received my transmissions. I know that for certain because I could hear the static buzz each time they replied to my transmission, but I couldn't hear anything other than the static. Which reminds me. We could run the engines—one engine, at least—for about five or ten minutes and transmit on the radios. That'll charge the batteries. If they can hear us—they should have over two ships out there searching for us—they can triangulate our position and come get us.

We find a sturdy tree to make notches on for each day we stay on the island. The sap feels right as I carve the first two notches on the trunk.

We still have our emergency rations, which should last us about three days if we eat carefully and one week if we eat sparingly. Good for me, good for my figure. Never was a big eater, anyway. Fred, once he finishes his cigarettes, will be ravenous. His body will demand more carbohydrates to compensate for the missing nicotine. I think I know this from being a former nurse!

Three days to rags. What am I going to do? I got a few TPs and some liners in my bag. I was hoping to get more by the time we arrived in Honolulu. If we don't get rescued from this infernal island in time, I'll be shedding into the sand or something. Gross, Amy. Gross. I also need more freckle cream when I get supplies in Honolulu. I wonder if they have Dr. Berry's brand there or only on the mainland?

I CHARGE THE AIRPLANE BATTERIES enough for another session of Mayday transmissions. I figure I can transmit for about five minutes and not discharge the batteries below the voltage required to start the engine. I switch off everything—rotating beacon, fuel pumps, HF and VHF radios, circuit breakers for the gyros, and vacuum pumps. I hit the master switch, and the instruments spring to life. The gyros whirr and tumble to life, the familiar screech of static. I allow about thirty seconds to warm up, then key the mike until the prolonged echo tells me the transmitter is ready. I make the same call as the previous day, on 3,105 cycles, repeating our position from Fred's sextant determination. I rotate the frequency knob to 6,210 kilocycles and broadcast the message several times.

No response.

Fred's plotted coordinates put us on an uncharted coral reef—most likely way southeast of Howland. I call out the coordinates in longitude and latitude, certain that the Coast Guard will fix our position once they get any of the transmissions. The maps we're using—those Fred had bought in Miami from Aeronautical and Marine Services—may be outdated and wrong. How else could Fred's plotting of our new location be 350 miles southeast of our intended destination? I don't believe it. A navigator of Fred's caliber does not make a navigational error of such magnitude!

I shut off the radio and kill the master switch when the ammeter shows a measurable discharge. I check the voltmeter to ensure enough charge to start the engine next time.

It's too hot inside the airplane. We leave the Electra and seek shelter under the coconut trees and bamboo pines about thirty yards from the water's edge. We have no machete for cutting. There is no need to be braying about it: I get to work bending and breaking branches of young palm trees and from low-fallow bamboo pines. Fred joins me after a slight hesitation. Maybe he resents me taking the lead. I genuinely don't care. We have work to do before we get rescued. We make a pile. We interlock and bind them with creeping twine, then dig four-foot-deep holes on firm ground, into which we push in the large bamboo poles with grooved tops to form a rectangle. Another four bamboo sticks go across the top. I must trim the grooves with the bone handle knife until it holds the horizontal sticks. We place the leafy palm fronds across the top and the sides. We cut more palms and bamboo, and in less than three hours we had an acceptable alcove. It offers shelter from the sun.

We eat part of the emergency rations from the Electra and drink potable water from the airplane. The drinking water won't last over two days, three if we stretch it, so we need fresh water. The irony of being surrounded by water we can't drink is obvious. Drinking salt water would kill us faster than dehydration. With Fred's help, I construct two channels, stringing together large funicular leaves. They incline from the roof to channel rainwater into two metal containers from the airplane's galley. We both know that a human can survive without food for weeks, but without water, we won't last more than three or four days. Since our route was along the equator and this island lies athwart the equator, rain shouldn't be a problem—unless this is the dry season. Rain comes in spurts two or three times during the day, lasting only ten or fifteen minutes, before giving way to clear, cloud-dappled skies.

We listen for the sounds of a vessel or an airplane—anyone searching for us. Fred has the Very pistol primed and ready should we sight anything. More than once I hear the drone of airplane engines. I look upward, Fred doing the same, our eyes sweeping the rippled cloud formations. The sky is blue above the white puffs of cloud, overarching blue. After a while, the sound fades. Nothing. Sometimes, the sound remains like a prolonged echo, our necks cricked from looking skyward, long after it's clear we're hearing a phantom noise. Soon, white bulging cumulus clouds build, tinged with angry black edges—so much energy in there. Come late afternoon, perhaps earlier, it might rain.

Fred retrieves a small tarpaulin from the Electra, the one I use when crawling beneath the belly of the wing or fuse-lage to drain water from the fuel tanks. He spreads this on the reef floor, which seems an effective barrier against stinging insects. We haven't seen many biting insects so far, or stinging ones unless when cutting the palm fronds in the marshy bush. That doesn't mean there aren't any hiding underfoot in the sand.

I've never seen so many stone crabs. They scuttle across the white sands, their gait is peculiar, sideways yet forward, pincers held threateningly like armor-piercing javelin of jousters from the Crusades. Sometimes, Fred and I beat them away with long sticks before they get too close. They have no fear of humans, it seems. Fred thinks some South Pacific natives probably migrated here years ago. They died off or moved on to other islands. The wildlife has lost its fear of humans and—turtles aside—have probably never seen one. This has a depressing effect on me. It brings home, as nothing else has that we're marooned on an unin-habited part of the planet. The turtles also do not fear humans. Big, plodding, and utterly docile, with their crown lodge of a shell sitting on their backs like armor plating on a fighting tank. I figure some of them are at least seventy years old or more.

We shall sleep in the airplane again tonight if no help comes. Safer than the cramped leafy shelter. There is the fear of a reef tide flushing us into the ocean as we sleep. We sleep wearing our Mae Wests just in case. We think of pushing the airplane further inland and try this twice during high tide when the water beneath the airplane mass lessens the weight. Instead, the wheels dig into the soft sand so deep it isn't possible to shift them. For a while, we hope that a mighty wave will lift the Electra further inland than it is. A riptide comes; the airplane's wings rock a bit, and the fuselage appears to shift inward. But if it gained three inches inland in the daytime, by nightfall, it seems to have lost five inches seaward.

8

1

600 PENNSYLVANIA AVE: Oval Office

"MR. PRESIDENT, THE TELEX IS FROM Naval Command Pacific Fleet," said the Navy Secretary. "It confirms that we have lost contact with Amelia Earhart and her navigator. Nobody has sighted them, but we made radio contact with them yesterday."

President Franklin Delano Roosevelt rolled his wheelchair to his favored spot behind the Resolute desk. "How come? They were doing so well." He adjusted his monocle as he perused the telex. "What do you think happened, Meyers? Apart from the obvious?"

The Navy Secretary shrugged. "They probably ran out of fuel and ditched in the ocean. The Central Pacific is not a friendly place to put down a land airplane, but it's doable since the wheels are retractable. They have a life raft aboard, from what I understand."

"I see." The president grew pensive. "She's had quite a good run so far. Amelia Goodhart."

"Earhart, sir."

"Yes. Her luck has held for quite some time, you know. She's good at what she does, and that helps. Eleanor's quite fond of her. She'll get to hear it, eventually."

Meyers nodded. "That she would."

"Amelia represents some... women's movement, women's independence, if you know what I mean."

"I do know what you mean, sir."

"We must look for her."

"That is being done, Mr. President."

"Details?"

"The Itasca was in radio contact with her until we lost contact. They must have run out of fuel after that. They couldn't possibly still be airborne."

"Did Amelia and what's-his-name—Nungesser?—say where they were before they went down?"

"Nungesser?"

"There were two of them, weren't they Meyers? She and her avigator, or something."

"Noonan, sir. Fred Noonan. The navigator. The Itasca received her transmissions, saying they were flying a north-south grid. That's a prearranged maneuver they would have done to enable our ship to get a bearing on their position. They came up with nothing."

"Nothing?"

"Absolutely nothing, Mr. President."

"Meaning?"

"We think they lost their way. They're not within range to get a fix on our ship. We heard them because they were airborne, and there's better radio reception the higher up you are. We have no clue where they might be, other than that it may be within a three-hundred-mile radius of Howland Island in the Kiribati Republic."

"Kiribati? The Kiribati Islands?"

"The Kiribati Islands, Mr. President."

"Damn it. The Japs are all over the place, isn't that the place?"

"They are, sir. They have nothing on us. They keep their distance."

"What assets do we have over there?"

"Three frigates and one cutter, Mr. President. The battleship Colorado is in the vicinity. We can deploy a couple more assets from the Solomon Islands. We may have a sub or two in the area on stealth patrol."

The president removed his monocle, and his blue piercing eyes held Meyer's brown ones like field magnets. "Find them, Meyers," he boomed. "Do what you have to. Just find her. It's good PR for us, with that little Nazi martinet Hitler doing his goddamn pissing contest in Spain and the so-called Sudetenland. We need this to be successful. Do you understand?"

"Yes, Mr. President."

"I'll sign the authorizations when you bring them." Roosevelt paused, thinking. "Perhaps I'll break it to Eleanor this morning. Are you and your wife having dinner with us tonight in the Lincoln Room, Secretary Meyers?"

"We'd be honored, Mr. President."

"Good. A marvelous time to bring it up. Perhaps you'll have found Amelia Hartman alive and in good health by then."

"Earhart, sir. See you, Mr. President."

Meyers left the Oval.

∽

NEW YORK CITY

GEORGE PUTNAM'S SECRETARY BUZZED him again, urgently this time. "Call from the White House. Line one."

Putnam straightened his tie and gripped the phone with unsteady hands. "Yes, Mr. President?"

"He's not on yet." A woman's voice, suppressing laughter. "This is Carolyn Watts from the White House switchboard. Am I speaking to Mr. George P. Putnam?"

"This is George P. Putnam speaking."

"Hold on, please, for President Roosevelt."

The line clicked, and the well-known voice boomed, "George! Is that you George?"

"Yes, Mr. President. This is George Putnam."

"I can't say enough how sorry Eleanor and I are about the... about what's happened. Distressing. Very distressing."

"Thank you, Mr. President."

"Let me get this right, George. Your wife's airplane just vanished. She and her navigator are missing. Is that correct?"

"Right. All the ships have lost contact with her. There was some initial contact—there appeared to be—and then nothing. Nothing. We are still hoping, waiting for word."

FDR made a clucking sound over the line. Putnam thought maybe the President was pulling on his well-known briar pipe. "Well George, let me tell you that Eleanor and I and the American people share your anxiety about our missing aviators. I want to assure you that this government will do everything possible to find and retrieve them from the ocean's claws."

"Thank you, Mr. President. I can't say just how honored I am."

"I've ordered all available naval and coast guard vessels

in the vicinity to help in the search. From the figures they're giving me, we have six ships and several aircraft—almost thirty aircraft—involved in the search. We hope we can locate her."

"Mr. President, I appreciate what you are doing. My family appreciates what you're doing—the massive resources you are putting into the search for my wife and her navigator. I don't know how to thank you."

"Amelia represents the best in what is American, George. I want you to understand that. Eleanor and I and the American people are praying for her safe return."

9

F RED

HOW ON EARTH DID WE END UP HERE? I have that sickening feeling you get when you sense you're going off course, getting lost. It gets worse when you know for certain you're hopelessly, irrefutably lost. This is the middle of the largest ocean in the world. Boggles the mind. We could be within a hundred miles of Howland, or three hundred miles away. My calculations suggest we are about 289 miles from where we need to be: Howland. That's impossible! Unless the charts are wrong. A miss in the ocean is a damn big miss —nothing for orientation, especially at night. Those maps are suspect. I read them correctly; I took star sightings. I mean, I'm a goddamned instructor in the damn astral navigation business, so what in the hell happened? You tell me, Fred. Did I screw up? It couldn't be Amelia's fault. I tell her where to go, she steers. Damn Lindy bitch. If she could stop scratching her butt and quit picking her freckles long enough to fly straight, hold a course, we probably wouldn't be where we are!

Got to cadge a fag. I sure need it. I'll stock up when that Coast Guard cutter rescues us and gets us the hell out of here. They ought to have a commissary on board that ship. I'll load up in Honolulu. This trip's gone to shit, that's what. Seven thousand miles to go, and we flew maybe 2,600 miles of that. About 4,600 miles to Honolulu, and onto the mainland, Oakland. If the weather's bad, there's San Francisco, or Stockton, or even Fremont. Shit. So near, so far.

I think we'll get rescued today. Those transmissions were good. The *Itasca* must have heard them. Hope they can pinpoint our location. Christ, it feels good to be alive. Yesterday morning, I thought we were dead for sure. Ever had to land in the middle of the ocean, with nothing but water three thousand miles either side? — absolutely nothing—save a few specks of land in between? I thought I knew the Pacific, but nothing scared me this much. Heck, I thought the Indian Ocean was big, deep, and terrifying, but that was easy compared to this. The Pacific is the real deal, and I'm the supposed expert on it. Hell, I don't think even God is an expert on this sucker.

I hope Mary Bea's fine. We just got married—and look what happens! Almost widowed in less than two months. Wonder how she's doing. I know her. She'll be up in hysterics when they tell her our airplane went down, that they're looking for us. Josephine would have held up better, but hey, we couldn't hack it together. Divorce sucks. Worst experience I've been through. Never again, not if I have a say in it.

Back to the situation. When the *Itasca* gets to us, they must lower a skiff and come lift us out of here. If they get here in time, we can still dismantle the Electra and carry most of the pieces back to the States. Otherwise, she's a goner. Tide will wash her off the reef in, I reckon, two days, give or take either side. We've got to have a shelter before then. Yeah, if they don't pick us up today, I guess by tomorrow we ought to think night shelter, apart from the makeshift one for the daytime. Too goddamn hot to sit in the airplane during the day. Damn. Worse than Lae. Much worse than India and Java. In Lae, I thought for a while Amelia was doggone sick. She was so pale, flushed, waif-ish; I thought she might've come down with dysentery from all the stuff back in India and Java. Can't imagine what it feels like having the constant urge to crap, then going over to do the business and passing cruddy, phlegm-like bloody crap. Heck, I get better stuff out of my sneezes than that. And then I'd see her at the airstrip come to fuel the airplane and check the weather, accompanied by this faint fecal whiff masked somewhat by light perfume (I know she hates perfumes, girlish things)—sandalwood, the smell of her blondness, her body cavities. Yep, the one between her legs, I caught that too; I swear. We been cooped up in that darned airplane for a month now. Caught that during some stressful moments; you can't miss it—not if you're a man and know where it's coming from. I know she thinks my hygiene is atrocious, but hers just might be worse. Don't I know it? And she's earthy too, damn famous aviatrix she is. That obnoxious fart she laid on me during the tough instrument approach into Bangalore. She was concentrating so much she didn't even know she'd done it. Like an abrupt epithet. Damn lethal, too. I almost left the cockpit. Jeez, women. What was she eating? It couldn't be all cheese. Anyway, I think she's over most of it now, though she's been looking exhausted since Lae, tired and submissive. Yeah, quaint and submissive, like she's given up. Like she's just about ready to hop into the sack with the first guy that asks her.

Maybe.

Don't even go there, Fred. She's a married woman. George Putnam will have your hide, skin it good, and hang it up in Union Square for the hound dogs. By the time he's done with you, your name and reputation won't be worth one goddamn cent. You won't be navigating anything bigger than a skiff down the Mississippi.

This island's spooky. I don't get it. I feel we're insignificant, two specks one two heartbeats away from being washed into the ocean and never seen again. I am impressed by the vastness of this place. The ocean has its song. You can feel it. A swirling, the slap of the waves at riptide, the susurration of the ocean depths. I just want to surrender, be swept up, done with it, consumed by this giant force of nature that dominates three-fourths of this planet's available mass. Just kidding, Freddie, old boy. Got to fight it. Got to survive. I have a family: Mary Bea and the old man and my mother. Gee, I hope they haven't heard we're missing. We'll be on a US Coast Guard cutter sipping iced tea before the word even gets to them.

10

FRED

I REMEMBER ONCE READING AN ARMY Air Force survival manual. I can't remember much of what I read. I wish I'd paid more attention. It lists many edible plants, leaves, and animals a person might find in the habitat where they've gotten themselves stranded. Three-leaved plants, four-leaf clusters, palmate and non-palmate leaves, the whole gamut. Common poisonous plants, how to spot them, and how to avoid. Edible leaves, herbs. Characteristics common to those. Some things stick in my mind after all these years. One excellent test for a probably edible plant: first you scratch open any portion of skin with your fingernail to simulate a cut and then squeeze the leaf juice on it. Make sure first it's not poison ivy! Wait for some minutes. If no adverse reactions, and meeting the characteristics shown above, that leaf or plant is safe for consumption. Please don't quote me on that.

I make notes on a portion of the exercise book I use as a jotter for navigation. I list the edible plants I can recognize on the island, leaf clusters.

Amelia comes over and sits beside me. Her hair is all roughed up again. She leans over so she can read the notes.

"Green three-leaf clusters most times are safe to eat," she reads, squinting a bit in the sunlight coming in through the shelter rafters. "So are four-leaf clusters meeting the safety guidelines." She looks up. "Guidelines?"

I tell her about the few things I remember from the Army Air Force manual.

"As a general rule, ninety percent of all animals are edible. Only ten percent of all plants are."

"Lots of vegetation here on this island," she says. "So, ten percent of what's on this island we can consume without poisoning ourselves,"

I grunt in reply.

"So, we go about identifying the leaf clusters that are safe?"

"I guess so." Her breath smells of clam chowder, a bit stinky, but infused with a warmth I never noticed before. Strange about the clam chowder; I haven't seen one or eaten one in months, since LA. This must be a result of all the shellfish and mollusks we've been eating.

"We need to diversify our diet," she says, looking me directly in the eye. I notice the green specks in the irises of her eyes. She has hazel eyes which at times morph into a lucent green. She is a beautiful woman in a tall-framed, tomboyish way, even in our present situation. And the freckles on her left cheek have sprouted again. I love them; they give her an earthy look. I know she hates those freckles.

Why, I don't know. They're responsible for a substantial portion of her charm.

Maybe she reads my thoughts. She leans toward me and the warm clam chowder Santa Ana winds pour from her mouth onto my face. "We've been eating mostly fish and sea products, Fred. We need to explore other possibilities, don't you agree?"

"Yes." I cough loudly.

There's a strange movement in my loins, the crackling of my boxers inside the trousers. I know that feeling, know what is happening. She mustn't see it, mustn't know she affects me that way. I think of baseball scores. Maybe I can recite verses from *The Bhagavad Vita*.

She is staring at me, pushing her hair back from her face, the straight patrician nose perfectly cut, almost pert, thrust in my direction. At such times, you notice strange oddities. Like when you are making love to your wife and trying not to let the people in the next room know what is happening. We amplify sounds; a car going past the house seems outlandish, magnified, and a car horn seems to be right outside. I notice for the first time the fine blond hairs on her face, almost invisible unless the sun angle is right. I glimpse the small tufts of pale-brown nostril hair. The hair on her right ear sticks out like weed tufts.

She smells of gilded sandalwood, an effusion of all-American gilded lily if ever there was one, bringing me back home to the pleasant, parched heat of southern California and its beautiful women. This is as close to humanity as I will get for now; she's the only human being next to me in this castaway world, and the warmth of her just being this close, with her imperfections, is indescribable.

Amelia springs up suddenly. "I'll go check out the leaves. Find the edible ones."

"You going alone?"

"Yes."

She walks away.

I'm left there, shielding my excitement, which is now of magnificent proportions and awkward. I call out to her, "Here, Meeley. Don't you want the notes I made?"

This is a mistake, because she hesitates, turns around, and now I must get up to hand her the scrapbook. I try staying sitting, hoping she'll come to get the jotter from me, but she is expecting me to do the gentlemanly thing and bring it to her. No way to escape this. I rise, covering my zipper front with the lowered book and waddle over to her. "Lizard seems to be in my leg," I smiled. "It's an expression. Peripheral neuropathy, I think it's called."

"You have my sympathy," she snaps. "I hope I don't get it."

"Get what?"

"The lizard legs."

She takes the scrapbook from me and without another word strides off toward the low ferns to match and compare leaves.

"From sitting too long," I call out. "You won't get it if you don't sit too long in one spot."

I don't think she hears me. My boner remains strong, and I can't figure a way to drive it down short of drinking hemlock. I don't even think I could find it on this damn island. With my luck, it would do the opposite—drive me to priapism.

Oh, well.

11

A MELIA

FRED'S CARRYING A HOT ROD FOR ME. No doubt about that. He's on his own. Poor sailor. Those maps? I know he got us into this. Plus, we didn't know how to operate that radio thing. We're on this infernal island, and Fred's got the hots for me. Did he plan all this? Absurd. I had to leave him right then. My prenup notwithstanding, you could feel the adultery in the air.

You left right then because your knees came together, and... you lubricated.

No!

Time out. You left Fred back there. Think where you're going. Watch for snakes! Snakes, yikes! Why didn't I remember them before I left? Can't go back now. Not after I've deflated Fred and his thing. Haha.

George Palmer Putnam, how I miss you right now. How I

miss your predictable, patrician ways, your hairy arms stretching out for me, covering me, protecting me from extant evil. I wonder how you are dealing with my absence, my being "lost at sea," or whatever designation they assigned. I know how much you love me, you poor dear. I love you too, honey. I know it now as never before. What wouldn't I give to feel your big, uxorious arms around me? Your privileged New England breath (what's that?) descending on me, your thick mustache (you had one briefly; it made you look like a tall Chaplin) bristling against my cheek. Your authentic aura of corporate East Side rolled Cuban cigars, expensive two-Martini lunches. What will you do without me, George? I see you weeping during my wake. Empty casket. Weird thought. Well, God gave you two hands. Use them! Think of me as you do it. What was it Jesus Christ said to his disciples? Take ye, eat. Drink this, and as oft as ye do this, do it in remembrance of me—something like that. I've got closets full of lingerie and undergarments in two drawers in the apartment. Use 'em George. *Drink this, and as oft ye do this, do it in remembrance of me.*

This is blasphemy. Forgive me, God. This island, our predicament, is hurtling me into insanity.

Poor Fred Noonan must take care of his problem. I can't help him with it. Was that... thing meant for me? God, how big it looked. He's been getting a lot of those lately. This morning, too, he woke up turgid from some blissful dream and almost poured from whatever damsel's orifice he worshipped. He's getting more animated each day. Must be the shellfish we've been eating. More reason to diversify our diet!

I need to concentrate on the scrapbook. Our lives could depend upon it. The way we're eating fish, I'm liable to upchuck them by the pint any day now. I mean, I love eating fish. At Los Angeles, on the Sunset Strip, those marvelous restaurants on the Boulevard. 'Frisco had them. Now try 'Frisco for fish. Nowhere else I know comes close. I miss even the meat dishes: a good Swiss steak, medium rare, sizzling in its juices, mashed potatoes, thick gravy on the side. For an appetizer, I would choose a spicy mushroom soup with garlic breadsticks for dipping, a slice of white butternut bread, and sautéed onions on the side. A half-slice of strawberry cheesecake and some real dark chocolate milk for dessert. That should do it. It's funny how I think about food all the time. I never was into gastronomy and all that stuff. When Fred and I get back to civilization, I'll pay a lot more attention to the food I eat, the things we take for granted. There's a bit of rationing over in Spain. Generalissimo Franco and the problem with the separatists. I'll remember to donate toward the food drive. Don't care which side—just help the common folk who don't have enough to eat.

Starvation is a terrible thing.

We tried walking around the island yesterday. Pooh. We turned back about a third of the way. Hard to tell. Tide came in near about one o'clock by the sun's shadow, and we couldn't go through the rising wall of water. Too much risk. We walked back the way we came. We'll try another day if we don't get rescued by then. Just before we made our forced landing, the island looked small enough. But from the air, distance can be deceptive. Relative, you understand. But we'll do it for the challenge—go around the island, I mean. Hey, it's our island, remember? Earhart and Noonan Island, somewhere in the Central Pacific, about two thousand miles south of Honolulu. Sounds better if it's just Earhart Island—Fred's my copilot and navigator. It is my island. I'll stake my fanny on that. Hey, good idea.

I look for Fred. He's nowhere in sight and the vegetation obscures him from where I am. This is my island. Thank God I'm not wearing those dreadful overalls—the flight outfit. I pick a suitable spot, a clear sandy patch untouched by vegetation. I lift my dress, squat. Long and messy stream. My urine is pale yellow and frothy. Feels good, though. I've anointed the soil. Do women mark territory? What a man can do, etc. My soil.

Take that, Fred.

~

RAGS.

Fact of life.

Who says you must be polite and ladylike about it? Here I am, stuck in God-knows-where in the middle of the Pacific and I worry about gender indispositions? Get a life, Meeley. This is becoming a life-and-death proposition. There's a genuine possibility they may never find us. Shocking, isn't it? Never in my most vivid dreams.... Well, don't you go off again.

Back to my issue. The cramps. I think there's some codeine in the first-aid kit. I'll take that. No aspirin. Makes you a bleeder. That'll take care of it. Fred's got to wonder. The guilt of the cramps isn't visible in gold script on our faces. Men could never tell unless you mention it. Or they see a telltale underpants bulge. Women probably could. They know coppery whiffs.

My main issue: no supplies. I'll plasma the sand if I had to.

I'm getting scared. Our window for rescue is closing. Does the US Navy even have a clue where we are? Fred thinks we're in one of the Phoenix Islands of Kiribati. Probably Gardner Island. He keeps coming up with that name. Says it must be. But why aren't the rescuers seeing us, or the distinctive red-and-white paint of the Electra? They can spot a person in a flotation vest from two thousand feet. I'm getting a grim feeling about our situation. Our emergency food rations are zilch. We're down to a few granola bars, two cans of corned beef, one packet of crackers, and some beef jerky. If we skimp on rations, we can last two or three days more before we have to eat turtles, crabs and, more fish. You can feel the tension. You could—

An airplane engine drones some distance away, above the broken cloud layers. It gets closer. It's all Fred and I can do to stop from jumping up and down in joy. He grabs the Very pistol, aims at the sky, and pops a round he hopes will vault the cloud layer where the searching airmen can see it. We both underestimate the power of the Very light. It's only a pistol and pistols rarely have spectacular range. Even with an explosive cartridge propelling the pyrotechnics, it falls far short of the clouds. All I see is a thick trail of smoke rise in an arc about a hundred yards from us and burst upward, showering the firmament with a burst of sparks and incandescent light. We wait, not daring to breathe, gazing skyward, straining our ears for the increasing throb of aircraft engines racing toward our just-revealed position.

Nothing.

The engine sounds fade, surge briefly, then silence. If it were nighttime, the Very signal would be more visible. The disappointment is crushing. I see Fred looking suddenly haggard in his three-day stubble and uncombed hair. He seems much older than his forty-four years. He's only four years older than I am. This reminds me of my hygiene. I need a bath.

I mention it to Fred.

"Do you a world of good," he says. "And nobody's watching,"

"You are."

"Tell me when you're ready and I'll turn the other direction. I won't look back until you give the okay."

"I've just got to have a bath. Too humid. I feel clammy. My pores can't breathe."

"I feel the same way."

"You do?"

"We're in the tropics, in case you haven't noticed. California is heaven compared to this."

"Fred?"

He looks up. "I hear you."

"Call me Amelia or Meeley for now, okay?"

"I sure will, Mrs. Putna—Amelia."

"Go on, say it, Fred. Missus Puta? You were gonna call me a puta."

"No, I wasn't."

"Go on. *Say it!*"

"I wasn't too!"

"You won't own up, right. Coward! Now, turn around. I wish to undress for my bath that's overdue."

His smile is pasty. "I'll turn around. Just take your time."

"Listen. Do you think I care?"

He gives me a funny look as if to say, What's there to look at, you waif? "Scout's honor," he says.

"Sailor's dishonor is more like it."

Fred ignores me. "And don't worry, if the rescue planes show up, I'll warn you in time for you to throw a robe over yourself. Or something."

Or something. Fred can insult you without seeming to.

I walk to the water's edge. I undress without haste (time stands still in this island) and pile my clothes on the sand, away from the waterline at high tide. I must remember to check underneath for crustaceans or arthropods before I put my clothes back on. The ocean is refreshing, and I'm careful where I step to avoid crabs, turtles, or jellyfish. Using both hands, I scoop water onto my body. The ocean shore has that musty character of mussels and pebbly seashells, but this feels almost like clean spring water. Perhaps because, as has become clear to us, Fred and I are the first people to inhabit this island in a very long time. When we leave here, we must make sure they name the island after us. Earhart and Noonan Island would be appropriate. Finder's keepers. I lather my body with a bit of toilet soap left from the three I stole from the guesthouse in Bandung. Guests can do that, couldn't they? Only with the small dispensable toiletries—never with the towels or bed sheets. I rinse with the wonderfully clean water and dunk myself twice for beneficial effect. I'm scared to wade deeper, be swept into mid-ocean, and perhaps never seen again. That would be ironic, wouldn't it? Fred gets rescued, and I go missing again, and a new search begins for my body. What the sharks don't eat, that is.

My hair is dirty and needs washing. These nine-cylinder Wasp Junior engines leave you wafting avgas and engine oil. So I wash my hair. In this climate, drying will be a breeze. Pun intended.

"I'm done, Fred," I call out when I'm finished. "You can open your eyes now."

He pivots around. Searches his shirt pockets for his pack of cigarettes. I know the ritual by now. "I've got eight sticks left," he says. "Want one?"

"You know I don't smoke."

"Thought you might now. Being bored and all."

"No, thanks."

What will he do when he runs out of cigarettes? I've seen him using my tweezers to pick up discarded cigarette butts. He relights them, holding the short stub, and smokes the stub down till the heat chaffs his lips. I dread the day he runs out, and we're still on this island, no rescue in sight.

He stares at me. He knows what I'm thinking. Then he shrugs. "Delay the inevitable, you know? It's still like cold turkey, whichever way. Unless those shit-picking rescuers find us."

I don't like his language. No, I don't. But I nod.

ANOTHER ENGINE RUN-UP TO CHARGE the batteries and make radio transmissions. I get excited when a radio operator from some ship answers. Fred runs over when he hears the transmission. Someone out there has heard us and is replying.

I tried repeatedly, hoping the operator would call back. Nothing but static.

Just what is going on out there? By now, I've concluded that we were so far off course that we aren't even near Howland. Our best bet—and Fred agrees with me on this — is giving out the coordinates from his sextant sightings. His sightings put us in the exact location three times —which seems accurate. Unfortunately, it shows us nowhere near Howland. Unless the earth has shifted, we are three hundred miles southeast of Howland. This is beyond despair. If the searchers can get bearings on our transmissions, they might zero in on our location.

I shut down the engine and switched off the battery master. I jump down onto the wet sandbar. The Electra has sunk perhaps two inches deeper into the sand, submerging the tailwheel and the locking arm. So is part of the twin empennage. The rear fuselage rests partly on the sand, and stepping out from the rear entry doorway, the sand is level with the airplane's interior. It's best to use the forward top hatch from now on. Clearance from the Hamilton propellers is just over one foot, and the flaps and ailerons on the left wing are inches from the water. I've been alternating the starts between the left and the right engines. But I see now that the airplane lists more to the left, putting the left prop nearer the sand than the right one. At high tide, ocean water probably washed over the port nacelles and into the left air intake. I'll run only the right engine to avoid curling the prop tips. Until now, with each engine start, I've never advanced the throttle beyond idle power with the props unfeathered. I fear the Electra might nose over, even with the yoke fully back against my chest.

We retreat to the shade of the temporary shelter. We are hungry, both of us. I can tell. The emergency rations are meager; the preservatives in the tinned food give us heartburn and still leave us hungry. It skews the ratio of protein to carbs in favor of protein, so the heartburn is a surprise.

I DECIDE TO KILL A TURTLE. I PICK A STURDY stick from the brush and search places with sun cover. Soon, I spot one resting placidly in the leafy shade. The turtle probably has never seen a human being until now and has no reason to fear one. I hide the stick behind my back. One barnacled leg reaches out in peace, seeking friendship, its short serpentine neck probing, two hazy eyes regarding the visitor warily—this is his island. It's a lovely turtle, and I almost spared his life. I hate to do this. Hunger drives me. So when, without warning, the stick emerges and I whack the turtle on the neck, two things happen. The neck disappears inside the shell. The turtle itself becomes a bowl-shaped carapace of rock. It happens in less than an instant. I hammer again and again on the turtle's armor to no avail. I turn the turtle over, trying to get at the soft underbelly. But the legs have retreated, sheathed inside the turtle's hardened castle, and nothing coaxes it out. My stick splinters in pieces.

I've had enough for now.

I'll go for the land crabs. Much easier. There's almost always one visible at all hours—gamely trudging across the sand from the water's edge to the leafy reef vegetation. I grab another stick. I hold the stick against the crab. Her powerful, pincer-like claws latch onto the stick and don't let go. I get about six this way and deposit them inside a cardboard container from the airplane. Next problem: how to eat them.

The island is full of leafy green foliage and there isn't enough dried deadwood we can use for fires. We gather some wet pieces and string them out to dry for future use, out of reach of the surf. It has rained three times since we became castaways, but when it looks as though rain is imminent, we'll get our pile into a protected space to keep it dry. We haven't eaten heated food in days. The version of the Lockheed Model 10 Electra supplied to the airlines—Eastern and Braniff, I think—has a hotplate or a small oven in the galley so the stewardesses can serve hot snacks. I had mine removed to save weight. I almost regret it, but I remind myself that even if we had it, we'd have to start one engine to provide power for the oven. And we don't have the fuel!

Anyway, using the strainer cup, I siphon a little avgas from the wing drain. Fred has assembled the dried twigs and rotted wood beneath three blocks of wood to make a makeshift pod for the pot. The "pot" is the aluminum can we use for replenishing the Wasp's engine oil; we sanded and washed it thoroughly to remove all traces of gunk. The oil whiff is just noticeable—if you insist on sniffing. We sprinkle the avgas over the slightly wet wood, light a match, and throw it on the pile. It instantly makes a healthy fire, and despite our precautions, we both leap back as the flame explodes toward us. Everyone knows that fuel is highly flammable, but the reach of the hungry flame surprises both of us. Unspoken between us is the thought we shall have to watch our matches. We have only two boxes, each containing twenty matches, so we can only light so many fires over so many days or weeks before we run out. How on earth we shall make fires when the matches run out is for another time. Rubbing two stones together as cavemen did —we've all tried that in high school—never seemed to work for me. Knowing what they say about watched pots never boiling, I walk away and do other things, like check on the health of the airplane (the waves are lashing both main wheel tires now and rocking the airplane). It doesn't take long for Fred to call, saying the water is boiling. I return just as he throws the first crabs into the cauldron.

I look away. Hunger has forced us to do this. I feel for the crustaceans—a flash of excruciating pain followed by instant death. I hope it is brief, and I feel guilty that they have to undergo this process so I can eat their meat to survive while they surrender their own lives. I shudder. Fred is the cook. He takes my bone-handled pocketknife and strings and scallops the succulent meat beneath the hard shell. We spread a little corned beef on the side, forming the bulk of our late afternoon meal. It serves as both lunch and dinner. By the time we finish, the turtle I whacked so hard with the stick has vanished! I'm secretly pleased it got away; the attack was brutal, and the turtle walking away testifies to its ruggedness. I suppose that's one reason they live so long; few predators can get at them once they recede inside their armor shells.

12

F RED

DAY FIVE AND COUNTING. WHERE THE hell are our guys? Call it Day Six if you start from the day we crash-landed on the atoll. Why the hell can't they find us? US Coast Guard, huh? They couldn't find a lit marker buoy in a harbor entrance if their lives depended on it. I have a grim feeling about this. I mean, the maps show the British Solomon Islands and the American Solomon Islands. Even the Japs have a big presence in these waters. Between us and them and the airstrips and the ships, there ought to be a sizable contingent out there looking for us. So why in hell aren't we hearing airplanes and ships' engines? Spooks me. Something's not right. Either I'm a total clod, and my navigation was way off, or the maps are not current (I checked, and they looked current. I now know they are not. Somebody in India or Indonesia changed the effective date). The maps are inaccurate by default; many of these waters are uncharted. Heck, I helped chart them for the Clipper flying boats. Was she paying attention to flying the headings I gave her? She's done well since we left Miami two weeks ago. We made excellent time and didn't get lost. Just this last stretch to Howland, then to Honolulu and the mainland, and we would have made history. Now, I hope we don't make history the wrong way...

I feel for her. She's a tough broad, no doubt about that. And she's so goddamn self-conscious. We've been here—what? — five days, and she hasn't taken a crap since that first day in the airplane. At least I ain't seen it. With all this tension, getting lost, getting down safely on this island, becoming castaways—heck, I would have crapped in my goddamn pants before I even left the goddamn airplane. I haven't seen her go near the potty. She's holding it. That can't be healthy. Let it flow, is what I say. Push the crappy stuff out. Maybe I ought to walk around the island—from the air, it didn't look that significant—and she ought to have done her business by the time I get back. Give her some privacy.

Yeah, I'll try that in a minute.

Jeez, what'll I do when my cigarettes run out? Never gone cold turkey before. Bad enough not having a drink in as many days. I finished the last of the brandy in my suit-case. We got some medicinal brandy or something inside the first-aid box. If nobody gets injured and we don't need it, I'll probably dilute it with a bit of water, which ought to go down well. Thank God drinking water is not a colossal problem for now. We'd be dead suckers otherwise.

I've got an idea. The rear cargo bin net in the Electra. I shall rip it off, weave it around a sturdy stick, and presto: a fishing net. That should improve the variety of our menu.

Lots of fish, mollusks, and shellfish around here. This place is overflowing with all kinds of fish.

From the air, before we landed, I noted the general layout of the island. Looking southeastward, the entire island is pear-shaped, with the broader end facing northwest. A dry, flat reef surrounds the atoll, and there are two sandy inlets, but for which the island would have also had its lake. The lagoon is emerald green, beautiful, and shaped like a handgun pointing southeast. The wider inlet at the northwest lets in the water at high tide, as does the smaller southeastern inlet, and a substantial body inhabits the large, Paramecium-shaped interior of the island. That body of water is surrounded by vegetation thicker in the northeast than in the southwest. I know I could walk around the entire island, wading through sections of water and sand, though it might take the better part of three or four hours to do that. Maybe half a day. Judging walking distance from the air is deceptive.

"I aim to walk around the island," I tell Amelia. "Might take a few hours to make it all the way 'round. I—"

"No!"

That was almost a scream. Startles me.

"What?"

"No, no, Fred. You just can't. It's too dangerous. We go everywhere together, okay?" She brushes sand off her overalls furiously. "How could you even think of doing that?"

She's not taking the opportunity I'm trying to present. Maybe she's genuinely constipated. We have eaten no solid food with fiber since we landed. It's been this high-energy calorific diet of survival bars, corned beef and crackers, and a few crabs and smoked fish from Lae—all of which make you thirsty.

"Okay," I say, "suits me. We'll go by you. Let's explore. We won't lose sight of the airplane. If it takes longer than we figured, we'll head back."

"That sounds much better," she says. "I can't bear being alone on this horrid island. Don't you forget that."

"I won't."

I borrow her pocketknife again, the bone-handled one, and strap it to a long stick I've cut from a limber tree branch. I tie the handle nice and strong with rope from the airplane mooring line (for land airport tie-downs, not sea moorings). It's only a crude spear, but it's better than going close quarters with any animal we may meet.

We hold hands as we begin. This feels natural, holding hands. Still, it's quite a shock to me. Her palm is soft like a woman's (Gee, Fred, she is a woman, in case you hadn't noticed. Sensational one at that). With those flight suits and mechanic's overalls she loves to wear, I'd somehow imagined callused hands, a bone-tight grip, and Jackie Robinson muscles. None of that. The electricity that jolts my arm as we interlock hands excites me yet frightens me. We are both married, with dependent spouses waiting for our safe return. I need the comfort of another human being just as much as she needs me. It's probably just a security thing for her; Meeley feels safer clinging to my hand as we leave our camp to explore the island. She is a tough woman, is Meeley. I know that. But we have only ourselves in this vast, unforgiving territory with no human in sight for thousands of miles.

She reads my mind. "Are there caimans here?"

"You'll find alligators in the Florida Everglades. What you have here is mostly crocodiles. Crocs like rivers mostly, but saltwater ones exist for sure."

"Are there crocs here or not?"

"No crocs." Don't ask how I know that for sure.

"Good to know."

Walking in the sand throws sand particles inside our shoes and sometimes inside our socks as we walk, avoiding the waterlogged edges. It seems easier to remove our shoes and proceed on bare feet. But we both know the dangers— chiggers, sunburned feet, including scorched soles, lurking sand scorpions . . . God knows what else is out there that might come ramping up at us. The wind comes off the ocean from the southwest and is a refreshing foil to the clinging humidity. The beach stretches before us as we trudge south. In the distance, we can see the curve to the west, and the green ocean swells if one does not make the curve. I like this feeling: holding hands with Meeley, the sense of infinite resources, finite humans, and our fragility in the broader sense of the cosmos. The music of the oceans mingled with the wind's caress is a good counterpoint. I bet she doesn't know I'm poetic. Thinks I'm some drunken-ass navigator who got his act straightened out. Well, you tomboyish maiden from hell, get a life! I could ream her, of course. Right here on the island. No one would see us. If we get rescued, it might be a problem later, and she might mention it in her memoirs. Te-he-he! She would, too—don't most women love this 'kiss and tell' stuff? It's all about them. Something was done to their bodies—inserted or with-drawn, deposited or withdrawn, draw your conclusions.

I see all these funny creatures ahead of us, and it thrills me that they don't scurry into the ocean or bury themselves in the sand at the sight of us. Polynesians or Samoans or Aborigines—I don't believe any of those tribes have gotten here yet. Noonan Island, that ought to be the name. No, it must include her, since she's here also. Noonan Earhart Island? Noonan Earhart Atoll?

What the hell?

We'll sort out ownership issues much later.

AS AMELIA RUNS THE STARBOARD engine of the
Electra the next day, our sixth day on the island, we both
know this could be the last time. While the engine sputters,
she transfers all the usable fuel from the left wing to the
right wing. Even at that, it doesn't register on the fuel gauge.
I helped her siphon fuel through the drain valve the day
before, as the increasing list to port and the wing drain
valve's proximity to the sandy floor made the valve almost
inaccessible. We won't be able to insert a slide rule in the
remaining space tomorrow. I drained out roughly two and a
half gallons—all we can get for the increasingly uncertain
future. The fuel left in the tanks wouldn't support further
engine runs.

Amelia makes the usual transmissions while the engine
is running. Her voice is listless, resigned, devoid of hope.
She goes through the motions. "KHAQQ calling Itasca . . ."
She repeats our estimated position for twenty minutes,
stating that she and I are still alive, awaiting rescue. She
reads out the coordinates of the island twice for clarity. The
engine coughs twice and sputters. We wince, knowing the
last fuel is entering the combustion chambers. Still no
response from any rescue vessel, so she shuts down the
engine for what will probably be the last time. The sudden
silence is awful.

She alights from the Electra without another word.
Nothing else will be said. We have three or four days' worth
of transmissions on battery power alone before the lead-
acid juices peter out. Where in the hell is everyone? Sometimes, through atmospheric propagation, we've caught

snatches of conversation between the searchers—especially the airborne planes, since they're up there and have line-of-sight range. Yet nobody answers Amelia's transmissions. Weird.

I can't believe it.

Neither could Amelia.

We still sleep inside the airplane—both on the starboard side now since the ship lists dangerously to port. We sleep head to toe in the cabin space. We sleep with one eye open, hearing the waves dash against the sandy reefs and the whisper and crash of the ocean swell, both a threat and a powerful lullaby. We cuddle in individual blankets. It's not cold enough to warrant the blankets—except early in the morning or after it has rained and the chill spreads from the ocean breeze. Our bodies never touch, as if by unspoken consent. We scrupulously keep it so. Sometimes, our bodies migrate toward one another during the eeriness of night, with the occasional accidental touch. By morning, we are only inches apart.

Something weird happened this morning. I was dreaming, wrestling with demons in my sleep. I'm in a yogi center in Honolulu, sitting opposite the Linue woman. I'm in deep meditation, and so is she, one ankle of each leg resting on the knee of the other leg. She is tall, like Amelia, and has faintly Asiatic features. Since we sit facing each other in this position, I have an unimpeded view of the Linue woman's shaved, clean, oddly protuberant pudendum. I find the sight disturbing. I meditate on those protuberances, the gonadal aspects, and her visible succulence. I can't help myself. I reach over to give her a friendly pat. She pushes me away. "Go away! You know I'm married," the Linue woman says. I yell back at her, "So what? I'm married, too." I thrust my fingers inside her. As expected, she's gushing, and I sense carnal excitement in succulent cavities. I toss and turn to meet her, knowing I will have the sensation of my life.

A shout. Someone shouts.

I wake up, startled. Amelia, who must have woken earlier, is staring at me in horror. The eyes— her eyes were frighteningly huge, two hazel orbs swimming in a sea of white. And I mean huge. The whites were everywhere. I take three seconds to understand the source of her amazement: a rock-solid "morning wood" pushing through my Panama pajamas.

She looks away—not quick enough—and even in my groggy state; I am helpless to do anything. I've never been embarrassed by an erection, and being a sailor, I would say, "Hoist away!" or some such holler, and the hell with that.

Much silence after that. Awkward silence. I am still awed at the enormity of Amelia's eyes, the starkness of the whites which had enlarged to proportions I had never seen before. If you know Amelia you would agree she has narrow squinty eyes, a bit of crow's feet, and more suited for the outback. But now I had glimpsed the raw sensual woman behind all the West-of-the-Rockies ruggedness and it was full head-on allure.

She pretends to go back to sleep. After some time, I do likewise. Linue girl? Where in the heck? Then I remember. I had met Linue women during our first ill-fated attempt at a westward round-the-world trip when we aborted the journey in Honolulu because of the Electra ground-looping. The lady was tall, and resembled Amelia, with a touch of Asian features. I can't explain it, but there it is.

This morning's event doesn't form a wall between us. We go about our normal castaway duties, eating the last remnants of the emergency rations. Then, we go out to fish and look for crabs between switching on the Electra's battery and radio master and trying to contact USCGC *Itasca*. I notice that Amelia avoids eye contact with me. Twice, though, I catch her surreptitiously staring at me, a questioning, faraway look in her eyes.

I cut off the fishnet baggage restraint in the cargo bin for the fishing, then tied it to two sturdy long-branched sticks. It's a crude fishing net. From an angle, it resembles a basketball hoop more than a fishing tool, but it works well. Perhaps because the island is uninhabited and the fish unused to human predation, the fish trust us and swim willingly—almost fondly — into the snare. All I do is wade in to my knees on the sandbank and cast the net. Only twenty minutes of trawling and I have enough catch for the day's food. For land crabs, I pick them off the sand with a stick, careful to avoid those pincer claws. Shellfish and oysters are just as abundant.

After we finish the morning's affairs, and with nothing else left to do before the wilting heat becomes unbearable, I decide I need a shave. I glimpsed my face in the shiny aluminum wing and knew I didn't want the straggly look. I borrow Amelia's compact and stare at the face of a bedraggled stranger. The lean, well-defined face I know now looks worn, haggard, tired—hollowed cheeks made monstrous by an atrocious stubble. Amelia watches as I retrieve my shaving tackle from the airplane.

"See something funny?"

"I see a cagey Father Christmas," Amelia says.

"Father Christmas never gets to shave. I do."

"I'm not stopping you."

I strip to my boxer shorts and carry my tackle to the water's edge. I drop the equipment north of the watermark and swim, immersing my head in the water several times to loosen up the beard. When I surface, I notice Amelia watching with trepidation. She might wonder what would happen if a sudden sea pussy sweeps ol' Fred away, leaving her alone on this infernal island. She'd probably drink glycol from the engine and end it right then. I'm hale and hearty when I leave the water, retrieve my tackle, and wade back into where the ocean is knee deep. I lather generously and apply the tackle to my face. When I'm done, I dip again to wash off foam remnants and leave a squeaky-clean visage. Then a victory swim, coming up on the sandbar and rising like a Visigoth king from the sea, wading ashore in long, loping strides. Well, I'm hoping Amelia sees it that way.

A shadow darkens the water.

Shark! Shark!" Amelia shouts.

I'm startled. I recognize the urgency in her voice and leap out of the water in huge, desperate jumps onto firm sand, swiveling in time to see a dark shape curving into the blue water. The fin-shape is unmistakable.

I stand there, winded. Breathing hard.

"A hammerhead. Damn."

"Could be a tiger shark," she says. "Or a great white."

"Could be." My breath comes out in loud rasps. I focus on her. She is shaking, too. "You saved me. Thanks for the warning."

She waves it aside. "You would have done the same for me. You were already on firm sand, anyway."

"Oh, it could have got me. Make no mistake about that."

"And beach herself? I don't think so."

"You rarely see them until you get hit. They come so fast."

I walk over and hug her. She stiffens. She doesn't offer her cheek or neck, and probably thinks her body is rigid, ironclad. In my arms briefly, she is fragile and malleable, all bones and recessed sinews.

"Thank you, ace."

"You're welcome." She frees herself and runs a hand through her blond locks.

After some painful silence, she says, "Why do I feel intruded upon?"

"Are you?"

"Yes." Her eyes shift. Down, up, and down again.

"You mean that we're no longer alone? Our island bliss now threatened by an additional shark species?"

"What do you think attracted it?"

"Blood. Probably nicked myself shaving. Sharks detect the scent of blood miles away. That was close."

"It was close."

"You shouldn't go near the water during your... Um..."

She smiles brightly at me. "During my monthly indisposition?"

"Yeah."

"Thank you for the great insight, Fred."

I get up and walk away.

Near the shelter, I turn back to look. Her smile is pasty.

13

 MELIA

DAY SEVEN. WE BOTH ARE DESPONDENT. The searchers are either looking in the wrong place or they've scaled down the search. More unsettling, they may have called off the search. I enter the Electra cockpit and enable the master switch. The radio beeps to life, and I listen for several minutes. The airwaves are strangely silent. Just one transmission from a merchant ship on its way to Australia. I am using battery power, so I turn off the master switch again after only a few minutes. Leaving the cockpit, I step outside the airplane.

Right into knee-deep water.

The shock of wet feet sobers me. The Electra has migrated further from the sandbar! That, or the tide has not receded. Maybe it was time to stop turning on the master switch. If water had entered the battery bay, and I switched the battery on....

Something is different about the search now. I know this. I'm sure Fred does as well. Even if we don't discuss it, we hope this afternoon might be different.

Fred walks over to our tree, where we notch how many days we've been marooned on the island. He carves another mark in the trunk.

"What's for breakfast?" he asks.

"Scrambled eggs and toast. Crisp bacon on the side. A mug of steaming hot coffee."

He spins around. Fast.

I smile at his obvious disappointment.

"I smelled the coffee."

"How nice. When we return to civilization Fred, I'll scramble three eggs and serve them with fried sausage and two pieces of toast laced with strawberry jam. And proper coffee. Like Folgers."

"No kidding."

"Nope. I'll serve them to you. Fresh steaming coffee. Squeezed orange juice as well."

"I prefer Maxwell's. Hash browns with my scrambled eggs."

I sit on the makeshift stool Fred has fashioned from twigs and stems. "You mean grits?"

"What?"

"Where I'm from, we call them grits. Anyway, hash browns and grits are two distinct things. It took me a while to get that."

"Where do you think *I'm* from?"

"Would that be Atchison, Kansas?"

He laughs. "You wish."

"Yeah, I know. Chicago, right? The Windy urban slop."

"Not my Chicago. But yeah, whatever you do, never forget that I'm from Chicago. Cook County, Captain Earhart. Got that?"

"I get that you were born right up Capone's alley."

"Something like that."

"That a threat?"

"Nope. Just wondering what's with the 'grits' thing. I'm not from the frickin' South. Alabama or Mississippi or whichever place calls them grits."

Our conversations drift like this, aimless and quite frequent. There's nothing else to talk about. Is there?

Yesterday, I removed the navigator's seat and table from the Electra and brought it to the shelter. We removed all the seats except one from the Electra cabin to save weight. I left the cockpit seats intact. I have the tools with me—I am a rated airplane mechanic, which Fred is not. Now, Fred is sitting on the airplane seat, which looks funny with no back prop. We do what castaways do when there is nothing to do, which is 90 percent of the time—look out at the ocean, dream, let the mind roam. Fred's back is half-turned as he stares at the western horizon as if willing the rescuers to come. If willpower alone could drive armies, I'm sure the search fleet would be steaming full-bore toward our island.

He's not aware I'm examining him. The angular head stares off in the distance. Fred has a magnificent head of hair, and I imagine the black cowlick like an inverted comma on his forehead, its habitual place. His face in profile is almost aristocratic, though as far as I know, his ancestors hadn't arrived with the Mayflower or anything— just regular folks from the suburban Midwest. The nose is aquiline straight, the face narrow, the forehead high and intelligent, and two deep furrows on either side of a strong jaw. His brown flannel shirt with the button-down collar is fading, and he is tieless. He shaved yesterday, but already I can make out dark bristles on his cheeks and chin. If we must stay on this island and Fred's shaving cream runs out and his tackle becomes blunted, it will only be days for Fred to resemble a cardboard version of Robinson Crusoe. Would he be as attractive as now, with his thin-lipped, gaunt face denoting extreme churlishness or light gentrification? It must be somewhere in between, somewhere up on the side of transformation. Fred is too shallow to be aristocratic. I watch the brown-flannel-clad torso moving on each breath, a thick vein on the right side of his neck throbbing. His narrow head cants to the left, amid the formidable black locks, the subtle hint of strength. Fred must have sensed something. He starts to turn.

I am gazing out to sea when his eyes rest on me.

He says something.

"What?"

"I said, 'Dog day, ain't it?'"

I nod, not trusting my voice yet. After a while, "Why do you say that?"

He shrugs. "In the air. Everything's quiet. We're out here listening to the ocean—the music of the ocean. It's weird."

"Weird?"

"Yeah, soulless. If you know what I mean. It's sort of an ongoing kind of celestial music—day in, day out. It seems to have soul, but doesn't. It couldn't care less. Nothing seems to matter beyond the immediate, yet everything matters in some sense." He looks at me. "Do you think I make sense?"

"No, you don't. Celestial? How on earth do you connect the skies to the ocean? You must mean the flow of life, the symphony of the waves in perpetual motion?"

"Yes, I suppose that's what I mean." He reflects. "You also

know that ocean tides and full moons somehow affect people?"

"I am aware, yes."

We listen to the ocean, each aware that something is happening and unsure what. Not just the technical bond between the pilot and her navigator. What started as a minor discomfort at waiting for the expected rescue has turned into alarm. This is the seventh day, and nobody has even acknowledged our transmissions. There's growing horror that, just possibly, the Fates have abandoned us on this island. The only human connection I have on this side of the planet Earth is Fred Noonan. I am married to a prom-inent New York publisher over seven thousand miles away: George might as well be on another planet now.

On a whim, I ask Fred, "What's your wife's name again?"

"Mary Beatrice. The current one. Who wants to know?"

"I do."

"Do you know her?"

"Nope."

"You ever had a divorce?"

"No."

He gives an abrupt laugh.

"I have. With my ex-wife. Worst type you can get into."

"Nice way to talk about a former spouse."

"That's crap, Amy. Utter crap. Sure, we ground pelvises, and she was a good poke even if I say so, but let me tell you something: divorce isn't something you ever want to get into. It turns your life upside-down. It's bad for the soul."

"How long ago was this?"

"Barely—what? — four months." He counted on his fingers. "Yeah. Four months."

"That quick? And you're already married again?"

"She went to Mexico and got a quick one. Juárez." He

shrugged. "I married Beatrice almost immediately after. Fine woman, Bea. We're still in the honeymoon phase." He gave another cough that doubled as laughter. "I'm still finding out things about her, about her body."

"How do you think she is? Beatrice, I mean. You've been missing for seven days now. How do you imagine she'll take it? If we don't get back, I mean."

"I've been missing her for five weeks now," he said. "It's been five weeks since we left Miami."

"That's what I meant. The time you've been away."

"Are you thinking along those lines?"

"We can't pretend otherwise."

He grunted—or laughed. "I prefer to take a more optimistic view."

"You know what I mean. Just from a hypothetical point of view. Come on, Freddie, humor me."

He reflected. "She would miss me," he said. "Fine, gifted woman Mary Bea."

"Do you love her?" I feel a blush coming on and fight it.

He glances sharply at me. "I wouldn't marry her if I didn't. It's hard to spend the rest of your life with someone you didn't love or couldn't stand. That's why Josephine and I went our ways. The marriage ran out of steam."

"That was a stupid question. Sorry."

"Forgiven. Do you love your husband?"

"I do. He's the major love of my life."

He says nothing. Something in my voice?

"He'll be beside himself by now," I go on, "wondering if we're still alive, where we are. I know one thing."

"What's that?"

"Even if the authorities stop looking for us, George Palmer Putnam won't. That's just him. Tenacious."

"That's good to know. Really."

After a lengthy silence, I say, "We made mistakes."

"I knew you'd get to that, eventually. Look, I plotted us down—"

"No, I don't mean that. I mean the radios. We've been transmitting an SOS for six days—now the seventh. And unless I'm dumber than I think I am, they were trying to reply. They transmitted back. It should be easy—ridiculously easy! —for a radioman to triangulate our position. I finally figured it out. They can't plot us with the radio we have because we cut off a good portion of the antenna trailing wire. Back in Lae, do you remember? But we could have plotted their position—the Itasca's position from their transmissions. We didn't know how to use the RDF."

He seems stunned. But it was obvious all along.

"I just couldn't work that radio. It's that simple."

He sits there, breathing hard. "Me neither. Me neither."

"We never expected we'd make an off-airport landing. We never expected that. Every pilot, including myself, knows we're immortal."

"We cooked our goose," he whispers.

"You could say that."

Our gazes meet. The unspoken thought passes between us. We're never, ever going to be found. The Pacific is way too big. This is one tiny island among twenty or more in the area. It's not just looking for a needle in a haystack—there are too many haystacks.

"If they heard any of our transmissions," Fred says, "they should have a reasonable idea of where we landed. In the general vicinity, they—"

"They what?"

"Goddamnit, those are Coast Guard vessels. They should have sonar and whatnot. If they can ping hostile subs, they should be able to home in on a transmission that repeats in the same direction every day."

He is silent. Then his hands get the palsy. The fingers, rather. They shake visibly, and Fred looks down at them and tries to control them. That makes the trembling worse. I look away. Fred gets up and walks toward the treeline.

"Going to pee?"

"Fetch some firewood."

"Be careful, Fred."

"Oh, I shall."

I don't know. Delirium tremens? Fear about our situation?

Still trying to figure out which.

14

F*RED*

DAMN BROAD. WHAT GAME IS SHE PLAYING? The bitch is trying to blame me for us being off course? Heck, I was the chief navigator for Pan Am. You don't get to be that if you're anything but stellar. I charted the Pacific route for them, and it's been a genuine money-spinner for the airline. Maybe she should blame her poor piloting skills. She couldn't hold a heading for ten minutes if her goddamn brassiere depended on it. After that first round-the-world-at-the-equator attempt—the westbound one, when she ground-looped the sumbitch Electra in Honolulu—Paul Mantz, her copilot, pulled out. There were two navigators: myself and Harry Manning. Mantz did the right thing—excused himself from the flight and returned to California. Said he had movie commitments. The hell he did. He couldn't bluff his way out of an Honolulu brothel if he met his parish priest in there. That left me and Manning. Manning had to return to his ship—he's still ship's captain on an oceangoing vessel right now.

I kind of liked Amelia. Still do. That's why I came on the trip in the first place — plus the publicity from the trip, going around the world, would help the navigation school I started. Lend it authenticity. Should have listened to my gut. Two decades on the high seas and you develop a gut meter. Most sea masters do. But heck, I got to give it to her—she did a fine job getting us down in one piece on this island. Mighty, wonderful job. I'm not sure I could have pulled it off myself.

I need a drink so bad I can taste it. Jesus, what's happening to me? The shakes. The weirdest thing. I can't control myself or the craving. What's there to do on this godforsaken island? I can only gather firewood so many times. This place is so verdant and ripe, with hardly any dead branches or rotting trunks. Yeah, I need a drink.

I'll go on over to the airplane. It's now partially submerged in water. She'll go under any day now. The left engine's practically underwater. I was thinking: we got de-icing boots, right? On the wing leading edges. You select them when you're icing up in the clouds, and those black rubber boots expand and contract and break away the ice. You have to wait until there's enough ice accumulation before activating them. This engine is air-cooled—or is it? Never found out. If not, it should have ethylene glycol for de-icing the windshield. Amelia should know. Can't ask her, though. She'll know in an instant what I want it for. Just a sip. All right, maybe a tot. Dilute with a bit of water so I don't pucker off.

I reach the airplane. Clamber over the wing to the overhead hatch. Inside the cockpit, I putter around looking for the reservoir for the glycol. Maybe somewhere behind the instrument panel, inside the radome. After a while, I give up. There's a grapevine rumor that you can fill it from the glare shield panel, through a funnel-like device. Tales of passenger airplanes getting all iced up and the anti-icing and de-icing glycol all gone, and the stewardesses asking the passengers to hand over their whiskeys, so the pilots can pour them down the funnel into the reservoir and keep the airplane wings free of ice to remain airborne. That must be in the DC-2s and DC-3s, maybe the Boeing 340s. Lockheed Electra? If it's there, I haven't seen it.

"Looking for something?"

I didn't hear her come in. She squints her eyes against the sun, highlighting the crow's feet around them. She looks so vulnerable and girlish. Freckles dot her face, almost in a concentric arc around her upturned nose. It's disconcerting, like a puerile teenager, rebuked by her parents but not relenting.

"Not really."

"Something I can help with?"

"Nah."

She studies me for a while. Says nothing.

"Where's the de-icing fluid, Meeley?"

"I took care of it."

"You... took care of it?"

"A precaution. I figured it might get to this."

I am losing my mind. Now I'm angry. "You took care of it! A precaution." I advance on her as I speak. "So you think I want a drink, do you? You think I'm a lush, don't you?"

She stands where she is. "Fred, I—"

"We've been fucking stuck on this fucking misbegotten island for eight fucking days, and you are so fucking proper and prim and ladylike you have deemed it proper to take a shit only once. And you had to hide to do it, for God's sake. Everyone shits, drinks, spits, belches, and occasionally cuts loose a good cheesy fart. Not you. No. You're so prim and proper the fucking ethylene glycol will run off your hide."

"Fred?" I can't describe her face.

"What in hell—"

"Fred? Can I say something?"

"Go ahead."

"I've got to whisper it to you." She moves closer.

"Well, what is it?"

"This." She slaps me hard. I didn't see it coming. Only feel the sting and the scrape of her wedding band on my face.

~

1600 PENNSYLVANIA AVE

ELEANOR ROOSEVELT SAT DOWN across the Oval Office desk. She fingered the ornate oak, remembering that the wood came from the superannuated timbers of HMS Resolute, a gift from Queen Victoria to Rutherford B. Hayes. She looked up again at her husband.

"Have they found Amelia, Frank? Don't tell me you will order them to quit searching for her."

"For them, my dear," Roosevelt said. "There are two of them, not just your Amelia."

"Yes, the navigator man, Allred... whatever his name is."

"Fred. Frederick Goodman." The president pushed his monocle back to the preferred position over his eye. "The cost to the taxpayers, my dear. We can't continue indefinitely. We've committed sizable resources, and so has

Australia. The British are helping where they can. But if we don't find them, we must pull the plug at some point."

"Noonan. Her navigator's name is Frederick Noonan."

"What?"

"I can't believe you'd leave them out there to die," said the First Lady.

"What was that, dear?"

"You'll check with me before you stop the search, won't you? I want to make sure they have exhausted all avenues. We can't pull off the troops on that poor woman out there shivering in the middle of the Pacific, waiting for us, knowing in her heart that we'll come. This is America."

The president grunted. He adjusted his monocle.

"You hear me, dear?"

"I heard."

"Don't forget what I said." The first lady walked toward the door. Her secretary stood poised in the doorway, a steno pad clutched to her breast, feigning innocence. She disappeared down the hallway behind Mrs. Roosevelt.

15

A MELIA

I MISS GEORGE. I DO. HE'S ALWAYS BEEN comforting, a manly presence. From the time he chose me to be the first woman to fly across the Atlantic back in 1932 (he didn't tell me then I was to be a passenger!) until we kissed goodbye on my way to Miami in 1937 to begin the eastbound round-the-world trip, he's always given me that sense of power, of being in control. I'm sure George is out there leading the search for us. He'll be in charge, directing things, moving the troops, funding the extended search.

Fred is not in good shape. He's had nothing to drink since we've been on this island. His hands shake a lot. The DTs? No idea. It's not like he's acute; I've seen much worse. The shaking should disappear with time. The urge will be there for a while.

Maybe I'm just angry with Fred. He got our navigation

all screwed up. There, I've said it. I should have stuck with Paul Mantz—got George to plead, cajole, whatever it took to get Paul to come with me on this trip. The navigation may have yielded better results. Somehow, Fred screwed up this sector. The maps look funny. Too many uncharted areas. It's not like I was flying the Amazon or anything. I'm the pilot on this flight, so I get the blame for the flight going wrong, but Fred must share the blame.

No privacy on this island. Here we are in the remotest part of the Pacific, two castaways on an unknown island. We should have absolute privacy, but we don't. We are in constant view of one another. I can't lose sight of him for more than a few minutes, and neither can he of me. Strange thing. A woman needs absolute privacy sometimes. Getting on me. I need to stretch my labia, rub my devil's doorbell a bit, do things normal people do. Didn't expect that bit about the labia from me, did you, reader? Did you forget I'm an Atchison, Kansas, girl? The farm is a great learning place, all those animals and haystacks. People have considered me a women's leader since I began pioneering aviation activities. Being a leader applies in more ways than one! Ask Gertrude Stein. Or Dorothy Parker. I know where my clit is, and I tell you, it has gotten no exercise since we got deposited on this remote island. And Fred's roguish man smell intrudes sometimes, and I know it triggers my hormones. A woman, even a famous aviatrix, does what she must do.

I go back to the shelter and get inside the leafy enclosure. Some relief from the heat. I can see Fred out by the water's edge. By unspoken agreement, we don't look whenever the other is bathing. The night would be ideal, but we are both afraid of entering the ocean and being seized by some strange nocturnal creature. So we bathe in the daytime; this is the third time Fred is doing it in five days. I suspect this is because of the insufferable tropical heat. I do it daily. Fred gets ripe in this humid tropical air, and I have no desire to be whiffy like him. I see him through the rafters of the shelter on the sandbar; his clothes tucked out of reach of the swinging tide. He's baby naked and knee-deep in the ocean, scooping water onto his body, lathering his tall, bony physique with what remains of the bath soap from my suit-case. After this, he dips into the water and does a vigorous breaststroke up and down the shoreline, never venturing far into the water. I think he's afraid of box jellyfish or some-thing. The advantage is that the water is crystal clear over the white sands of the atoll, so you should be able to see any approaching creature in time to vamoose.

Anyway, the point is I have privacy for the moment. I've discarded the flight overalls because of the heat, so I've been wearing my white-and-red print dress. The one with the hem that stops about half a foot from my ankles. Many people see my photos where I always wear flight gear, goggles, a flight suit, and a scarf. It surprises them to see me in a dress; I've noticed this in my interactions with the press and citizenry.

My fingers get busy. My effluvium reaches me, interest-ing, suffusing, curiously mephitic. Given our major fish and crab diet, not surprising. A lady's orifice is self-cleansing anyhow. I'm copiously wet down there. I engorge my happy button to thrice its normal size, while my nipples erect. I try to imagine George doing this to me. It doesn't work. My thoughts turn to Fred. Again, it is all wrong. The excitement peters off. Yeah, okay. Let's try Gene Vidal. Bingo! The tempo picks up; I feel the rush. It's coming. I arch my back and oh, oh, oh!

I squeeze out three more earth-shakers before Fred finishes his noontime swim.

Fred returns after I've tidied myself up and pretends to be studying the survival booklet. He pauses as he enters the shelter. He wrinkles his nose, gives me a sharp look.

"You all right?"

"I am. Why?"

"You looked flushed."

"We are somewhere around the equator, Fred. Perhaps I should look white?"

"You drive a hard bargain, lady."

"I love to do that, Mister Sailor. What's with your beeswax?"

"Nothing. I feel zapped."

"Why would that be?"

"I don't know. I feel like zapping something. Anything, so long as it remains zapped after I zap it."

"You're not making sense."

"This remote island sure is getting to me. I feel it."

"I got an idea. Go and zap a Jap whore. East is that way." I point him the way.

His pale blue eyes light up. "A Jap whore? Where'd that come from? See any around here?"

"Came from the top of my head," I tell him.

"Couldn't be any Jap zaps around here. We're some-where between the British Solomon Islands and the Phoenix Islands. Japs are way up north and to the east. I know I got my orientation right."

"Okay, Fred."

He gives me another weird look, and shrugs. His hair looks like a mop just out of the bucket. You never towel yourself on this island. You'll dry soon enough. The torpid heat does a better job. He picks up the stick to which we've lashed my pearl-handled knife, turning it into a makeshift spear. "I'm going fishing," he says, looking lost.

"I was just wondering," I say, "if I should build a net for us. Just haven't got around to it."

"Want me to make one?"

"We should have, ages ago. We just knew they would rescue us any minute. Never thought we'd still be out here this long."

"I saw some schools of bright-colored fish. Seems they were having a field day."

He steals another rueful glance at me, undecided about something. His trouser pleats has an odd jut, and he's twisted up like someone shielding a bad ague.

Fred's missing Mary Bea a lot.

I yawn as he leaves. That was a good punishment for him. Let him stew in his semen. I'll swim in mine, thank you. Estrogen, I mean. Let's see who needs it more, who gets that hangdog look of absolute yearning that every woman knows too well.

～

USCGC ITASCA

"'TION!"

The Third Mate's yell got the entire room scrambling to their feet

The captain burst in and nodded absently. "Ease." He peered over the radioman's shoulder. "Anything yet on the Electra?"

"We're getting transmissions again, sir," said the radioman. "We can't triangulate or get a fix on her. We just can't, sir."

"What we talked about the other day?"

"Yes, sir."

"What's your gut tell you?"

"My hunch, sir, is they're using the low frequency radio?"

"HF radio?"

"Yes sir. But it's impossible to get a fix on whoever's transmitting. It's just not possible—at least not with the poor quality of the transmitter. I bet the antenna wire is too short—assuming they're still airborne, which, again, is impossible."

"Out of the question, Sparky. They're missing six—what, seven-- days now? Not a chance. Unless they landed on some island and transmitted from there."

"I agree, sir."

"Are you monitoring the VHF emergency frequency?"

The petty officer pointed to a band of switches on the left side. "We've got 121.5 permanent on one radio."

The captain nodded. Every ship at sea monitored the emergency frequency 121.5.

Standard protocol.

The petty went on, "Also on the Hotel Fox emergency frequency, as she has made transmissions on that one. But no way to fix her—just not possible, sir."

The captain said, "Why would they dispatch on a long over-water trip like this and not have the proper radio equipment? Would there be a technical reason for that?"

"To save weight, maybe. I'd carry more gas to stretch my range and leave a few things behind, sir."

"But not the essential radio."

"They took the wrong one, sir. A VHF radio would have been better for direction finding. Maybe they had one on board, and it packed up. Since Nukumanu we've only received their transmissions, they haven't received ours. All the frequencies used since departure have been on Hotel Fox."

"They couldn't possibly be alive," the captain mused. "If

they ditched successfully ... seven days on the open ocean. Transmitting from a raft radio all this time?" He shook his head. "Batteries should have run down."

"Aye, sir," said the petty officer. "No way they'd be making these strong transmissions from an emergency radio. The frequency and wavelength signature of those transmissions appear to be from a normal ship's radio."

The captain couldn't hide his puzzlement. "Our kind of ship? Our radios?"

"Aye, sir. The signature could be maritime or aviation. The signal strength shows it could not be from a raft. Sir."

"Some ship's radioman being mischievous, or what?"

"Could be, sir. Lots of ships and airplanes out there involved in the search. The chatter is continuous, lots of static. Squelch, too. The signal, when it comes, is consistent. Only in the daytime, two or three times at night—moonlit nights, I noticed—and the transmissions last about twenty to thirty minutes before the station signs off. Strange."

"Petty, explain what you mean by 'signs off.'"

"Like, go off the air, sir."

"Can we get a fix on the source?"

"Negative, sir. I've tried. The other ships have tried. No luck. Same problem. Source radio is not the type from which we can build a fix. If it's the Electra, they're transmitting on Hotel Fox. If they could even just once use VHF, we'd get a tracer on them, find them. The ditching could have disabled the radio, or they left it behind at takeoff."

"I see." The commander's face furrowed in thought. He turned to the second petty officer. "Take dictation."

The man scrambled for pen and paper. "Go ahead, sir."

"USCGC ITASCA to CINCPACFLT. Message Log One-Eight slash Earhart slash Noonan. Request check origin of flight Lae, Papua New Guinea. Possible Electra left crucial radio behind. Victor Hotel Fox radio. Over. Unable to gain fixes on rogue transmissions. Over. Advise ASAP. USCGC ITASCA. Over and out."

The second petty officer read back the telegram to the captain's satisfaction. As the captain headed for the door, the third petty shouted, "A'tion!"

"Carry on," barked the captain over his shoulder.

16

A MELIA

WE SPEARFISH IN A CLEAR WATER lagoon near the beached Electra. We use my bone-handled pocketknife strapped to the end of a sturdy tree branch. Awkward, but it works. There's a heart-stopping moment when the knife comes loose, drops to the sandy bottom. Fred dives under, makes a grab, loses it, and the knife floats away with the partial tide that had come crashing in, mucking the waters. Fred scrabbles desperately in all directions until some part of his body encounters the knife which he corrals.

That was not funny at all. We need that knife.

So now we are careful to fish in calm, transparent water —Fred doing the fishing, while I keep watching for shark fins or the flat, ominous cape of a stingray shadow. We alternate positions. We collect shellfish, oysters, and fish we speared into a makeshift bag woven from the airplane's cargo hold tarpaulin. Fish aren't too enthusiastic about coming close to the beach and are experts at darting away from our improvised spear. We learn to thrust ahead or behind or athwart the fish, guessing which way it would dart. Mostly we fail. On average, we snag one fish per fifty or sixty thrusts.

The wave comes and there are no breakers on the atoll except the rock on which the island stands, which appears to be of volcanic origin. The atoll consists primarily of sandy loam and fauna populating the flat apex of an age-long formation. The waves get bigger and threatening. We cease fishing then. The wind rises, frothing, the submerged rock slowing its momentum, whilst the top-water muddies and foams. We gather our paltry catch for the day: three tropical carp or kingfish and a trapezoid-shaped multicolored species we couldn't identify, flat like a pancake, with oversized fins. We head back to the shelter.

I stop.

Fred sees it too and stops. The third wave, like a rolling hillside, approaches the island. It resembles one of those spectacular waves you see in the Hawaii islands, but this is bigger, more threatening. Already the waters on the beach dance in anticipation. The Electra waltzes in the water. We scramble further inland, clinging to our precious cargo, then clamber up a tree, knocking away several fierce-looking tree crabs in haste. No time to run to the opposite side of the island. No time at all.

The wave hits, her power mitigated by the atoll's underwater rock fortress. It slams the Electra, juggling it like a cork in a bathtub. The waterline comes about four feet up the tree trunk. We cling to our leafy perch in fear, wearing our Mae West in case we get dragged into the water. The monster lifts the Electra, tosses it about, an aluminum rag-doll. There would be several more waves after this one, and the sky has that ominous, dark-brown cast that heralds a squall. But the rain doesn't fall as the waves continue to lash the atoll. Some raindrops plop on us from the periphery of the inky clouds. But the thunder and lightning and the high winds crash less than a mile away. A typical conventional rainfall; not much rain where we are but raining like the devil's bath half a mile away.

When the wind and the waves recede, our beloved steed, the silver-and-red Electra, is half-submerged at a crazy tilt some sixty yards from the shore. Nothing we do would bring it back.

Nothing.

November Romeo 16020 is gone forever.

"She's gone," Fred whispers. "She's gone."

I don't quite hear him. I'm in a trance. The Electra bobs in the waves. Each movement takes the ship further and deeper into the ocean. I imagine a flooded cabin, the Electra's precious instruments sinking to the bottom of the reef. The twin-tail boom is underwater, some red paint visible through the clear green of the reef atoll. In time the wreck would host its unique ecosystem.

We are now irrevocably, pitifully alone. The Lockheed Electra somehow shielded us from total despair—a feeling that in future somehow, the bird could be floated, rolled onto a flat stretch, fueled up, and flown away. Not now. As in Honolulu, the airplane might have been hauled aboard the rescue vessel, and shipped to Australia or back to the US mainland. We have flown over three-quarters of the way on this round-the-world attempt. The Electra faithfully transported us the entire distance, through heat and dust and unusually stormy weather along the equator. Around massive cumulonimbus and boiling thunderheads, over desert and ocean, hills and vales, and around mountains and some of the most inhospitable terrain this side of Hell. From Miami to Puerto Rico to South America, then on to Africa, the Middle East, India, Asia, Indonesia, Australia, then Papua New Guinea, to our present position. The Electra—on whose proud silvery wings we soared and slipped the earth's surly bonds—now suffers the indignity of listing on her side, submerged, broken, shifted by the tides, a sunken relic.

I hang the fish bag on a tree branch. I need both hands to steady myself on the tree limb I'm sitting on. The tears come freely. I don't know for how long I sit in that position. Fred says nothing. He understands. His gaze is far away, even beyond the green ocean swells. I weep for my baby, my airplane. I've never had a biological child. This is the closest I've come to having one, bonding with a mesh of sheet aluminum and stringers and propellers and grease, the smell of cockpit instruments and electric wiring, of avgas and oil tar.

 MELIA

THE LAND CRABS ARE EVERYWHERE. I mean everywhere. Whenever I look up, I see them clawing across the sand or climbing or descending a tree. Sometimes you have to beat them back with a stick. They've never had human visitors, not recently anyway, so they don't fear us or understand that we don't want them, except as food. Even then, I got nauseous the first time we ate a land crab and so did Fred. Fred says most land crabs are safe to eat, but some of them may have consumed toxic plants or algae, and that would by default render them toxic. So we eat them only sparingly. The crabs soon learn to avoid our little shelter— not unless they want to get their crustacean shells smashed in, courtesy of the enormous stone Fred uses during one of his tempers. We build a fire once a day to cook our food.

The hot embers and ashes linger for half the day and keep them away from our makeshift shelter of twines and leaf kelp.

We shall run out of matches soon enough. I can't imagine not being able to start fires to cook with. We'd better come up with other fire-starting ideas or we would soon eat sushi and raw turtle salad until we drop.

Mechanically, I use the pearl-handled pocketknife to carve another notch on the tree. This tells us it's our ninth day on this island. Hard to believe. Nine days. And they haven't found us yet? Airplanes have shrunk the world, no doubt about that, but we seem to have landed on the most desolate spot in the middle of the Pacific. I mean, it's not like we're in the South Pole or anything. Amundsen, Scott, those pioneers... they found them, or their bodies. And we're on an island on which Fred tells me a modern steamer—the SS *Norwich City*—ran aground. Fred tells me her wreck is charted in maritime archives. Just what is going on with the supposed rescuers?

Eleanor, are you listening?

Hey, it's me, Amelia. I'm trying to communicate with you via telepathy. Can you read me? Do you read me, Eleanor? We need your help. We're out here in mid-Pacific and I'm thinking this is no longer a joke—that the Coast Guard may never find us, ever. Better get your husband Mr. President to juice up the troops. We can't last out here much longer.

Fred and I speak little. We're lost in our thoughts. That we have just lost our only means of communicating with the outside world weighs on us. The Electra extended ourselves —our reach to the searchers and, by extension, to the rest of the world. We can only hope that they copied our last position reports and might still home in on us or triangulate and find us. It's not such a long shot; we just can't understand why they haven't done so already.

The surf is receding. The water no longer laps at the base of the trees and is not threatening to wash away our camp. In this climate, everything—soil and shrubbery included — dries quickly, and by afternoon it's difficult to see any signs of the monstrous wave that swamped us this morning. I pick at the fish I have grilled over the open fire, and Fred is trying his hand at another mollusk. I think he eats up to six of those things daily. Oysters. Yuck! Can't blame him, though. Even to me, they have lost the icky factor, and I just might consider eating one of those quaint birds that pick young turtles off the beach when the reptiles molt. I believe the mother turtles lay eggs beneath the sand on the beach. When the hatchlings are a few days old, they make what seems to be a mandatory journey from their beach dugout to the ocean. Some pristine force of nature drives them, though I cannot guess which. Under the sand, while they incubate, they are safe from nearly all predators. When they hatch, they would still be safe if they would just remain underground but come out they must and make the perilous journey to the water. Perilous because during molting season the predators—birds and other big lizards— are waiting to grab them. It's only a quick hop from their beach dugout to the safety of the waters, perhaps twenty steps for an average human, but I'd say only about 15 to 20 percent of the baby turtles make it to the water. Waiting predators gobble up the rest. Even in the water, a few fish specialize in snatching baby turtles, so their ranks deplete further. But they're hatched in many batches, so nature helps in this way by volume. Once they make it past this stage and grow their armor carapace, they can live to be a hundred years old.

All this thinking about losing our last means of contact with the outside world depresses me. By late evening, after sitting around listlessly listening to the music of the ocean and imagining sounds of airplane engines in the sky, I am sick with a terror of the unknown.

If we can just hang on a few more days, surely they will find us.

I am supposed to be a well-known figure and pioneer aviatrix—even if I brag, which I do not—and it seems inconceivable to me that my husband and my friends and the entire aviation community, which is strong and loyal, would stop short of doing everything possible to locate Fred and me. All this rumination gives me a queasy stomach—or rather, an uneasy one—and I must go to the toilet. Since our modest poop bucket in the Electra is no more, I have no choice other than to do the deed in the bushes nearby. Fred is off sharpening the bone-handled knife with two stones, so I figure I'll have some privacy. I grab some toilet paper from the last roll rescued from the Electra and head for the bushes in my rubber thongs. Straight into the path of the flickering forked tongue and red belly of the biggest iguana I've ever seen.

Fred says later that I screamed like a banshee. I recall little of anything. By the time I've calmed down, the lizard is a dismembered, bloody mess, belly up in the way of dead monitor lizards, and Fred is bending over me. The stick with which he'd beaten the iguana is itself in several pieces. He says he pushed me aside (I froze in shock) when he rushed to attack the iguana. "Damned aggressive thing," he says. "Tried to bite me. Had to beat it to death. Tough hide, too."

"I didn't know they had iguanas here."

He gives me a strange look. "That's a monitor lizard. A big one."

"Could you tell?"

"Hell, I could."

"How?"

"Iguanas have large spines on the back." He takes my hand. "Come on."

He leads me toward a clearer patch of the atoll.

"There may be more of them," I whisper, still not quite with my breath yet.

"Yes. But they're solitary, if I remember correctly. There may be others, but probably on the other side of the atoll."

"That one looked like a Gila monster. That was a close one, Fred."

"Not really. They have a vicious bite that can fester. The real danger is from the infection that follows. But they're only aggressive if attacked. They generally avoid humans."

"This one has probably never seen a human."

Fred studies me. "You okay?"

"I am."

"Take a deep breath," he says. "Gather yourself. Then we'll go take a pee."

"We?"

"Didn't I tell you? You've got company now."

"Fred, I know you've been an angel about this, but—"

"There might be others like him—" He gestures toward the dead lizard. "Would you?"

I stare at the dead lizard.

That settles it.

He takes hold of my hand. I shake it off angrily. The notion I screamed at the sight of a lizard unsettles me. I find it impossible to be kind to myself. A weakness of any kind disgusts me. Hatred of cruelty to animals or humans I do not consider a weakness. The lizard just looked so... frightening, with its forked tongue and red underbelly. Like some ancient mini-dragon. It's dusk now, the sun a pale red blob smack on the western horizon. Breezy, not cold. Just pleasant. I consider myself a liberated woman, always have, but if my suffragettes were around to witness Fred leading me inside the bush so I can do a bowel movement, I would die of shame. Yet I must do it or risk a messier one later. Any job done too close to the shelter would haunt us around the clock. So I have to bury the darn thing. Truth is, I wouldn't want Fred walking around, navigating my poop dump, and thinking to himself, "There's Amelia's deposit" or something like that. I don't think I would want anything like that connected with me. Yeah, we've all done it since birth, and I believe my dad once told me that he was the one to change my first diaper after my birth.

This island is a world away from worlds!

After the lizard, I develop a curious disregard for propriety. My inhibitions vanish. The thought of stepping on a monitor lizard or land crab frightens me beyond measure. Or worse, a snake. In the gathering dusk, I squat down to do my business. I haven't squatted like this for years, except at Girl Scout camp, and in Japan, where I believe it's the only way they do it in their unorthodox toilets. I know how it's done. Fred stands some distance away, looking everywhere else but at me. I'm sure he hears the hissing sound, and the cathartic plops into the sagebrush. The perfect gentleman never blanches or chuckles. He can't even use a cigarette to lighten his mood because he ran out some days ago. His hand tremor is still there—it worsens when he consciously tries to control it.

I am almost done when I hear some scuttling underbrush.

"Fred!"

He scoots over, braving the stench.

"You okay?"

I point vaguely. "Something moved. In that bush!"

He looks around, hunting for the culprit. He pokes around with his foot. This is dangerous, and I don't like him doing it. We have no antivenin, so if he gets bitten by a venomous snake, he will die. From my little knowledge of equatorial islands, most of the snakes on the island have lethal bites.

"I see nothing," he says.

"Where were you when I had my encounter?" I say, just to make conversation.

"Over by the inside lagoon catching shellfish. Snagged a few."

"You did?"

"Yep. We'll head on over after you finish and get them inside the pot."

Almost done now. When nothing comes out after another minute, I'm done. For now.

Clean-up time. I wrinkle the tissue and wipe front to back as we've been taught. I do it twice, thrice to be sure I've got everything and stick the tissue on the pile. I peer down at the mound, which looks like a misplaced crown from some Halloween ghoul.

Tut, tut. The horrors of being a castaway.

Worse challenges for female castaways.

"Better throw some leaves, some soil over the stuff," Fred says. "Flies will have a field day in the morning."

"Maybe the dung beetles will move it before morning," I say. "Do they have dung beetles here?"

I extend my left arm, and he grabs it. Just to help me up. No entitlement there. He hangs onto my hand, but I wrestle it off him. I don't need the fragile damsel-in-distress bit.

"Dung beetles?" He shrugs. "Heck, I don't know." His

voice sounds hoarse and strained. For a second I wonder if I've said something bad.

He's right. I shuffle some dead leaves over the poop pile using my feet.

"I've got to wash my hands," I say. "In any pool of water."

He isn't looking at me at all. Something's happening to him, and I hope it's not the tremors again. He turns his body away from me. My poop stink isn't too encouraging. I hike up my thrift-store skirt and lead the way up the brief trip to the shallow waters of the island lagoon. Fred scoots up alongside and seizes my hand again as we navigate the clearing and come out on the natural path that leads to the lagoon. But he strikes a right turn and heads for the ocean sands. I'm confused for a moment. Did he see something on the path to the lagoon? A large lizard or snake? Something he'd rather I didn't see?

"Fred?"

He doesn't answer. His steps are quick and purposeful. His grip on my arm is firm, rock firm, and I quicken my steps to keep up. It agitates him. Whatever the reason, he must be quite frightened of it. I glance at his face. He stares straight ahead.

"Fred? I thought you said... the lagoon fish."

He doesn't answer.

"It's the other way. Where are we going?"

He's not talking. Won't even look at me. I steal another glance at him. His face is not Fred's face—his features are rigid, his eyes staring straight ahead, a dark vein throbbing in his right temple. I can't even guess what this is all about. On a whim, I glance down at the pleat of his trousers and everything becomes clear at once. They distend at least six inches, sticking out grotesquely, making a mockery of West Coast tailoring standards, turning his once-proud Macy's trousers into an odd-angle pantaloon. I try to pull away, but his grip is an iron vice. He pulls me inside the shelter roughly. I panic, fearing what might be next.

"I don't believe this! What do you think you're doing?"

My navigator is deaf.

Fred Noonan, please tell me this is not happening.

18

F*RED*

I MUST WAKE HER UP. SHE'S BEEN screaming.

"Wh-What?" Her eyes dart wildly. "What happened?"

I tell her gently. "You were having a nightmare. You seemed quite upset about something."

She stares at me, uncomprehending. Or trying to comprehend.

"Was it bad?"

She blushes. Two prime spots of red. "Oh."

"Frightful dream?"

"Yes." The wildness comes into her eyes again. "Fred, I...I didn't think it was a dream. So real."

"Want to tell me about it?"

She gazes into the distance.

"You okay, Amy?"

"It was a dreadful dream Fred, it was about us. So real."

"You could share if it makes you feel better."

"I don't think we will ever leave this island. The dream was so real."

"Well, tell me."

She isn't talking.

FINDING WATER PURE ENOUGH TO drink is a problem. We both know it. It has rained little since we became castaways. Our water cache, stored in water bottles from the Electra, has diminished to low levels. Now we must ration potable water. Difficult when your principal diet comprises oysters and fish. Whilst serving in the British Navy years ago, I remember reading a survival manual that set out means of collecting condensed water droplets overnight. I think I could modify one technique by using conch shells, or any container capable of catching paltry amounts of water. Overnight, coalesced water drops into the oyster shell or bottle beneath. Slow and frustrating, but when faced with an unquenchable thirst, this bit is much better than nothing. We also set out to hunt for edible fruits, berries, and flowers, with the little I remember from the manual.

"Look for blueberries, dark purple berries, or the like. They're safe. Boysenberries will be just fine."

Amelia squints. "Do they have those here? I thought they only grow in temperate climates."

"Let's look, anyway. We may find something."

It's as if she didn't have that dream. And I didn't have mine.

That night we share the same side of the shelter tarpaulin. We used to sleep apart, as if by unwritten code—

she on the tarpaulin, me on the dry bed leaves atop a burlap sack we used as a disposal bag in the Electra. In the morning, when the first rays of the sun illuminate the shelter, I wake up to another strong erection. These infernal things have a mind of their own. I nudge my body against hers by accident; I think. She responds instinctively, absently, then recoils.

She rolls over, weaves her body farther away from me. She has small breasts, almost boyish. I risk a peek at her face. She's shut her eyes tight. I see determination there. The blond eyelashes look eerie in the half-light. Her towhead, unkempt, is thrown back, her mouth slow-drooling. The famous gap-tooth is brown-stained. The freckled nose angles upward, straight and aristocratic, revealing brown nose hair I haven't noticed before. She looks helpless, and I have the odd impression that moving in on her would be akin to foisting myself on someone much younger.

Well, about time I had my dream event.

I must dismiss the innocence. I mean, she's a married woman? There could be innocence in absolute fidelity after marriage. I have no one to take of insistent Wood, so I must dream, fantasize. I crush my lips on hers, my tongue probing, sliding in and out, seeking the toothy gap. She lets me roll my tongue, try to slide it in between the gap. The men she's known throughout her life probably tried that at least once. Did Gene Vidal leap through the gap? It's smaller than everybody thinks. She almost smiles as I experiment with it. Her breath spools on my face, dank, fishy. Same as mine, perhaps—we are on the same diet.

I turn my attention to her nose, as she knew I would. I try to bite off the tip of her nose. All her lovers did that before, I'm sure. Her upturned nose does all kinds of things to me she would never understand. I keep my bite gentle, hesitant, then grip hard until she tells me with a jerk it's painful. I stop. I suck her nostrils with gusto. Where there was no mucus or phlegm before, I excavate some crud deep inside using my mouth and an index finger. My member nudges her thighs, her pelvis, rod-like. She reaches out to determine. Her fingers close around a massive shaft, steel-hard. Mine. Though a bit alarmed, she holds on, not wishing to let go such huge testimony to her desirability. Her thumb flicks over the frenulum, caressing it. My firmness remains ramrod stiff, a naval baton.

I now focus on her neck. She has a lovely, slender neck, another draw, and I won't disappoint. She clings to me, licks my forehead, traces her index finger over the ridge which is a scar above my right eyebrow. A legacy of my sailing days. I've noticed over the years women like touching my scar. I move from her neck, after giving her a satisfactory hickey-to-be. I kiss the space between her breasts, down to her navel, suck it, plugged her belly button with my thumb. Down lower to more sensitive areas. She jerks when my rough three-day stubble contacts her tight-woven mons hair. I part her legs, wider than she thinks necessary. She understands when my mouth descends on her.

She's shocked, I can see. People know her as a liberated woman, but she doesn't think it's hygienic down there. I can tell from the way she flinches, waiting for me to rise in disgust after the first few seconds. Instead, I do the opposite. Go for it with gusto. I flick my tongue over everything in there, drinking it in, feeding on it, inhaling her nether regions. Her clit stands erect, pulsating, faced with my relentless assault. She makes sounds she didn't know she was capable of. I work hard for what seems forever. Then she could feel it coming, and both her hands come down, pinning my head to her groin. She drives her pelvis into my face. EAT ME, goddamnit, Fred, EAT ME! She knows I can hardly breathe in that position; she doesn't care anymore. All she wants is for me to be there, doing what I'm doing for as long as she can hold out. I oblige her, obedient navigator that I am. She whoops and comes in my face, thighs clamping hard, in convulsive spasms, her pelvis jerking uncontrollably as she comes and comes again.

And again.

End of dream, Fred. Now wake up, you sonofabitch.

I am the one that has squirted.

Bad, nasty dream. Oddly pleasant and satisfying though.

AMELIA LEADS THE HUNT AGAIN FOR edible berries. She's too bossy, opinionated, unfeminine. I could hate her if I put my mind to it. We note the sun's position for orientation before setting out. I follow her around the island, not bothering to put on fresh clothes. Who else on the island to worry about the reek? Amelia cradles a one-yard solid club that she can swing freely at anything she deems a threat. I follow with the bone-handled knife and another club.

"We won't go inside the brush much," she says. "Safer all 'round. Seeing we don't have antivenin. Keep a sharp lookout, will you, Fred?"

"Sure thing."

"Let me get this right. If we see berries of any color, before eating we should squeeze the juice on our arm. Make a minor cut before? If there's a reaction, it's not edible. If no reaction, it's a good bet for eating?"

"That's what I remember the survival manual said."

Our search yields nothing but a few coconut husks fallen from trees. Massive coconut crabs and their land crab cousins appear to be the main denizens of the island. There are also migrating white birds of a species neither of us could identify, using the island as a transit stop on their great migratory routes. I guessed the birds are seagulls, yet their bills appear shorter. A dense bunch of them cluster on the sandbar. Their screeching rises above the sounds of the ocean lapping the sandbar, a continuous hum and wheedle that, if you didn't know what it was, would be unsettling.

I have an idea. The birds are so closely bunched there's no way I could miss. I find a low-hanging tree branch and snap it down to the length of a sturdy baton. I creep up to within fifteen feet of the birds. I'm sure the birds see me. They are aware of me and don't seem overly concerned. I draw back my right hand and wait. I hurl the stick with ferocious force at the center of the bunch. It cripples one bird, another staggers skyward dragging a foot and wing. The others rise as one bunch and fly to the opposite end of the island. I walk over to the crippled bird which is dancing in circles, wondering why her once dependable wings could no longer lift her into the skies and to safety. I dispatch the bird with two blows from the homemade spear. I wonder how far the bird dragging its foot has gone.

Amelia drags the seagull back to the shelter for lunch. No wild berries of any kind found. So much for the sailor's survival manual.

19

M *ANHATTAN, NY.*

THE PRESS CONFERENCE HELD IN A conference
room at the New York office of Brewer & Warren publishers.
The wire agencies, Reuters, and AP were there, as were the
nationals and the locals. Walter Winchell was among the
newsmen who poked microphones at the podium. Behind
the table clad in gray worsted three-piece suit sat George
Putnam. Beside him sat the vice president of Brewer &
Warren, next to Gene Vidal, an aeronautics instructor at
West Point. The mayor of New York glowered next to Vidal.
Behind them stood several important state and national
figures. Some newsmen had erroneously gone to the
Manhattan offices of G. P. Putnam & Sons, thinking that was
the venue.

"No, we have not found my wife and her navigator,"
Putnam says in response to a reporter's question. Putnam is

tall, patrician, bespectacled, and about him is the assured, subdued air of old money. "The US Navy and the US Coast Guard are doing their best. The White House says they have nine ships and sixty-six airplanes involved in the search. I am grateful to President Roosevelt and to our men and women in the navy and coast guard who are out looking for my wife and her navigator."

"Mr. Putnam—"

"Sir! — "

"Mr. Putnam, could you confirm—"

Putnam raised a hand. "One at a time, please. Yes, Mr. Winchell?"

The CBS anchor said, "There's been no word at all? No word from your wife or her navigator?"

"I don't understand you, Walter. Where would the word come from?"

"Our sources tell us there have been strange transmissions from around the area where Amelia Earhart and her navigator went down. Have they investigated those radio transmissions, and if not, why not?"

"Which sources?" Putnam's voice is acid. He adds in a softer tone, "The Itasca is there, and yes, I believe they have been receiving transmissions for some days now, from an unknown source. That source could be my wife and Fred. I sincerely hope so. I'm informed that the radio operators onboard the search ships have identified them and labeled them as 'rogue' transmissions."

"Rogue?"

"I believe that is the term they used."

"The so-called transmissions—was it Amelia's voice? I presume they would know if it was a woman speaking?"

"I presume they would know." Putnam locked eyes with Winchell. The man was a bulldog. "They must have investigated those calls to come up with the idea that the calls were bogus. I'm not a seaman, nor a radioman. But I have full confidence in the men who man our ships and airplanes, and if they determine that my wife cannot possibly be alive after ditching in the Pacific Ocean four days ago... well, that would be their opinion." He shrugged his massive shoulders. "I am prepared to challenge such findings. I know Amelia well. If anyone could pull off a ditching in the middle of the Central Pacific and survive, I'd lay bets on my wife."

Putnam moved aside to let Gene Vidal take the podium.

Vidal cleared his throat. "President Roosevelt has deployed enormous assets in the area that have no equal in recent memory. I can tell you we have involved no less than sixty airplanes in the search for the Electra. Even two Japanese naval ships are helping in the search. Every square grid of ocean in that area is being gone over with a fine-tooth comb. If they're still alive, and we sincerely hope they are, we'll find them."

An AP reporter raised his pen for attention.

"Yes, sir?"

"How long do the coast guard and the navy intend to continue searching?"

Gene Vidal said, "I believe the president will not give the order to stop the search until the navy is sure that Amelia and her navigator cannot possibly be alive."

"Is she alive then? I mean, are they alive, both she and her navigator?"

"We don't know. We hope they are."

"Are there indications from your White House sources that they might be alive and somewhere on a raft in the Pacific?"

"We are exploring all avenues related to the search for Amelia and her navigator." Vidal looked around. "Next?"

The press conference continued for another ten minutes, before the three gentlemen rose from the dais, excused themselves, and hurried from the room. The press corps hurried outside to wire their dispatches.

PART II

BACK STORY

1932

20

H ARBOR GRACE 1932

IT IS THE EVENING OF MAY 20, 1932. I'M IN Harbour Grace, Newfoundland. NR7952, my sleek, red Lockheed Vega 5B monoplane is about to transport me into history—or death. Less than twenty hours from now, I shall alight on English soil, French soil, or be drowned somewhere in the unforgiving depths of the North Atlantic Ocean. I'll either be the famous aviatrix Amelia Earhart or the late aviatrix Amelia Earhart Putnam. The Vega's empty weight is 4,938 pounds, with a useful load of 1,630 pounds. She has a new upgraded 500 hp Wasp radial engine instead of the stock 450 hp. With the extra fuel tanks and the main and auxiliary filled up, the airplane is substantially over gross weight, but I need every drop of fuel for the transatlantic hop. It would be preferable to depart from Harbor Grace in the morning, when the temperatures are colder, for better airplane performance: I should arrive over the English coast during daytime hours and avoid the hazards of picking a landing field at night. A spring evening in Newfoundland is still okay at 60 degrees Fahrenheit. I've sent a telegram to my husband informing him that we're set for departure this afternoon. George himself departs for California today on a business trip.

I shake hands with Bernt Balchen and Eddie Gorski, who both accompanied me from Teterboro to St. Johns, New Brunswick, and from there to Harbor Grace. Bernie flew the Vega—he's a superb pilot—so I could snatch some sleep lying on the Vega's cramped fuselage with Eddie Gorski beside me. There is moisture in Bernie's eyes, but he says audibly enough, "Okay. So long. Good luck!"

I run through my checklist and crank the starter. The Pratt & Whitney Wasp 500 horsepower engine roars into life. I do all the pre-taxi checks right where I am: ailerons, rudder, elevators, full and free, all axes. I give a thumbs-up to Bernie and Eddie. Eddie salutes while Bernie nods. Two newspapermen watch warily from the aerodrome terminal. It's as if they resent being there to cover a silly woman's escapade, desperate for publicity or attention or both. Can't say I blame them. Low, fluffy clouds dot the Newfoundland sky, but I'm happy with it.

I taxi to the very end of the grass strip to use every available inch of the grass runway. This airport layout favors a heavy takeoff—flat, undulating, breaking off sharply to the frothy ocean. I'll have miles of open ocean in which to accelerate and climb if the weight proves ponderous for the Vega. I'm strapped to a flying gasoline tank, and I understand exactly how Lucky Lindy felt on that chilly morning on May 21, 1927 in Long Island when he rolled for takeoff on the flight to Paris. Luck has little to do with it; diligence and meticulous planning and good airmanship are everything. That was barely five years ago. Since then no one—man or woman—has replicated that flight solo. Now a woman will attempt an eastward crossing.

I check the magnetos. The drops are acceptable on both engines. I'm all set, and I line up with the southeasterly runway. The heading indicator shows we're aligned on the correct runway. Now the moment of dire truth. Feet on the brakes, I push in the throttles about halfway to the stops while holding the wheel all the way back to my chest. It wouldn't do to have the Vega tip on her nose just then. The engine noise is deafening. The airplane bucks and shakes, and even at that weight it's rearing to go. We have good readings on all instruments. I release the brakes and push in the throttles all the way.

The Vega accelerates relatively rapidly, considering the weight. The extra weight means she stays on the ground longer than usual. Finally, we lift off, and I gently bank the airplane on course. Now airborne, I can relax in my element. But watching the coastline drop behind me, a certain panic sets in. Panic at the magnitude of my quest. Ahead of me lies over two thousand miles of open ocean. Unlike the Friendship with her three motors, my humble Vega has only one engine. No redundancy. No welcoming strip of land, no familiar windsock, or beveled grassland where I can put this thing down if the motor goes south. It's not even a seaplane wherein we may attempt a dead-stick water landing. I get a sudden overpowering urge to turn the airplane around and be back among human folk in less than ten minutes. I seriously consider this. In my imagination, the motor runs rough; the magnetos are bad—any flimsy excuse to swing the nose back to Harbor Grace. As my feet itch to kick the rudder pedals and begin the return to land, another part of me fights back. I've been here before, I tell myself, as part of a threesome: two men and myself. Now I am alone, and the sense of the vastness of the Atlantic — of the universe—opens up before me. If I hold a rough easterly heading, at some point I should make land-fall—be it Ireland, the English coast, even South Wales, as we did with the Friendship. My original plan is to reach Paris, as Lucky Lindy did. We'll see how it goes. I am deter-mined to reach the English coastline somewhere and then take it from there. I would then have crossed the Atlantic solo. Ireland or Scotland, perhaps even London, are destina-tions to keep in mind if my compass plotting is inaccurate. Scotland is far north for me, and I fear if I miss it I might end up on the North Sea.

I fight the itch to return to Harbor Grace. I grit my teeth, focus on flying the airplane, on maintaining a straight course, avoiding the uncoordinated sideslip. It takes forever to reach eleven thousand feet on the altimeter. By now we are doing about 120 knots. I have lowered the nose for better engine cooling and also for better all-round cruise-climb at this weight. As the airplane burns off fuel and gets lighter, the speed should increase a bit.

Having leveled off at eleven thousand feet, I check my watch. Forty minutes have elapsed since the departure from Harbor Grace. I am now about ninety miles into a journey of over two thousand. The airspeed indicator creeps up to 130 knots. The adrenaline of the departure, of making the trip, keeps me firing on all cylinders, and I check and recheck my route. The lighthouse I am supposed to see on the left—a promontory somewhere out there—I cannot see. There's a smudge in the distance, the momentary white flash of a beacon. I am supposed to be closer than that to the beacon. Much closer. It is tempting to swing the wheel left and align closer to the checkpoint, but I resist this. I know that unscheduled course changes burn more fuel, distort the original flight plan, and many times cause confusion. Especially if you're not sure you even have the correct checkpoint. If I hold my compass heading—calculated from the wind aloft charts—for fourteen to fifteen hours, I should hit the coast of Europe somewhere, and I will have crossed the Atlantic.

A daunting thought, but not undoable.

I bring the power back and synchronize and adjust the mixture for optimum burn. I adjust the propeller pitch. The din settles down to an acceptable level. Even with my ear mufflers, the throaty roar of the Pratt & Whitney Wasp engine is deafening. But it's a reassuring din. Rather that than the sudden wheeze and silence of a dead engine. I am praying the engine will hold to Europe. Looking down, I see wisps of cloud, a cerulean-green ocean, frothy on the surface, suggesting substantial wind. I am winning the fight against the urge to turn back, awed by the ocean vastness. I'm sure many explorers face such moments of fear and panic, wondering if embarking on the journey isn't all a monumental mistake. Wondering if they are trekking into an abyss. I think one early explorer believed he and his team would fall off the edge of the earth if he sailed beyond a certain point. With each second of flight, the option to turn back lessens just that little. I hold heading and altitude steady and trim the airplane until it is no longer necessary, for at least the best part of half an hour, to hold the controls.

Even though I took off from Newfoundland at 7:12 p.m., I'm flying east and therefore into a prolonged sunset. I took off on wing tanks, and they recommend switching to the auxiliaries soon after takeoff and burn off that fuel first. It improves the longitudinal stability of the airplane and lessens the chance of a fuel leak, and the danger of having tanks full of gas in the fuselage. But I fly on the wing tanks for now. At least I know they are working since the engine is running. Most fuel transfers are routine, but there is always the one-in-a-million chance of the fuel line getting blocked or something going wrong with the transfer. I'm over a seemingly limitless ocean, with night approaching, and I prefer not to tamper with anything I don't have to. At least not until daylight. I listen for any change in the sound of the engines, any abnormalities. None. The engine is running fine. One has to land on the wing tanks, not the auxiliaries.

NR7952. I can read the registration number of the Vega beneath the gleaming red wing. The Vega is a high-wing monoplane, so I can look down and to the front, but it limits my vision up and behind. A VHF radio is in the cockpit, but I'm loath to use it, because of all the extra fuel tanks and fuel in the airplane. I can smell the fumes, this being a radial engine, and I dare not risk an errant spark from a transmitting radio setting us aflame. My life, my adventure, my entire family's fortunes are riding on the integrity of Pratt & Whitney. The reassuring throb-throb of the cylinders seems to tell me, It's okay. Relax, lady. Let us do what we were born to do: convert fuel to noise.

The cabin is cold. I am wearing my suede flight coat and leather Abercrombie flight jacket. A helmet with earflap covers my head. My gloves are thick and warm. The outside air temperature gauge shows minus 9 degrees Centigrade. (That's 16 degrees Fahrenheit.) On the ground at Harbor Grace, the temperature had been 60 degrees Fahrenheit. I know it will only get colder during the night. Colder too, when the airplane is lighter and able to climb higher. Just kidding. I am at eleven thousand feet, which is just over the legal limit without breathing supplemental oxygen. You need to breathe supplemental oxygen after thirty minutes above ten thousand feet.

Yes, in my memoirs I stated that I flew at twelve thousand feet for the eastward crossing. Dear reader, I wouldn't make that mistake now. For aviation regulations dictate that east is least while the west is best. Heading east you fly at odd levels, and westward you fly at even levels.

Enough of that!

I am flying over the ocean. Layered clouds obscure my view of the whitecaps. It offers comfort, as I don't like the constant reminder that if the engine fails, I'm only minutes away from being submerged in deep, frigid waters. I glance around again to make sure my Mae West and the orange collapsible raft are right there behind me, ready for whenever I might need them. They are. We drone on.

Two hours pass. I am fully over the ocean, immersed in a cocoon of airborne aluminum, suspended in the sky between moon and water, seemingly motionless, but I know from my instruments and the barely perceptible shift in the dark contours of the earth that I'm in motion. I do some calculations in my head and on a piece of paper and come up with something closer to 158 knots groundspeed. This being an eastbound flight, I expect tailwinds. One has to fly much higher up to see large tailwind components. The ASI (airspeed indicator) is rock steady at 135 knots. The five hundred horses housed in the engine are galloping, the nine cylinders whirling away as they were born to whirl, through lentil clouds and azure skies and moon-illuminated airspace. I am one with the stars and the wind and the air a mile and a half above the ocean waves. I am one with the reek of airplane grease and engine oil and the rush of the slipstream through the fuselage nooks and crevices. The engines putter on. I fly into a cloud bank and lose all outside references. Completely. My eyes stay in the cockpit, scanning the instruments, making sure we are upright, and remain so. It is easy to fly solely by reference to the instruments once you learn how and maintain proficiency. It becomes second nature, you never really forget—like riding a bicycle. You might get rusty and perhaps become dangerous if you don't practice for a lengthy while, but once you do and fly a few range letdowns, you'll get back to your groove.

The third hour. By now it is dark. Come morning, the sun will rise right in my face. There's a nice moon, which I glimpse through a break in the clouds. I am on instruments. I have trained for this in the months before making this flight—training in New Jersey with the help of Bernt Balchen, the Norwegian pilot, and my trip advisor. I knew from my experience with the Friendship that flying on instruments for lengthy periods is inescapable on a flight across the North Atlantic. So I decided that if I can get above the clouds, I will sit with the moon and elevate my mood. I do not give a thought for the effects of hypoxia. Not good, I know—I just can't resist going higher, even if for a brief period, to parley with the moon.

My altimeter has failed.

Just like that. The needle is frozen in its dial. Kaput. It's been reading 10,900 feet for some time with a rigidity I know is not normal.

The engine note doesn't change, nor the sound of the slipstream. So I know for sure I'm in level flight. If I climb a little or descend likewise, the engine note and slipstream tell me, but the altimeter is stuck at 10,900 feet. I resolve to stay level based on the vertical speed indicator, artificial horizon, and airspeed indicator.

By now it is dark. Clouds swallow the airplane and

without warning, I am swinging and buffeting around in turbulence. I maintain altitude with some difficulty, as we dance through the storm. Occasional lightning punctuates the maelstrom, and I try not to look outside to avoid being blinded. I am still flying partial panel—that is, without a working altimeter—and I think I'm doing okay while being bounced around in such weather. It is then I notice for the first time that the airplane is icing up. First, I notice that the rpm has dropped by about fifty units. It was steady at 2,300 rpm before; now it is 2,200 and will probably drop more. The manifold pressure isn't where it should be. Both gauges can't be lying. What could have caused this? Ice! I glance up and see at once the buildup of rime ice on the windshield poster and corners. The ice looks ragged and milky. It is building up over the intake or the carburetor air scoops. If we continue, it will surely choke the life out of the engine— the only engine I've got out here at night over the lonely Atlantic. I've got to watch the rpm gauge closely. If it drops to 2,100 or below, engine power will diminish considerably. I hope I'll fly out of it soon. I have little experience flying in ice, but the dictum I've heard from veterans of the airmail routes such as Lindbergh and Mantz and Stultz is to get out of it fast. The outside air temperature gauge reads −15 degrees Celsius (5 degrees Fahrenheit). Maybe I'll fly out of it.

I'm not flying out of it. Now my airspeed indicator wobbles. The pitot tube icing up! If the airspeed goes, then I'll have a harder time flying the airplane by instruments, as I will have no airspeed. The panic sets in rapidly. I'm no longer flying straight and level but in a series of Yo-Yo climb-and-descent profiles that have no meaningful aeronautical function. Without warning, the airspeed indicator drops alarmingly. Sixty knots! Impossible! And I'm still airborne? Or am I? The stall horn squeaks once, twice, startling me. I have never known such terror. Here I am in the middle of the North Atlantic at night, with an airplane near stall, and nothing but the violent waves and hungry sharks beneath. I push down on the nose and add more power to fly out of the stall. This is no ordinary stall; I'm on instruments, I have an artificial horizon instrument, but the altimeter is immobile. I can't even tell how high we are. We could be at nine thousand feet (I doubt it) or nine hundred feet in the cloud-obscured night. Or even ninety feet!

I yell and yank back on the wheel. I might have descended to a low level without knowing it since the altimeter is unserviceable. I could just fly into the water without even knowing it. No, no, no! I have to get back up. I hold the control wheel way back and begin what I think is a laborious climb to altitude. The airplane is quiet, unnaturally quiet, with a higher than normal upward pitch. But speed! Speed, what is happening to my speed? Bleeding off. Eighty knot—seventy—sixty knots. These are speeds that only dead pilots have seen flying at that altitude. And with all that ice? We should have stalled at eighty knots. Yet I'm seeing sixty knots on the airspeed indicator and the airplane appears to be stationary. The stall warning is still blaring. Since I don't know my altitude because of the failed altimeter, I just feel safer climbing. With a sickening lurch, the bottom drops out of the airplane. That helpless feeling of instant weightlessness; I feel my internal senses in a whorl of sensation. I immediately chop the power so as not to aggravate the situation. The airplane has stopped flying, robbed of speed and therefore of lift, and the laws of gravity have taken over.

Few things inspire terror in pilots more than the thought of spinning an aircraft at night. The fear doubles if you're flying on partial panel. I believe it kills more Army Air Corps pilots than is generally acknowledged. There is no horizon save the one on your instrument panel. To survive, I have to remain detached and let go of the controls or push them down. This seems counterintuitive. But it's the right thing to do in such circumstances. The airplane, like most, is inherently stable or seeks stability. Letting go the stick unloads the elevators and ailerons. I am in clouds, have no view of the horizon to help me judge my attitude relative to the sky and the water, except the artificial one created by the instruments. In instrument flying, it's always drummed into you to believe your instruments, to disregard what your body is telling you. I know from experience that this is true. Your body can lie to you. Try sitting on a chair with both eyes closed while you're spun around in a circle. Stop the chair suddenly, and in your mind you'll still be turning, or falling, and you may even put out a hand to break your fall. Your inner ear deceives you in such situations. So here I am, my instruments in disarray, my stomach plus my inner ear telling me I am falling and turning to the right. The instruments tell me I am less than a minute from certain death, spinning to the left and the heading indicator spinning like a top. To top off all the weirdness, the altimeter stays glued at nearly eleven thousand feet, even though in a spin you could be descending at a horrendous rate. The vertical speed indicator pegs downward. That means I am falling toward earth anywhere from four thousand to six thousand feet per minute. I have spun aircraft before and recovered but all were under clear azure skies and with a working altimeter. I want to live!

I push down aggressively on the wheel to unstall the wings. I note from the turn coordinator and heading indicator that we are turning to the left. I push the right rudder opposite the turn and hold my foot there. The crazy spinning of the heading indicator slows, then stops. As it stops, I neutralize the rudder and note that the turn coordinator is level, though the attitude indicator is showing over ten degrees of negative pitch. Now I am in a steady-state dive, freed from the deadly spin, but things are not yet kosher. The airspeed finally increases from the almost stationary fifty knots up toward normal parameters. Ninety knots, increasing to one hundred...130...140. The moment of truth. I have to pull the Vega out of the dive before the speed gets excessive. Too much speed in the Vne (never exceed speed) regime and the wings will shed. But pull back I must, and I do this slowly. Slowly but steadily, pull, pull, pull. The Gs build up; I can feel my jaws and my hand getting heavy. My body weighs twice what it normally weighs, and an air of unreality suffuses the entire experience. But the airplane pulls out of the dive, albeit lethargic. The artificial horizon returns to the horizon bar, and I go above it a bit to about five degrees of pitch to continue a shallow climb out. I add power as the nose comes through the horizon, as the speed has dropped to 100 knots and dropping further. The Wasp roars again, and we're in business, just as I break out of the clouds and see the murky opaque waters of the Atlantic opening its giant maws for me. No thanks — no. I don't know how far I descended in the spin. Still, it's a major shock seeing those whitecaps just below as I began the shallow climb back to altitude. God, it was that close! I know you lose altitude at an incredible rate in a spin, but even I am impressed. Ten more seconds in that spin and I wouldn't be writing this journal. I mouth a silent thanks to John Montijo, my second flight instructor who took over where Neta Snook left off and made sure I did spins and stunts before he allowed me to solo.

I climb out slowly at 110 knots, the heavily iced airplane clawing for altitude. I think of George and the headlines in the New York Times. "Famous Aviatrix Vanishes—Feared Dead." I know exactly how distraught George would be. But not yet, hon. Not yet. I'm back on course, still among the living and the able. I'm carrying about an inch of ice on the vulnerable parts of the airplane, enough to change the flying characteristics of the Vega, but if we can hang on another seven hours, we should strike the English coast. I feel whipped and battered as from a grueling fight. I level off again, just short of entering the cloud bases. I resolve to fly on at this level, staying clear of cold clouds and moisture and precipitation patches to avoid icing conditions. It's 2 degrees Celsius (35 degrees Fahrenheit) on the OAT. Cold for a May night, but then this is the Northern Hemisphere and the North Atlantic Oceanic currents.

My left knee shakes. At first, it's a mild shake, an annoyance—then it continues, beating a weird tattoo against the side of the cockpit. I can feel the rattling on the rudder caused by my shaking foot. I attempt to arrest the shaking, but this makes it worse, and the palsy transfers to the other foot. Now both feet are quivering on the rudder. Just what is going on? My heart palpitates; my breath comes in quick, shallow gasps. I recognize it for what it is: a delayed reaction to the events leading up to and including the spin in the dark—being only seconds removed from becoming the late Amelia Earhart Putnam. Yes, it was close. Hey, I tell myself; you deserve the jitters, girl. You earned it. You survived and recovered the airplane, and you're still flying. A good number of aviators would have lost the airplane—and themselves—right then. I analyze the situation. Yes, I know some male pilots have a less-than-stellar opinion of my raw stick and rudder skills. They think I'm all slick and glamour, lacking the right stuff that molds flying aces. Well, to them I say, Hogwash. They should all walk into a spinning Hamilton Standard propeller blade. I can hold my own, and I've nothing to prove to anybody anymore.

Another hour stretches by. My leg is no longer shaking, but I'm still in a heightened state of alert.

Then another hour. The Vega is holding her own, the rhythmic throb-throb of the nine-cylinder Wasp the most comforting sound in my life. Over five hours since airborne and now nature demands I go to the bathroom. I've been taking sips from my bottle of chocolate milk and some water, so I expect this. It's still ten or more hours at least to go, so I know there'll be several bathroom visits before reaching Europe. Now, as I think about it, the urgency increases. I am in an awkward position; one mile above the inhospitable North Atlantic waters in a cramped, noisy cockpit reeking of oil and needing desperately to go to the bathroom. We break out of the cloud bank and the night is resplendent and enchanting, even if just briefly. I catch a sliver of moon between a dark cloud table, the rippling opaqueness of the ocean, and the white, moisture-laden clouds ahead. Thankfully, the lightning flashes are coming at longer intervals. I seem to have left the worst of the storm behind. I have been in the storm with the icing and turbulence on and off for about four hours now.

All that tension and now I have to go to the toilet. It builds up. I cough phlegmatically and a spurt of urine escapes into my panty liner. I'm startled by it. The term medics use is stress incontinence. It tells me I cannot wait much longer. You know what they say nowadays: when you got to go, you got to go. Something along those lines. I trim the airplane once again and find that the Vega holds well. Ten minutes later, I'm all but bursting, and I decide it's now.

Medics who treat patients on the battlefields (and I worked with wounded soldiers returning from the Great War in Toronto, Canada) and even in peacetime say that uremic poisoning is a pleasant way to go. No pain. At that moment, I must disagree. Not if you're alive and craving to piss everything out and your plumbing is not defective.

So then I do it.

I bet you'd like to know how I did it?

That'll be for another day!

The airplane drones on after I'm finished. I feel several pounds lighter and the gargantuan pressure down on my waist has eased beautifully. Ah, relief! Still a slight wet patch from the incontinence, but it'll soon dry in this dry, cold cockpit. The heater is on, but I leave it low so I don't fall asleep, which I do when I'm too warm. Seven hours into the flight and it is fully night now. I am flying solely by reference to instruments. For lengthy periods, I have no visual reference to earth or sky. Sometimes even the stars appear to be beneath me and the ocean up where the stars should be. It's all an illusion as the instruments in front of my knees tell me the airplane is upright and perfectly stable, not inverted. *Believe your instruments!* How true those words. I focus inside, not daring to look outside, waiting for the illusion to fade or pass, whichever occurs first. Inside are the familiar instruments, representing sanity and life and orderliness, telling me I am moving across the Atlantic Ocean at 130 knots indicated airspeed, and probably a groundspeed of close to 150 nautical miles per hour. Lucky Lindy's trip from Roosevelt Field, Long Island, to Paris, France, took over thirty-three hours, and only seven hours into this thing I already have a grudging respect for the man. I have enormous respect for what he's accomplished, and I got a superb idea what it was all about in 1928 when I was a passenger in

the Fokker Trimotor that Wilmer Stultz piloted across the
Atlantic with Lou Gordon as a mechanic. The Friendship
had pontoons and could land on water if the need arose.
And it had three engines. Presumably, it could run on two
engines if one failed. If two failed, and we came down on the
water, I imagine the idea was to have Lou get out on the
wing or something and try to fix the engine. We would have
taken off again to continue the journey to Europe. Even
landing in rough Atlantic swells and Lou trying to manipu-
late a wrench while the airplane bobbed, perhaps losing a
screwdriver or pair of pliers to the depths, makes me smile.
But this, my Vega, has wheels instead, and there's no way of
landing normally in the water except for a chancy ditching.
It would be very abrupt, and the airplane would likely flip
over. Assuming I survived the impact and still conscious,
getting out from the wreckage would be interesting.

Better not to think about these things. The initial excitement of making a record-setting attempt wears off as reality
sets in. I'll be passing through five time zones, and already
my circadian rhythm is reeling. I am getting tired just about
halfway to Europe. Somewhere in the darkness to my left,
many hundreds of miles north lies Greenland, and further
on will be Iceland. I can't see them, nor do I think it is
possible to see them with the naked eye from this position. I
have no desire to see them. To do so would mean I am so far
north of my track that the possibility of missing the Irish or
English coast is there, putting me somewhere in the North
Sea. I must stick to my plan and my compass heading, all
corrected beforehand on the ground for prevailing wind.
Once it is daylight and I see the first hint of land, I'll be able
to orient myself from the surface charts, which I have pored
over until I almost know them by heart. I stifle another yawn
—about the fifth since takeoff. Something about the

engines, their energetic, unwavering song of power, and sky-borne freedom. I can relate. We are alone up here. Just the stars and us, part of the firmament, yet suspended in it, a comfy warm cocoon a mile up and away from the frightful, unforgiving waters of the North Atlantic. We have enough gas in the tanks. I topped up the engine oil and double-checked before the flight. If everything holds, we should be okay.

The engine sound changes. The sound of wind rushing past the empennage increases to a shrill hiss. In a biplane with its two wings and struts and braces, the sound would be unmistakable. The slipstream sound changes as the airplane departs a straight-and-level flight. This cues the pilot that his attitude has changed. In the Vega, with her monoplane wing, there are no wires to thrum in the slipstream; the change in slipstream noise is noticeable. I know immediately the airplane is diving. Whoa! And where have I been? I didn't notice it; I'd fallen asleep. A slow, insidious sleep that I didn't even know was there—a loss of consciousness that might have lasted seconds or perhaps as much as fifteen minutes. I'll glance at my watch later to determine how long I've been out, but my first need is to recover the airplane back to straight and level. I level the airplane. Somehow in my sleep apnea, I have lost nearly four hundred feet in altitude and strayed thirty degrees off course. I climb back up to five thousand feet, steering back on course. I fly a heading of 040 degrees for about ten minutes to reclaim my lost course before turning back to heading 060. I reset the directional gyro once again with the standby compass. I have been doing this every fifteen minutes since takeoff when I remember. This is vital, as this instrument is prone to precession. Otherwise, it is very reliable and important, and I have to rely on it completely to get me headed in the right direction.

The yawns are coming at lesser intervals as I fight sleep. I look for my bottle of chocolate milk. I'm rarely hungry when I fly, and this flight is no exception. I sip through a straw. I feel my body being reinvigorated, my lethargic cells awakening, sleep being driven away. I've heard that milk and chocolate make you sleepy. For me, it does the opposite.

We drone on through the night. I am suspended in the firmament, an engine failure away from becoming the firmament itself. At this height, tonight, I feel this power surge, this outstanding feeling that I own the skies, that I'm the lord of the heavens. Sheer nonsense. Pilots know what I'm talking about. It is an enlightening feeling, yet humbling. The potential for catastrophe is inherent in every flight. Once you pass sixty knots on the ground and levitate into the skies, you are in a pact with the laws of physics while holding hands with God. Anyone of many things—three things, chiefly—could kill you. The speed, the height, or the lack of oxygen. You must maintain airspeed above a certain value from takeoff to touchdown, else you fall out of the skies. Climbing out of fifty feet on takeoff, any uncontrolled contact with the ground above that level would most likely be lethal. And the aforementioned hypoxia, if you fly above twelve thousand feet for any length of time.

I look down and glimpse the red stern lights of a ship bound for Europe. It reassures me I'm on the right track—the same great circle route used by the cruise ships from New York to Southampton. I think it was Lucky Lindy who saw a ship and dived alongside and leaned out to ask, "Which way is Ireland?" Anyway, I fight the impulse to dive and ride alongside the Cunard liner or whatever ship it is just for the comfort it would offer. Still, I'm not so alone anymore. If the engine holds up, I'll get to Europe before they do. I have six hours to Europe and they have a few more days. They are doing so in comfort, at a leisurely pace, and have warm cabins to retire to and port and sherry to quaff in bulbous wine glasses. I have a noisy cockpit smelling of gas to reckon with.

We fly on. The airspeed settles on 120 knots. I do some calculations and determine that we ate averaging about 144 knots ground speed. The ice-induced drag will also increase my fuel burn, lessening endurance. It has slowed us down by about six or seven knots, but that's okay. Maybe if we get into warmer currents before Ireland, the ice will melt away. If I fly below the moisture-laden clouds, I should avoid taking on more ice. The smell of exhaust gas and fuel grows stronger. Along the line, a little after the icing and spin event, the exhaust collector ring in the engine sprung a leak. Orange-bluish flame leaks out, and the noise is much louder, something of a racket. I've been watching it, and so far it hasn't disintegrated. I remain apprehensive about how long it will hold.

Daylight pecks the horizon. It's a brilliant orgy of spectacular colors in the Northern Hemisphere. The white carpet of clouds below looks like snow in winter in Kansas or Nebraska, and the brilliance of the emerging sun is awe-inspiring—and too bright! I fumble for my sunglasses and put them on. There is such a thing as too-brilliant color.

Just as I relax a bit and another cruise ship disappears behind me, the sharp reek of aviation gasoline assaults my nostrils. Fuel leak. I know it instantly. You don't have to be a mechanic to know it. The fumes fill the cockpit, coming from behind me where the extra tank with its intricate piping and check valves are. I need that fuel to reach Europe, and if too much of it leaks out, it will compromise my endurance and my ability to do so. From now until the end of the flight, no lighting of matches or anything like that. Even the sparks from the exhaust manifold are cause for concern; if a spark should migrate to meet leaked fuel fumes.... Not taking chances, I switch again to the wings, which still have a good number of hours left.

I look in the side compartment and find earmuffs, which I stuff inside my flight helmet. I have to remove the helmet before I can put on the earmuffs. My hair feels damp and matted, as if blow-dried with frigid Arctic air. I add another layer of fluff to the helmet's earmuff. Now the roar of the exhaust lessens, though not inaudible. I could not have done this in an open-cockpit airplane. The heater in the Vega warms my feet while freezing my upper torso. Sometimes I think the process is reversed, and I am bathed in sweat, though that might be because of the stressful events accompanying the airplane icing.

An orange glow illumines the canopy top where it meets the horizon. For a startling moment, I imagine the cowling is on fire, the exhaust flame shards having finally taken hold. But the glow is serene, no dancing flames—just a pendant arc too pure to be a rainbow, suffused though it is by a purple halo. I recognize it for what it is: sunrise. Despite the problems besetting the flight, I am encouraged by this sight. I soldier on. What's a girl to do? Especially a farm girl from rural Atchison, Kansas? I learned to milk cows at an early age, and I've birthed sows and she-goats. What am I doing in the middle of the Atlantic, at dawn, suspended in space, the theories of physics and geography telling me that each passing minute draws me closer to my destination— and history as the first female to cross the Atlantic solo? The fuel leak bothers me, the blown exhaust stack bothers me, the icing bothers me. When your plate is full, you crash and die. Not me. Haha. You must watch out for the sneaky effects of carbon monoxide poisoning. You get warm, euphoric, and gradually slip off. So gradual you don't even notice. You're alert for that scenario. As for the fuel leak, I can't very well leave the important task of flying the airplane to go look for the leak and plug it. Probably from a washer somewhere—not much I can do. So I sing. Yes, really. I break into song, more to stay awake and convince myself that I'm not succumbing to the fatal slumber of carbon monoxide intoxication. And it's so nice to have your voice keep you company one mile above cold, raging waters as the sun rises in the east. By now, my heading is almost directly east, 090 degrees, so the sun will ascend in my face. Soon, a compass correction to heading 075 puts the orange-red orb fifteen degrees to my right, still close enough to become a direct glare when it's full up. I enjoy the elation that comes from being aloft all night and rising with the sun. Few sensations like it, I assure you. Even though I yawn and stretch my arms and body and itch to kick my boots either which way just to exercise them. Even though I could trade, well, my little pink toe (just kidding) for a long undisturbed sleep, I feel a sense of accomplishment coming this far. If the Vega doesn't implode from all the issues she's having, come daylight and better visibility, I'll surely spot the coast-line of some territory on the other side of the Atlantic. Oh, the joys of daylight. So many options open up!

They say the hardest time to stay awake is just before dawn. How right! I enjoy the iridescent orange beauty of the earth waking up from deep slumber while I fight not to succumb to the sleep I missed while suspended above the Atlantic. After the fourth jaw-breaking yawn in as many minutes, I long for a warm, cozy bed and hours and hours of uninterrupted sleep. Instead, I sip more chocolate milk. I'm also regaled by the sharp sting of aviation fuel. The fumes are invisible, but the sting makes it real. All it needs is just one spark. This thought scares me and drives me awake. I give silent thanks that aviation gasoline has a higher flash point than automobile gas. Fear makes things look worse perhaps than they are. I imagine the Vega blowing up mid-air and spiraling down to the Atlantic with me in it, my screams and desperation lost in the eerie night winds. I have to soldier on. You cannot stop the airplane in flight to trou-bleshoot and solve whatever problem is afflicting it. You are along for the ride. The trick is to remain in control at all times so that the airplane takes you where you want to go.

And I want to reach any part of the English coastline. Only a few people know my intended destination: my husband George, Doc Kimball, Bernt Balchen, and Eddie Gorst. A replication of Lindbergh's flight, except that he took off from Long Island and I departed from Harbor Grace. But now, saddled by problems with the leaking auxil-iary tank, the disintegrating exhaust manifold, and a frozen altimeter, I have resolved to set down on the first available pasture once I hit the coastline, be it Ireland or England. Did you also notice that I took off from Harbor Grace exactly five years to the day Lindbergh took off on his epic flight?

So now you know.

I sip the last of the chocolate milk and then some cold potable water from my water bottle to assuage the thirst. I feel better, though still worried about the fuel leak meeting the exposed exhaust manifold. All these issues—fear, icing, manifold leak, engine noise—combine to raise my adren-aline. Soon it's time for another bathroom visit. I have to do it again, closer this time to England than where I was the first time. Ask me again how I go to the bathroom in the cramped cockpit of the Vega, with the exhaust port thrashing around my ear and the smell of avgas petrifying my nostrils?

Keep dreaming!

Did anyone ask Lindbergh how he managed his bathroom visits during his thirty-three-and-a-half hour flight? Did he mention he wore an adult diaper beneath his flight suit? I'm not saying either!

I can see ripples of dark-green ocean water from gaps in the clouds. The clouds seem to be everywhere, and I know this is a characteristic of northern Europe. Proof that I'm closer to my destination. If the exhaust holds. If the fuel doesn't ignite. My frozen altimeter problem subsumed by more dangerous issues. After recovering from a near-lethal spin on a partial panel at night in icing conditions without the benefit of an altimeter, I dare any pilot to look me in the eye and say I am incompetent.

Eleven hours have gone. Somehow I have stayed awake, even when asleep, whatever that means. I can't swear for sure I've been awake all the time. There are moments I cannot account for, blank periods of which I have no recollection but which must have been there because time passed. Weird. Hallucinations are part of the equation when fatigue and sleep-deprivation cohabit. I've lived with them through the course of the night. A giant cloud reaches out to swallow the tiny Vega in her maws and takes on the shape of a gargoyle spitting furious venom at me. Cloud wisps take on the shape of striking cobras as they float by. At one point, skating above a solid cloud deck, I have the feeling I am no longer in control of my life, sliding down instead into some bottomless cavern without light or purpose. Weird. Daylight is better. As it comes, I welcome another day and new beginnings. Time seems motionless. I am still upright and trying to count the minutes as we cross into the twelfth and thir-teenth hours.

I haven't died yet from carbon monoxide poisoning or the inflammatory aftermath of an ignited fuel leak. Thank you, Lord. The thought of carbon monoxide poisoning scares me the most. The gas is invisible, has no smell. You just drift off into oblivion. There is no way to crack the window a bit and allow fresh air, just in case. The ram air vent for the cockpit is fully open, but I don't think it aerates the cockpit enough to forestall exhaust gas poisoning. It may be a pleasant way to die, but no thanks. Perhaps fortune will be kind and allow me to reach the coast before changing my deck of cards. This is a normal plea for pilots. Has been through the years. A barnstormer praying the elevators will hold up coming out of a 2G loop. A mail pilot watching ice build-up on his wings, the weather deterio-rating ahead, and the next beacon lost in the blizzard, as he prays for a neat pasture to set the biplane down on. I'm praying for my coastline, for the exhaust clatter not to dissolve into total disintegration and drown me in engine thunder. I'm praying for the fumes in the cabin behind me not to ignite spontaneously or by any non-spontaneous means. That's all I'm asking. Because this is May, I'm also hoping that the rotten English weather that everyone talks about will not adversely impede my arrival when I get there. Wouldn't it be terrible luck to get my coastline and have it disappear in a complete whiteout and zero-zero visibility throughout the countryside? I wouldn't be able to see anything and then I'd run out of fuel and have to crash somewhere. That happens mostly in the winter, not in the middle of spring. But then, they don't call the English weather fickle because they like the word.

Broken clouds intersperse with solid layers for as far as I

can see. It is daylight, and though I am about one mile up in the air by my estimate, I imagine walking out to the barn to milk and tend the dairy cows back in Kansas. But I must focus on the present. I think the worst things are behind me, and daylight promises no fresh surprises I can't handle. I check my fuel. Endurance remaining should be about four hours, plus or minus one hour. Because of the leak, I cannot tell how much fuel I've lost or how much left in the tanks. I figure about two hours remain on the main tanks, and I'll run the reserve almost dry before I switch to the leaking tank. Common sense dictates you draw fuel from the leaking tank first before it all leaks away, but the sparks from the leaking exhaust manifold scare me. Leaking fuel from the cabin could ignite from a spark, then what? So I remain on wing tanks.

Sleep. Sleep never seemed so blissful. How on earth did Lucky Lindy stay awake for thirty-three-and-a-half hours? How I wish I could have just one hour to sleep. Just enough to recharge my internal batteries and continue my trip. It's impossible on an airplane. You can't park the Vega on a cloud top, shut down the engine, and take a nap. That would be a permanent nap. I force myself to go on, shaking my head vigorously whenever I feel the stupor creeping into my senses. It all seems unreal: the monotonous drone of the engines, sounding like hallowed music of the spheres, and at others as if a cylinder flywheel is about to break off. It seems unreal being suspended above the waters of the North Atlantic, seemingly motionless, yet undoubtedly making progress. I dwell on the mystique of it all, the harmony and aggregation of sundry events, each distinctive in its effort, all calculated to lift me above terra firma and transport me across a big ocean into another continent. If only I didn't have to worry about leaking fuel tanks and blown exhaust stacks.

The sun has come up fully now. My body aches. For sleep. For rest. For relief from anxiety. For chocolate. I love chocolate. Most women do. I promise myself a nice warm bed, warm milk, and a bar of the best chocolate you can find in the hotel commissary or whatever accommodation is available for me in England. In England! That assumes I make it to the English Isles. Time stands still. The airplane drones on, as if destined to an eternity of banging gears and cylinders and torn exhaust stacks. The Wasp engine had been born to run on aviation gasoline. I silently thank the Pratt & Whitney engineers whose expertise and extraordinary workmanship have kept me aloft and safe from the ocean creatures waiting below.

The minutes crawl agonizingly slowly. My fears about the frozen altimeter, the ice on the wings, and the leaking exhaust have not abated. But at least I have hope the entire contraption will hold together until we hit the coast. Another interminable hour slips beneath the airplane. But a strange thing is happening. Tired beyond measure, I am getting a seventh, even an eighth wind—I've lost count of how many windups I've had in the past few hours. The atmosphere undergoes a subtle change. I sense it. I know the smell of America, on the ground and in the air, having flown in open-cockpit airplanes. Mid-western America smells of wooden barns and smoke mixed with a certain summer hayfield smell I know and loved even as a kid. I know that aroma as surely as I was born in Kansas, and I catch snatches of it all over the country, from New York to California. Now, fourteen plus hours into the flight, I am certain I have caught a distinct scent, something continental and distinguished, like aged wine—centuries old, with textured history. Even in the closed cockpit of the Vega, I am certain of it. I remember it well from my flight across the Atlantic with Bill Stultz and Lou Gordon. It hit my nostrils the moment we emerged from the trusted Fokker Trimotor in the bay at New South Wales and knew we were surely on another continent. The smell of wood smoke and coal, a thousand chimneys choked by ash deposits. The doorways waft sizzling bacon, poached eggs, and baked beans. Drifts of white smoke or mist caress incongruous wet grass. Probably smoke, as even up here the acrid tang of burning peat moss reaches my nostrils. Even the texture of the sky seems to have changed. The clouds are low and broken, through which I can see occasional glimpses of the ocean, now dark brown and suffused by deep green as if soiled by the detritus of approaching civilization. The cloud puffs drifting past are gray-white with brown edges as if charbroiled in giant industrial coal vats and unfurled skyward. This is not the smoke and grime of New York or Chicago or Los Angeles. You can sense the history in these clouds, sense that the people who once ruled the world and from whose empire America sprang forth left these sky trails in mute testimony to their land and her still-powerful culture. The air feels distinct; the water looks different, and even the skiffs and the ships—of which I'm seeing much more than usual—herald the approaching landfall.

My exhaustion melts away. Seeing these odd cloud shapes and strange boats, I know I'm on another continent, approaching the shores of another country. There's renewed vigor in my eyes, my bones. What is bone-tiredness with the goal in sight and the promise of a long shuteye? Well, Europe, here I come! British Isles, Scotland, Ireland, whichever territory I hit first shall have the bounty.

My eyes flicker several times before I take it in. Still far

away, but I know what it is. The brown smudge of a coastline. Unless I'm hallucinating, which I think I'm not, what
I'm seeing is a landmass—my first sight of land since the
shores and many inlets of Newfoundland. It's still way up
ahead, but the horizon meets the sea. Soon there is further
evidence I'm approaching a substantial human settlement.
The water is brown, muddied, and small fishing crafts,
which rarely venture over fifty miles from shore, are in
abundance. I have seen such brown efflux, almost conical,
many miles off-shore. Just following the tail of the cone
invariably leads to the shore, to human settlement. I push
the nose down a bit, converting height for speed and beginning initial descent. Rate of descent on the vertical speed
indicator is only a paltry 300 fpm, but that's the way I want
it. I still have the problem of the broken exhaust port and
frozen altimeter. Not knowing my exact altitude, I have to
remain visual. It's hard to gauge height by reference alone to
what is below you and the horizon unless you are landing
the aircraft. But I level off in what my oblique eye tells me is
about two thousand feet above the water. I still want to
climb if I sight a mountain range or elevated ground ahead.
I glance at my wristwatch. It has been fourteen hours and
some twenty minutes since the Vega lifted into the azure
skies above Harbor Grace.

I feel the excitement all over my body. While a noisy
radial engine throbs away inches from your face for hours
on end, anyone would become intimate with the waft of
aviation gasoline and with their sweat. My yawn alone terrifies me with its cascade of dank hyena breath.

To more enlightening thoughts. The few hours of
daylight and the descent to a lower altitude combine to
warm the airplane considerably. I can see the ice melting
and then being carried away in the slipstream: weak icicle

sticks trailed by water droplets. The wings and wheel struts shed their ice coats just as quickly. It seems a long time when finally the brown coastline slips beneath the airplane amidst some bucking and heaving. Mild turbulence will sometimes accompany crossing a coastline—especially one corrugated by high cliffs and uneven terrain. The air currents meeting at those points—one smooth, the other rough from passing over irregular terrain—mark the transition from ocean to land. Today, I feel the jar and bite of the winds as I struggle to keep sight of what is ahead of the Vega. The brown coastal mud turns to abundant acres of green slopes and brown culverts as the inhabited areas hove into view. The cliffs are green and the ground flat and sloping in areas. The countryside appears springlike; we're in the month of May, so this is no surprise. The buildings have that funny, upright, squeezed look that is the British Isles or Northern Europe. Brown brick buildings with staid chimneys in rows like toy houses on display for Santa Claus. I feel an exhilaration I have never felt before. Yes. With Wilmer Stultz and Lou Gordon back in 1928, I was merely a passenger. A woman observer. There had even been opposition to my going along in the sense I would be a distraction to the two men in what promised to be a difficult grueling flight. Now I have done it, solo. One up for the Ninety-Nines! The Ninety-Nines is an organization made up solely of women who fly. A certain Amelia Earhart is the pioneering chairwoman. Didn't I tell you?

The engine is singing. Even with the exhaust manifold torn and the slowly leaking fuel, I notice renewed energy by the horses. But how does it know—the Wasp engine, I mean—my desire to put down at the nearest pasture? It seems to know, somehow. And put down I must. For the better part of fifteen hours, I aviated over shark-infested waters at night, coping with icing, a frozen altimeter, a leaking fuel tank, and shredded engine exhaust manifold. Now that I'm over solid land, why take more chances than I have to? It would be ironic, wouldn't it, having made it this far to come hurtling down in a blazing conflagration, a spark from the exhaust having finally ignited the leaking fuel? Flying is mostly risk management—you realize this as soon as you leave the fledging aviator stage for serious flying. You mitigate risk and doing so comes mostly by training, common sense, and experience. You cannot make flying totally risk free.

Some hours ago, when I'd summoned the nerve, I'd switched to the auxiliary tanks out there in the Atlantic. The leak was not much more pronounced, feeding on the extra tank. I kept a wary eye on it. But it's poor practice to land while feeding the engine from the auxiliary tank. With a landing assured, I now switch to the main wing tanks again. I switch on the boost pumps just in case. But the transition is seamless, and the enormous Wasp engine drinks thirstily from its prime source. Scattered clouds provide uncommonly good visibility for what I assume to be a northern European clime. Acres and acres of pristine grazing land unfurl below. I choose a farm that looks adequate and free of obstacles. I descend to about eight hundred feet AGL using my inborn altimeter and make a pass down the field to gauge its suitability. Everything looks okay. No windsock, but if the grazing cows I see are any sign, I should land opposite the direction of my pass. I enter upwind instead, throttle back, and drop the first notch of flaps. In that configuration, I turn downwind, still visual with my chosen patch. At the right moment, I bank left, descending at the same time. When I level out, the field is straight ahead and I'm on profile for a landing. Full flaps come out, the props full forward. The snarl of the Wasp turns into a howl as I converge on the field. The ferns and furrow patterns differ from what I'm used to in the States, and this crosses my mind as I hurtle over the hedges, adjust power slightly, then chop it off fully for a passable three-pointer. You don't want to plant the main wheels first on grass that could be sodden, as that could cause a tip-over. Hard surface runways are best for that, and I had wanted to do just that because there may still be a little ice adhering to the surfaces, I cannot see. I cannot take a chance on stalling on short final. I don't want a prolonged rollout on a strange field.

It feels strange when the wheels touch ground fifteen hours after detaching on another continent. The sudden putter-putter of the engine after the din of a long evening and night and part of the morning seems positively like silence. I taxi toward a tall man I see; he's wearing a squire's wool cap and a spring coat over brown dungarees and wellingtons. I swing the Vega around and stop abreast of him. I cut the engine. The sudden hush comes as another shock. It takes some getting used to. I hop out, nearly falling over. The kinks in my legs have palsied them. I walk over on unsteady legs to the farmhand who reeks of cow manure and who stares at me with a mixture of wonder and wariness.

I smile at him. "Where am I?"

"In Gallagher's pasture." He studies me. "Have ye come far?"

"From America."

"I'll settle for Ireland anytime.

PART III

21

1 *937: MANHATTAN HOME OF GEORGE P. PUTNAM*

A SMALL CIRCLE OF GEORGE P. PUTNAM'S friends sat on the back porch of the apartment, facing the East River. The timepiece showed twelve minutes past 8 p.m., on July 19, 1937. The men had just heard Walter Winchell announce on the radio that President Roosevelt had called off the search for Amelia Earhart and her navigator. The long summer evening still had ample daylight left, and they could see the busy orchestrated East River pier with its warm humid harbor and depressing skyscape. The somber mood did not dampen the frequency with which they passed vintage port around. Thick, aromatic cigar contrails lingered in the balmy sweet air and the evening seemed endless.

"I tell you, George, it's a goddamn Republican thing," said one visitor, a Texas author on a book tour. "They lean a lil'bit on ole FDR about the cost, about programs awaiting budget approvals. They'll mention blocking future bills on the floor. It's a tactic thing, George. It's politics, that's what it is, son.What's a decent guy to do? The life of an important and decent American icon don't mean much to those government jackasses—and I don't excuse the phrase. I'm from East Texas, see."

George Palmer Putnam nodded, his face thoughtful.

"Why in the heck would Washington do a thing like that?" said a state legislator from New York. "What if those poor souls are still out there, hoping on hope for rescue—only the goddamned Coast Guard calls back the boats? That's damned heartbreaking."

Putnam buried his heads in his hands. He remained in that position for some time.

"I'm sorry, George," said the man from East Texas

Putnam raised his head, gathering himself, his pallor faint. "I would like to believe that Mrs. Roosevelt—would not have let President Roosevelt call off the search." His voice caught. He swiped his face with a white handkerchief. "If—if she hadn't satisfied herself that Amelia and her navigator drowned in the Pacific."

"Tragic if that's what happened."

"We don't know that for sure," said one Boston publisher.

"I believe they are still alive." Putnam seemed to gather strength. "Just a feeling. It's there."

"Is your wife real close to the first lady?"

"I'd say so. Eleanor was close to Amelia. That close. She was mighty hooked on Amelia."

"Puts a lid on things, I'd say," said the man from East Texas. "That's kind of final, ain't it? Not that I agree. No, sir."

"I still think they're out there. Count me in," said the state legislator.

"I think so too," said the senior man from Harper & Row. "Just don't give in yet, George."

Putnam blew a smoke curlicue across the hazy porch. "Gentlemen, I declare I am not giving up hope yet. I intend to continue the search for my wife with my resources, limited as they may be."

"Attaboy, George."

"I'll drink to that."

"Hear, hear!"

GEORGE P. PUTNAM WAS ON THE TELEphone all morning. He spoke to Gene Vidal over at West Point and they discussed possibilities for continuing the search for the missing Electra. Vidal offered his advice, and when he hung up, Putnam cranked up the long-distance operator and asked for a connection to California. He gave the operator the number.

"One moment," she said, and then, "lines are busy. You will be called back shortly, sir."

"That's fine."

He hung up. Less than five minutes later the telephone rang.

Paul Mantz out in Hollywood. Putnam spoke at length with Mantz, who promised to speak with merchant ship companies in San Francisco and also with ships out in the Central Pacific region. They could help by keeping a watch on certain sea lanes and by listening on aviation and maritime frequencies for any distress calls in the area. Mantz assured Putnam that as a matter of navigational etiquette, every ship monitored the emergency frequencies on a 24/7 basis, listening for SOS calls. Mantz promised to do the same with the Pan Am Clipper offices in LA. They were to advise crews on the Pacific routes to be on the alert for sightings or transmissions from the doomed Electra. Putnam hinted broadly there would be a financial reward for any crew that picked up a signal from Amelia and Noonan if those signals led to their rescue. Better yet, sighting the wreck of the monoplane or the two castaways— if they were still alive—would be the find of the decade.

Putnam hung up, satisfied that the search would go on— if on a reduced level. He next called his banker and his stockbroker to find out how much liquid cash he could sink into the search. FDR's New Deal hadn't eased the ravages of the Great Depression, just provided a lifeline. He stared out the window of his Manhattan office, out toward the Empire State Building and the majestic city's skyline. The same skyline from which, after Black Thursday in 1929, Wall Street stockbrokers in double-digit numbers had plunged to their deaths. The thought he might never see his beloved Amelia again was unthinkable. She had made it clear in the prenup that even if properly married in the eyes of the law, any proprietary notions of fidelity and monogamy would not bind her. Meeley was a free bird and always would be. She would not hold him accountable either for any lapses in sexual adventurism. George sighed heavily. He stared out at the cityscape, almost seeing the summer heat rising in waves from the narthex. The humidity pulsed between the steel towers of the giant buildings clear out to the corrugated steel piers of Hudson Bay in the pale glow of receding daylight.

He supposed that in any relationship one partner must love the other a little less. That was a given. It had taken him time to fall in love with Amelia. From the time when he had sought her out to invite her to be the first woman to cross the Atlantic, she had triggered something in him. She went on the flight as a passenger, though she wasn't too pleased about that. A few years later, she had done the same flight solo across the Atlantic, recreating Lindbergh's flight, but landing in a Londonderry, Ireland pasture, instead of Paris. She had crossed the Atlantic solo—a rare feat then for any aviator, let alone a woman. The publicity, the book deals, the product endorsements—he had managed her career well all these years. Somehow being close to her, appearing with her, dining with her, staying in the same hotels (different rooms then), he discovered a feeling he had never had for anyone. Even standing beside her on some platform, sharing her exploits with a rapt audience, he could feel the magnetic resonance she beamed at him. A sandalwood essence clear in some blond types, seen in quantity all over Scandinavia and here in Minnesota. Amelia could be tomboyish, a reputation not helped by the faded army-issue flight overalls she wore often. She was alluring in naïve fashion, fussing about her freckles, the manner she picked her pimples absently. She used perfume sparingly, rarely applied foundation and cold cream—all those pesky activities. Hers wasn't the in-your-face type of American womanhood. Amelia grew on you. She was fierce, independent, and ambitious. Putnam found her immensely desirable. Needed her. He suspected, and in due course knew, that the same independence and adventurism that marked her flying career would stretch to her bedroom culture.

He was right.

22

A MELIA

I SPEND NEARLY AN ENTIRE MORNING gathering stones and then laying them out on the sand in the form of an SOS. The call for help must be visible from a searching airplane, so the letters need to be big and wide. Getting enough stones and rocks is part of the process. Not enough stones that I could find or unearth, so I intermix with broken old tree stumps and twigs. I think the SOS is discernible from the air. Fred thinks so too.

We wait.

Fred believes that a raft just might get us back to civilization. The thought had occurred to me much earlier. Hadn't given it much thought as I had assumed, someone would rescue us in no time at all. Now that that assumption is looking more remote, the raft idea resurfaces. We consider our options for making one. We could use tree branches bound with rope twine and part of the tarpaulin from the Electra as matting. We know the sun rises in the east and sets in the west. We know the general direction of Australia and New Zealand. If we then strike west, we should hit Australia or the Papua New Guinea islands, eventually. If we drifted south, we could hit Guadalcanal, the Solomon Islands, or even New Zealand.

New Zealand?

I doubt that. The Tasmanian Sea is big enough and wide enough for us to miss Christchurch entirely and end up heading for the Antarctic. Though, who thinks we'll get that far anyway in that flimsy contraption? No water to drink, no food, dehydrating under the merciless sun. And that's without thinking of the ocean currents. It might sweep us toward South America, thousands of miles away, instead of toward the southern Pacific islands.

~

FRED

SHE'S BEEN STRANGELY QUIET ALL morning. I know that look. She's reliving her past triumphs. Record-setting flights, the paparazzi, the crowd adulation. All crap. Faraway, dreamy eyes moistening now and again. She has that distracted, zombie-like look. She looks every bit squeezable in a disheveled way. Her trousers hang on her as in those comic-book cartoons of castaways, except there are no cutoffs. She tied her blue cotton shirt in a bow-shape around her abdomen, exposing her bare midriff. She's recumbent on the tarpaulin in our tree shade, looking somewhat like a bag lady. Her decadence migrates to my nostrils. My instinct is to take her right there and then. There's unintended lewdness when a woman is a slob.

She must have said something.

"What?"

"We need to concentrate on building the raft," Amelia says.

"I hadn't forgotten."

"Let's get to it then."

We aim to use that very tarp she's recumbent on. First, I need to gather more twigs, branches, and strong twine to use as rope.

The only cutting tool we have is Amelia's bone-handled knife. It's blunted now, the bone handle shaky; I wouldn't trust it to slice a slab of butter in two. I need a sharp machete to bring down those boughs and bamboos that would make fine raft material. The mollusk shells are sharp enough but chip off with repeated pressure. We must think of better ways. These thoughts are depressing. I am thirsty. I also crave a smoke. No dice on the smoke. And the water is scarce. I walk back to the shelter, grab the container, take a nice big slug. I look around to see Amelia watching me anxiously.

"Relax. I only drank half the jug."

"We've got little."

My body is streaming in sweat. She can see that much.

"Yeah, that. Point is, see how humid it is. We're sweating pigs and bullets. In my experience, this kind of humidity presages rain."

"I hope so." She sighs. Drinks water from the jug, taking care to avoid the rim where my mouth had been. Sets down the jug. "Now back to work."

"Tired."

"It's an order," she snaps, grabbing the bone-handled knife from me and wading into the brush.

Got to say, she has more energy than I do. Shames me, the nimble way she hews down, prunes and marshals the boughs into oblong lengths which could go into making the raft. She almost has me convinced. I'm in favor of the raft. I had brought it up. The rafts of folklore are one thing. Makeshift rafts that can withstand Pacific gales are another. If we drift out mid-ocean and a minor gale even lifts us, they may never find our bodies.

In the distance, a swordfish or dolphin breaks water, flutters artfully in the air, before arcing back in the ocean. You can see to infinity in this humid, near cloudless sky. The clouds can build fast and bring rain in as little as two hours if the conditions are ripe.

I study her as she works up steam. A warm flame flickers in my loins. She draws in her breath, steps back a few paces.

"Did you say something, Fred?"

"Raft ain't going to work."

She pauses. "Why do you say that?"

"Just won't work. Am no pessimist, Amy, I just know it ain't going to work."

"What are we going to do—swim to Tahiti?"

"You could try. I'll pass."

"Fred, you quit? I can't believe you quit on me. Such a vital job. Our survival hinges on that."

"That's right, I quit. I was a master mariner long before I became an aviator. I can do more things with ropes and knives than you'll ever learn in a lifetime. I could tie knots in forty unique ways and never repeat a previous link. If I say I quit, believe me, it's not workable with what we've got. I would die quicker from frustration and heatstroke. If I had the proper tools, I might fashion something. It's no dice for now."

I leave her staring after me. I walk over to the shallow beach water to wash and soothe my clammy, heat-benumbed body. Behind me, she resumes hewing and pruning, but I sense less gusto in her activity than before.

~

AMELIA

FRED MUST BE RIGHT ABOUT THE RAFT thing. I am an optimist by nature, but I know his nautical experience far exceeds mine. I lay back in the shelter, while the sun's shadow lengthens, and the day seems listless bereft. The sound of the ocean is an accustomed noise. Part of the background, the repetitive crash and swish and slap of the surf. The humidity and the heat keep almost every living thing on the island under the shelter of trees or burrow or, in our case, a makeshift dwelling.

On this languid day, my mind wanders.

23

A MELIA

I DAYDREAM A LOT. MY BODY FEELS strange. Somehow, Fred is right. I have this glow. Maybe because I'm getting better orgasms than I ever did with George or Gene. And yes, I'm living in past glory these days. Like after that landing in Culmore, Ireland. The surprised farmer Gallahan out in his meadow. The gathering of the townsfolk. News that I'd arrived spreading like the Dust Bowl. The first woman (and second human being) to cross the Atlantic solo since Lindbergh's epic flight. The fete at the town center, thrown by the mayor. The next few days and weeks a blur. London, Paris, Italy. Ah, Italy.

Why am I smiling?

Italy's my favorite. George had canceled his scheduled business trip to the West Coast to come over in a steamer. We dined with Benito Mussolini, the first markedly diminu-

tive man I found charming and lewdly charismatic. Not that
I desired him, no. *Il Duce* had a carnal pull about him. I
wanted no part of it. At the state dinner, he stared at me with
a look every woman recognizes, and which most men don't
catch. George had no clue. I'm sure that state protocols and
perhaps his new mistress, Claretta Petacci, prevented Il
Duce from having his guards seize me there and then, and
take me to one of his vaulted bedrooms. The little runt. I
would like to break a Ming Dynasty vase on his Fascist
balding pate. I didn't like that look at all.

But if I thought he was openly flirting, then what could
I say for the antics of a famed poet? I will redact his name
because I respect my Italian hosts, and the man has a
family. Let's just say that celebrated writers, poets, painters,
including Gabriele D'Annunzio were present. I was
clutching a welcome bouquet delivered to me by a curt-
seying Italian schoolgirl with brown braids and an angelic
oval face. The ceremony had just ended, and we were
mingling during the reception, when from nowhere this
strange man, clean-shaven with a deep thinker's brow,
sidled close to me. One moment I thought he was
squeezing past me on his way to a different part of the
room when the crook of his elbow and arm nudged me
right in the solar plexus and his splayed fingers alit briefly,
but spot-on target, right on my vagina. More aptly, on my
long dress gown. His fingers were accurate. I gasped,
nearly dropping the bouquet. Despite the gown and the
protection of the underwear, his fingers alit unerringly on
target. Incredibly, no one else in the room saw any of this
because of the thickness of the crowd. In his effrontery,
too, his terrible fingers dug and groped in a flash,
desperate and evil. I wore garters, and I was so happy to
disappoint him. The buffoon turned and smiled brightly at

me. All this happened, incredible as it seems, in one second.

"Sorry," he leered. "Is accident, no?"

It was no accident, and he knew it, as did I. Nor was he sorry. His teeth had the rotted, devastated color of ochre parchment. I glared at him.

"I hope you enjoy yourself, Signora Earhart," he said, edging away.

"Putnam," I snapped at him—one of the rare instances I preferred my married name over my maiden. He knew my husband was around, yet he carried out a brazen assault right in the middle of a major reception party. If I'd shouted or dropped the flowers and made a scene, I'm sure he would have been in big trouble. I didn't, and I don't know why to this day. He had a reputation anyway. As a sexual mad dog. I heard talk much later back in New York that he slept with his house help several times a day. Maybe he drew inspiration from that. Italy was full of men who freaked out on women, and in that aspect, I found it worse than Paris. At least the French do it with finesse. The Italians go for the dessert first.

Those were memorable days. The media reporters couldn't get enough of me.

Now here I am, a castaway on a strange island. With an ex-sailor for a companion—a sailor living up to all the legends about... well, sailors. I feel sad about the fifty commemoration stamps in the nose of the Electra. Now they're at the bottom of the Pacific, creating a new reef ecosystem in the fuselage of the Electra.

I hear strange sounds from where I am recumbent on the sand, enjoying the coolness of after-rain. For it rained. The sounds are awful—as if Fred is beating something to death. I walk over, and Fred is hitting a medium-sized turtle with a piece of rock washed up from the ocean. The poor creature has curled up inside its shell, and Fred seems unable to split it. He beats it until the rock shatters, then picks another from the three or four he has handy and goes at it again. In frustration, he turns the turtle upside down and tries the bottom shell. This seems more effective, though the shell remains intact. He finds our bone-handled knife and slides it through the aperture where the turtle's neck had disappeared. He twists it. I hear a squeal or a sound, and I can't bear to watch anymore. I grimace, and walk away.

I know what Fred is doing. He'll drink the turtle's blood, which he has done before when we're short of water. But it just rained and we have good water from the dozens of mollusk shells we use to collect rain. So long as the lizards keep away from them, we have enough for three days if the weather remains cool, or two days if the heat becomes unbearable. But Fred also likes turtle meat. He told me they used to catch turtles in the water during his time in the navy, and the ship's cook had a special way of parting the turtle's body from his armor carapace—it wasn't with a well-wielded cudgel. I hate to even think about it.

24

 MELIA

THIS *NEVER* HAPPENED. I AM DREAMING about it. Another one of those horrid dream episodes. I guess it must be the sun. It affects you. Nothing to do all day except sit, ruminate and dream—when you aren't scrabbling for an edible dinner.

A woman needs to remember what it used to feel like, those indescribable junior adult years. You sort of never see that level of turgidity from men after the twenty-something years. It could be all the shellfish we've been eating. I read somewhere that Casanova used to devour twelve raw oysters daily. Ugh! Fred's not an eater, but hunger has made him one, and he's eating gobs of oysters. I do the same; it seems. I have to admit; I feel more...horny (is that the word?) since we've been on this infernal island. Like going on holiday abroad—you relax personal boundaries, inhibitions. I know friends of mine who visit the Caribbean Islands (they favor the Bahamas) and let down their guards. Yes, they sleep with natives, those Negroes with massive dicks you only hear about. Or they have serial one-night stands with any of the WASPish tourists hanging around for just such encounters. But my situation here with Fred is no holiday. Plus, there's a genuine possibility they might never rescue us from this island.

Hey! Where did you get that from, Meeley? You never were a pessimist. They'll come to rescue us. Knowing GP, he won't give up so soon. He's rock-solid in that aspect. No pun intended. I must remember when we get back to Rye, to make up for neglect he's suffered over the years on my behalf. Poor sod loves me to heaven and back. Don't worry, George. When I get back, I shall rescind that written "understanding" we have, at least for a year. I'm going to "musk" you till you squeal in disgust. You will have more Amelia than you'll be able to handle, you'll see. Only get me out of here! Do that and I'll not just let you sniff my armpits, I'll let you smell my pussy, and I'll fuck your bookish brains silly. I'll even take you in my mouth, see? What's the matter, George? Shocked, are you? Didn't imagine your Meeley had it in her? Women hide it out of choice and conditioning. But trust me, it's there. Thought it was only you that knew where that battered copy of The Kama Sutra hides in the attic? Think again.

Fred gave me head. I liked that. Gene Vidal never did that. Like most men I've known, he obsessed with touching me down under. He'd sniff his fingers afterward, unconsciously. I caught glimpses of him doing that. What a dick. Old hat, anyway. But gee, I came so fast after Fred put his tongue right on my electric button! That's what it felt like. If we get out of here and back to civilization, I shall demand it from George, from future men. I mean that. They just have to do it if they claim they love me, etc. I won't reciprocate. Duh! Don't like it, too humiliating. Not with Fred. He's an ex-sailor. His dick's been global. The wharf-side brothels from San Francisco to Bangkok to Jakarta, or Southampton to Cape Town, and Lagos. Surprised he didn't get syphilis. Maybe he did and got it treated. With his type of drinking behavior, he'd be a hit with the harlots in Rotterdam, or New York or Lisbon. I'm still current with my Krafft-Ebing and Havelock Ellis, you know, and I'm not in any mood to analyze what happened between Fred and me. If you enjoy it, then go for it, is my opinion. I never was one for guilt or strange hang-ups. I've always been me, Amelia, independent. I'll carry that trait to my grave. That said, you know what gets me? There was no thought of using a rubber with Fred. I just accepted it. What is it with me? Did dysentery in Asia affect my brains as well? If GP finds out what happened between Fred and me, he'll seek a divorce. He mustn't find out. He's a proud man and has been tolerant all these years, but to him, Fred's got to be somewhere near the bottom of the social barrel. He'll feel I've committed the ultimate act of betrayal: chosen a common lush and ex-sailor over an aristocratic top-five New York publisher. Once we get rescued and back on the mainland, I bet Fred will go on one of his drinking binges and blab everything about us.

In wine there is...lies. All lies!

See, I can make mine up, too.

End of the dreamscape.

It never happened. It will never happen! I'm from a respectable family, "good" middle-class American family.

～

BACK TO OUR DILEMMA. WATER. I NEVER knew
water could be so sweet. Just for a sip of clear delicious
mountain spring water on my lips! Oh, I long for those early
Midwestern spring days, when the snow has melted, but it's
still chilly enough to warrant a winter coat. Atchison,
Kansas is mostly flatland, but I remember chasing rabbits
across the fields, coming up against the clear brooks that
cross the hayfields and disappear into dark serpentine
creeks. Sometimes clear water runs down the side of the
elevated boulders like a faucet and pools at the bottom of a
small ravine where you could see tadpoles and strange
insects dart across the brook. That water is transparent,
clean, and safe to drink. I dream of it now, watching the
natural sandbar of our island ripple and quiver with each
assault from the Pacific Ocean waves. As mentioned before,
a large lagoon exists on the island. Surrounded by so much
water—yet here we are dying of thirst. It's tempting to scoop
up water and drink from the ocean. Not wise at all. It would
be fatal. The salt in the water would turn one's insides into...
ugh! Can't even imagine it. More pleasant to die of thirst
than to die of a salt-induced coma. We had some water left
from the Electra when we landed, but that's long gone. It
rained briefly several times, but now our hoarded supply is
less. It hasn't rained for three days, though the sky darkens
two or three times a day, and we prepare our conch shells
and little containers and leaves to catch the rain.

Nature is being mischievous with us. And because our
diet consists mostly of shellfish and fish, we are constantly
thirsty.

Despite all the surrounding water, my body seems to
have layers of dirt on it. We're out of soap, so we use the
sand as scrub or mudbath or something. We scoop up wet
sand and rub it down our bodies. It does two things: cleans

us a bit and exfoliates dead skin cells. Still, my body has a ripeness, which I recognize as unique and emanating from oneself. One time after a foraging hunt with scant success, we enter our little shelter. Soaked in sweat from the tropical sun, away from all those pesky bugs, I peel off my blouse for better cooling. Immediately I realize it's a mistake because the air around us changes with the swirl of the blouse. I glance at Fred. His face is expressionless, though I know he felt stung by the whiff. He may like it, for all I know. Sometimes I find him leaning toward me, distracted, when we're conversing, even though the subject isn't a matter that requires him to be almost at a thirty-degree angle, with his head bent toward my shoulder blades. As if he is intent on making my personal space part of his. I have no such compunctions toward him: Fred's efflux has an off-putting quality I associate with derelicts, bin-scavengers, sidewalk hobos. Perhaps that's not fair, but I can't help it. Why should I say I love his aura when he has the breath of a possum doe?

~

1600 PENNSYLVANIA AVE. July 18, 1937

FRANKLIN DELANO ROOSEVELT brooded over the reports on his desk. He grunted, pushed back his wheelchair, then motored over to the large, curved glass doors that overlooked the Rose Garden. This was July, and the magnolias looked tight and crestfallen. Fall was his favorite season, mid-October up to Thanksgiving Day in late November when the colors bloomed. Then the Rose Garden resembled

a fiery orb straight from the Elysian Fields. Possibilities
bloomed, and the scenery more than once likened to God's
own country seemed to weep of her own accord. Yes, the
land wept, Roosevelt believed, from joy, not bereavement, at
the incoming prodigious change from flowery, lustrous
bloom to the cold, leaf-bereft starkness of winter. Such
comfort and safety from the Oval Office. Yet, out there,
somewhere in the Pacific Ocean, a brave aviatrix and her
navigator were dead or awaiting rescue. He couldn't commit
a sizable portion of the nation's resources to that search
indefinitely. Not a simple choice to make, but then, that was
the purpose of the Oval Office: hard decisions made on
behalf of the American people. Amelia Earhart had once
given Eleanor an airplane ride and engaged to teach her to
fly. First Lady Eleanor Roosevelt was an ardent fan and
admirer. It made more difficult the decision he would have
to make.

After some minutes of contemplation, he wheeled back
to his desk. He rang the bell and his secretary appeared
almost immediately.

"Yes, Mr. President?"

Fala, his beloved Scottish terrier, jumped onto his lap
just then, upsetting his cigar ash onto the Oval floor. When
the moisture in the briar got too much, he switched to
cigars. The president carefully laid the cigar holder on the
ashtray. He reached out, stroked Fala's rough black fur. The
First Pooch gazed dolefully into his master's face, then
licked it vigorously. Roosevelt held his breath while Fala's
tongue worked over his cheeks. He pulled away and started
breathing again. His secretary waited. She had seen this
mime before.

"Send a POTUS telex to the navy secretary," Roosevelt

said, pinning Fala down on his lap. "Copy the Joint Chiefs chairman, Secretary of State, and the Air Force Secretary."

Call off the search for Amelia Earhart and Frederick Noonan. Effective immediately. All search units to return to base and resume activity interrupted by the search. The President of the United States and the American people appreciate the untiring efforts of all our men in uniform and all those involved in the search for the missing aviators. We thank them all for their sacrifice and selfless service. We continue to pray for the safe recovery of Amelia Earhart and Frederick Noonan through some miracle of God. All indicators point to the idea that they are inaccessible to us through misadventure or some untimely act of nature. We continue to hope and pray, but we can no longer commit our resources to a search that has lasted sixteen days and is the longest in the history of this nation."

25

F REDERICK

AMELIA'S GLOWING. SHE LOOKS RADIANT in a homely, disheveled way. There's smug entitlement in the way she sits contemplating the ocean. You can stare at the ocean for hours, I know that. It has a timeless susurrus, a carminative lullaby, the sense that these waters flowed deep before you were born and would still flow long and deep after you're six feet under.

Life feels wonderful. If only we can get out of this infernal place, then it will be a perfect world.

Water is our major problem. Potable water, I mean. I've got all kinds of trickle-down arrangements with local plant leaves that collect water in our makeshift can, but it sure hasn't rained for some days now. I get an idea and walk over to Amelia, where she's trying to knit a fishing net from the straps of the Electra's baggage hold netting.

"I got an idea," I tell her. "You want to hear it?"

"Not if it's about rafts."

"We'll talk about rafts later. I got something different. We barely have enough water to drink, do you agree?"

She stares at me. "Fred, that's obvious."

"How about we conserve it best way we can? We save our urine and drink it."

She squints at me. I think she's sure now that I'm batty. "Drink our urine? *Our* urine?"

"Yep. What I said."

"That's weird, isn't it?"

"Not as weird as dying of thirst and doing nothing about it."

"Oh no," she shakes her head emphatically. "No way. No."

I say nothing. No need to. I watch the waves ripple in the sunlight.

"You may have a point," she says finally. "I've heard some Indian mystics do that. It's not uncommon in India. Sort of recycling the water, or something."

Amelia always surprises me. She is smarter than I give her credit for. She has just spoken to my thoughts.

"Yeah. It should be okay," I say. "Nobody's died yet far, as I know, from drinking their piss. Maybe it'll keep us alive until they find us."

"You still think they'll find us? I don't think they have a clue where we are. They'd have given up the search by now."

"Well, let's continue hoping. No good beating on it."

Her right hand goes to her forehead fingers splayed; she brings it down again. She says without looking up, "It'll be difficult for me to pee into a bottle. You know that."

"You can pee into a bowl."

"Sorry?"

"You could pee into a bowl."

"You'll provide the bowl?"

"Yes."

She looks up. "I don't see any Ming Dynasty vases lying around."

"Don't need one. Just a bowl."

"I'll need better than an ordinary bowl for me."

"You can use the biggest conch shell we can find. Do it in spurts, you know? Three or four spurts ought to give you about a cupful."

"How nice. Will you make those...spurts for me?"

"Not much difference in color from a glass of whiskey. I'm not talking about bootleg whiskey. Bootleg has a bite. Your piss won't."

"Thank you very much, Dr. Noonan."

"You're welcome. From this moment we hold our piss until we've got a substantial amount. Then we shed it into a container and after the silt and whatever has settled, we drink the liquid above it. Got that?"

"Yes. Just don't ask me to drink your piss, Fred, because I won't."

I smile. "Not to worry. I don't have enough to share."

"Let's keep it that way."

"I'll drink yours, though, if it comes to that."

She rolls her eyes. "Perv."

26

A MELIA. (DREAMSCAPE)

TWO DAYS TO RAGS, AND I'M FEELING cross-eyed. That's what I said. Like a Siamese cat. Sometimes I see ships on the horizon, steaming toward our island to the rescue. Sometimes it's just the *Itasca*, a tiny dot in the distance, sailing away from us, missing the island completely. I would have asked Fred to shoot flares, except that we don't have any left. We fired them during the first five days when we thought we heard searching airplanes. Besides, asking Fred anything is an invitation to another haystack tryst. I suspect he's a sex maniac. I should certify him as one, and I'll make sure of that once we make it back to LA. Sometimes he makes love to me four times a day. It must be the oysters. That's the major food on this godforsaken island. That and the few birds we can catch and the turtles. I read somewhere that Casanova consumed twelve oysters daily to fuel his sexual acumen. No

old wives' tale about that. I believe it. I am the recipient of all
that pent-up energy unleashed on my poor hapless vagina.
My pelvis aches, I nurse an inflamed vulva, my insides throb
from bearing his weight, though he is much skinnier than he
was before. Now he resembles a rag doll. My entire body, head
to toe, feels as though I've been whipped in a fight where I'm
the only one getting pummeled. I wouldn't have it any other
way. There is unspoken satisfaction in two bodies slapping
against each other, torsos grinding, joined at the waist with
purpose. Now I understand why men love sex so much, and
they don't even have to be in love with the woman to enjoy the
act. Who says women can't be the same way? Well, we can't.
We have a much higher stake in the act and the outcome.

I don't love Fred. Even I know that. No way. To begin
with, he's a violent usurper of a woman's dignity. He's been
around the world several times. He was a sailor, and
everyone knows about sailors. There's the thin scar above
his right eyebrow, just beneath the hairline. I've never asked
him how he came by it. I suspect it's the result of one bar
fight too many. And there are certain dried-up features on
his skin that suggest to me he may have had syphilis at one
point. Sailors and whoremasters, one and the same.

No, I could never love Fred in the way of Gene, or even
of George. Now, what Gene and I share is passionate love.
But many times a woman marries not for love, but for
convenience, for opportunity, for money. There. I've said it! I
usually attract a certain type of man. I have almost non-exis-
tent boobs, am Lindbergh-thin, freckle-heavy, a so-called
Nordic type. Yet Gene finds something in me.

Gene's son, Gore Vidal, is the opposite. Though he's still
a child, he already has that look I recognize. I just know.
He'll end up liking men as a man does a woman and don't

ask me how I could tell. The way he looks at me, our conversations in Gene's car, I just know. He just has an alternate mind, I think. He's a brilliant boy with a sharp mind and caustic wit. I hope he takes up creative writing.

I know what will stop Fred. Temporarily, I mean. Rags. Ragtime is one of my favorite types of music. Al Joplin. Ironic, isn't it? And I'm two days to it. That'll be the only respite I get, probably. He couldn't possibly do it through the bloody mess. Not unless he's a dog. He might be, for all I know. He likes it doggie style, too. I go on the offensive to prepare him for the period of abstinence. I hit him with it as soon as he comes out of the shelter.

"I'll be taking some days off. I don't feel that good."

He barks out a belly laugh. "Well, look-it that. Look who wants a day off. What are we doing here, anyway? Are we not on permanent days off?"

"You know what I mean. I mean, let's have a time out."

"For how many hours?" he asks.

"About a week."

He stares at me. "Look, whose idea was it in the first place? Who got me going in the first place?"

"As I recall, it was you."

That hoarse bark again. "It was you, damn it. You and your dick-loving cunt, that's what started it all."

"Is that right? And who was it grabbed the other first without her consent? Who is the navigator who dared to strip his captain naked and have his way with her? You've got it all skewed, buddy. When the rescue boat gets here, one of us must explain to the rescuers why the two castaways are naked and not wanting to be rescued and why one of them has permanent morning and afternoon wood and just can't keep his hands off his captain's genitals. You explain that to the world. I was you, Freddie, I'd start composing authentic answers right now."

"You're shouting at me."

"Was I? It's not like we have neighbors."

He advances on me. "So who grabbed whose genitals first?"

"What?"

"You said I have to explain to the rescuers why I grabbed my captain's snatch."

"Didn't you?"

"What's there to grab? You tell me. There ain't piddling to grab." A strange light appears in Fred's eyes. He leans over to where I'm reclining on the tarp. Thrusts his unshaven face close to mine. I can spot individual white hairs on the cheek bristles, his rust-stained teeth, the smell of oysters on his lousy breath. Even his gray tufts of nostril hair.

"Tell me what there is to grab," he repeats. "It's a goddamn sink hole down there. A fucking musty pink crack with all kinds of smells emanating from it. Who in his right mind wants to insert his fingers down a goddamn wet piece of ass? Isn't it bad enough to have a hole right between your legs where your pee-wee ought to be, a hole so big a boy could put his fist through it—and for all I know a third base catcher could do the same thing with his mitt on. Isn't it bad enough not being able to pee into a bottle? Now I get flack about me grabbing crack and whatnot. Why would I grab a stinkhole, for Chrissakes? The goddamn place is a SEWER!"

I can't believe what I'm hearing.

I believe Fred has gone mad. Or intoxicated by some poisonous fish. This isn't going the way I envisioned.

"Did you hear me?" he repeats. "Now she colors on me, and I believe she's angry, or she's shaming. I'm sticking to my bulwark—the goddamn place is a stinking sewer."

I am annoyed that my face is reddening. I mustn't let this monster know he has upset me. "That's just fine with me. You've said how you feel about the entire thing. From now on, just stay away from my vagina. And I mean that."

"Oh? Now she snaps at me." That hated bark again. "Stay away from my vagina? I would advise YOU to stay away from my dick. Keep away, do you hear me?"

"I mean it, Fred. You stay away from my vagina and let's all mind our own business."

"That's easy. Who wants to dive inside a sewer?"

"If you find it so distasteful, why did you put your mouth down there? I didn't ask you to go down on me."

This gives him pause. He grins evilly. "You beguiled me, you dick-lover, you."

"No, I didn't."

"You love dick, admit it. You can't do without it."

"No, I don't."

"You do, too."

"No!"

"You love dick, come on, Meeley. You know it and I know it. That I swear. You never got it so good with your gallivanting giant of a publisher—"

He never finishes. I wade into him, screaming and yelling, anything to keep him off balance. I slap him hard on that feisty unshaven face, and it's like smacking your hand against a hairbrush. So, I repeat the slaps on those parts of his face and torso free of the engulfing hair, my hands splayed for maximum distribution, and I add a bit of rake with my fingernails. That should draw blood.

It does. He pushes back at me.

I don't reel. No way. Can't give him that satisfaction. I'm not one to wonder anymore where chivalry went with him. The fight is not one-sided by any means. Then he pushes me over and we are fighting on the sandy floor once again. I give him trouble where I can, but I can feel his penis rear its ugly monster head once again. I tighten my pelvic muscles and clamp my thighs tight. He tries and tries. Then he goes for a painful spot on my wrist, presses on it. It hurts, and I yell. Still no deal. He scrabbles for the bone-handled knife —my knife; the one we keep around in case one of those creatures from the ocean comes too close. He threatens me. He's trying to force his way inside, and I can tell I already have injuries from resisting and there'll be a hell of a hickey on the morrow. A friend once told me that if you don't allow a man to enter you, there's no way he would. I sort of believed her until now. With a knife held against my throat, I don't think I have a choice really.

He has his way.

I am angry enough at his words not to like it. But truth be told, his erection is massive, and once he gets underway his thrusts so earnest my involuntary wetness almost makes me puke. For an emaciated, near-starving castaway, his excitement is way out of proportion and his vigor enormous. He comes with an otherworldly yodel, squealing and gasping and spasming. I watch his late frenzy with some detachment. He slobbers onto my breasts, his head bent low, resting on my chest, spent.

Drained.

Milked out.

I push him away like a disjointed rag-doll and clamber to my feet.

Fred Noonan is an evil man.

I just know it. He mentioned something about sewers and other comments aimed at my body plumbing. Well, he's crazy. What else would you call somebody who has his snout and mouth up somebody else's ass? I've told him already. Stay out of my sewer, Fred. I warn you.

27

M ANHATTAN

GEORGE PUTNAM DRAINED HIS GLASS of Scotch on the rocks and put the tumbler down on the mantel. Through the window, he could see the buildings of Manhattan pushing into gray, dank skies. He wasn't losing his mind, but he was close to it. His wife was missing, presumed dead, along with her navigator. Everyone assumed she was dead. He just knew she wasn't. At least, he suspected she wasn't. Every bone in his body told him so. She was so—there. He would know it when she left this planet, wouldn't he? Not that he was superstitious or felt special or anything. That was just his life with Amelia. He was so connected to her. Somehow he felt—knew—she was marooned on a Pacific island. There was a string of islands in the area near Howland, and his best conjecture was that right now she and the ex-sailor were cohabiting one of them.

Eleanor Roosevelt—bless her heart—had called that morning to ask if there had been any further news on Amelia and her navigator. He told her no, none. Privately he fumed: how the hell would he know anything if the American government—with all its resources—didn't? Eleanor sounded apologetic about her husband calling off the search—blaming taxpayers' funds and all. He said he understood. He told her he would continue the search using his resources.

The call from his accountant had not been reassuring. A sizable chunk of his fortune was being channeled into the search. Soon he would have to call in some long-term notes with stiff penalties attached thereto. He had cashed in most of the short-term instruments. This was Amelia—his wife. Once she arrived back on American soil, he would market the hell out of her. Appearances, stamp exhibitions, book tours—the lot. She had always defied the odds, by instinct, or design, and Americans loved that. He would recoup his money in no time. He sighed, leaned back in his chair, his gaze far away. He picked up his Parker rolling tip and signed the dotted line releasing yet more funds targeted to finding his wife and her navigator.

When he got her back, he'd fuck the hell out of her. Payback. Maybe she'd let him try some anal.

He felt his face redden.

GEORGE P. PUTNAM SIGHED AS HE PUT his checkbook away. His banker sitting across from him made a notation on the check and laid it down on the desk.

"I shall wire the money at once to the West Coast," the banker said. "A second tranche will go to the shipping company in England for the services of the steamer in the Central Pacific involved in the search. The third tranche will go to the private Australian enterprise with another ship in the area."

Putnam nodded. "How large is our exposure?"

"Roughly two hundred and twenty thousand dollars as of now. If they remain on site—that is, engaged for the search another week—we'll be looking at three hundred thousand plus. You're still in the black, ledger-wise."

"Could I sell the Conrail stock on brief notice?" Putnam said.

"Yes. I would suggest that. The Treasury bonds—I would advise you to hold on to them as much as possible. Short-term expendables too—Conrail, American Airlines, will do for now. Leave the Connecticut farms and Long Island properties. Going forward, perhaps you should shed some real estate in the Bronx and Brooklyn. Your assets portfolio can survive that, no problem. It all depends how far you're prepared to go in funding the project." The banker coughed phlegmatically and added, "I hope we find her, Mr. Putnam."

"I pray for that, Kenneth. Even though I am not a pious man. If there is a God—and I believe there is—I pray he delivers my wife back to me."

"Isn't there another man? An avigator?"

"Navigator. Him too."

"I do hope we find them, Mr Putnam," the banker said again.

"I do hope so." Putnam shook hands with the banker, grabbed his hat, and rose.

Outside, he got into his 1937 Buick Special and told the driver to head back to the publishing office. He thought of his wife out there, probably dead from the airplane's impact with the ocean during ditching. If she'd survived the impact, he hoped that she'd been mercifully unconscious when she drowned. He wondered what her last thoughts had been as the fathomless waters of the Central Pacific closed over her head. Like most drowning people she would hold her breath, until the final intake of water that would cascade inside her mouth, fill her lungs, and the imploding fire as her lungs jerked for air and not getting it, her brain dying. In four minutes, everything about who she was would be irreversible, the brain forever silent, never firing synapses again, all the music lessons, flying lessons, and life's lessons gone. The same lucid female mind that had written him those strange but unforgettable words on the prenup letter: I will try to do my best in every way and give you that part of me you know and seem to want.

She read him like a book. That part of me you know and seem to want. He already had an erection and tried to squelch it before they arrived at the office of Brewer & Warren publishers, where he was vice president. His family-run company, G. P. Putnam, had merged with a conglomerate that had majority shares. They had forced him to resign as Chairman.

This was madness.

His excitement was beyond solid—no way it would wilt before he had to get out of the car, as they were already approaching the Manhattan office. He leaned forward and said hoarsely to the driver, "Take me back to the apartment. I'll be ready to come back to the office in about an hour." Time enough for a bath, and a refreshing slug of good bourbon.

The driver nodded and complied. He couldn't very well drive to Rye right now. Too far from the office, in

Connecticut even, his country house. At various times Rye had belonged to the states of Connecticut and New York. He kept the Manhattan pad for occasions when he needed to be close to the office, and in winter when sometimes snow and ice made the roads dangerous.

Putnam wondered if his wife and her navigator had survived. He wasn't superstitious and didn't believe in all that thought-transference business. Yet something kept telling him Amelia had survived the ditching and probably at that moment was clinging to a life preserver she had taken along for the flight. He wondered if her navigator Fred Noonan was also clinging to his. He had never liked that man and had, for once, agreed with Gene Vidal, who had warned her not to make that trip with Fred. Vidal had told her certain things about Fred, and though details of his parting ways with Pan Am were sketchy, it was general knowledge among insiders they booted him out for excessive boozing. Putnam and Vidal and Amelia had formed, in their way, what the French adroitly called a ménage à trois. It worked for them. He loved her and still did, and he wanted her solely for himself. But the conditions she gave provided the only avenue for him to become intimate with and ultimately wed her. He knew she was strong enough not to budge. So, he slept with her and enjoyed that part of her he liked, and the West Point guy also got his on the side, and both men tolerated one another and tried to pretend it wasn't happening. But each man knew. Putnam now had a horrid thought: what if they'd both survived? Amelia and Fred floating on their life preservers or life raft onto an uninhabited island? A warm, curious feeling came over him, and he recalled the telex he'd gotten from a trusted source in the government that the USCGC *Itasca* had continued to receive transmissions for days after the Electra supposedly ran out of fuel and went down. He just sensed that she was out there, just as he had sensed years ago when he'd seen her and chosen her to join the Friendship crew over many others to become the first woman to cross the Atlantic in an airplane. He had sensed a common destiny with hers. Was she and Fred marooned on an island? He wondered, as so often happens when a man and a woman are thrust into such situations if they would develop an intimacy from circumstance? Doctors and nurses on battlefields knew that phenomenon. Survivors of natural disasters marooned for weeks before being rescued had become intimate in the darkest days of despair. He wondered if that meant Fred had had carnal knowledge of Amelia. Again, that warm anger creeping down his back. That sometimes happened on early mornings when he awoke prematurely and thought about things and had those sudden eureka moments. Some things were better not known.

George Putnam felt rage then. Pure unadulterated rage. He trusted his wife. The West Point instructor was an exception: he had influential military friends, he was head of the aviation program at West Point, and Amelia was passionate about aviation and the people associated with it. The man was now a powerful government official in Washington, DC. George could just barely tolerate that. But if, after we rescued them—and he thought this was still possible—he learned that the two castaways had been....

He pushed his mind to other thoughts.

Inside his two-bedroom pad on Manhattan's Upper West Side, Putnam felt better. He took off his tie and lay on the quilted sheets of the king-sized bed.

That part of me you seem to know and want.

George Palmer Putnam had always found his wife exciting. The allure remained because she was so... unpredictable. His excitement grew. He dug deeper and faster into the pillow propped on the bed at his waist. He imagined her face, that favorite picture of his where her then-youthful looks and upturned nose got him going.

He lay there afterward, panting, exhausted. A brief image of Fred Noonan doing the same thing to Amelia flashed through his mind. He dismissed it as quickly as it had come. They were both probably at the bottom of the Pacific, most like.

Hardly fair to her, thinking of his wife that way.

28

A *MELIA*

WE HAD PICKED A PALM COCONUT sapling, and each day we cut a notch on the trunk to keep track of the days we spent here before being rescued. I think the notches stopped on the sixteenth or nineteenth day of our being marooned on the island. Who cares now anyway? We just forgot to add a notch one day. Same thing the next day. Now I do it, or Fred does it when we remember. It doesn't reflect the true number of days we have spent on the island. We've stayed much longer than that. Life on the island has taken on an endless ennui. We tilt our heads, listening to imagined sounds of airplane engines, crane our necks to peer into cloudless skies for the pinpoint glint of metal. Sometimes I think we'll end up with early cataracts from staring at the sky so much and peering at the horizon, seeing ships' masts and superstructures that aren't there. We must be careful. There's a thin line between hallucinations and madness. The first could be a harbinger of the latter, and both could merge as one in full manifestation of the latter.

We are aground on one of the remotest corners of the planet. It's a shipping corridor as the wreck of the rusted SS *Norwich City* attests. We know for sure it's the Norwich City because twice now we have tried to approach the wreck. Her ochre-rusted hull is beached on volcanic rocks beneath the surface of the island. Her bottom and sides gutted by sharp rocks, she lists markedly where she's beached on the island. A shallow section of water separates us from the wreck. The green water looks knee deep, but halfway there, we were up to our thighs, then waist water. We thought of swimming across to another knee-deep area we could see but decided against it. A fresh reef with a flourishing ecosystem had sprung up in and around the Norwich City, and with two box jellyfish stings between us, we decided against going further and headed back to our shelter. So much for exploration. It would be ironic to have one or both of us die from a shark attack or jellyfish sting on the eve of our rescuers showing up. I think we sort of hoped for some human companionship in searching the Norwich City. Not in the sense that any humans remained aboard. All the sailors died abandoning ship or were rescued. Perhaps another ship heard her distress calls and came close enough to evacuate everyone on board by boat to the bigger ship. They then scuttled the Norwich. I think Fred and I had the quaint idea of somehow getting on board the wreck, perhaps finding livable quarters somewhere. Not food or anything, since the ship's larder would have long rotted. Rather, there's enough of the ship's superstructure still above water, even if tilted at a crazy angle, for us to make a crude shelter. The ship just being a manmade structure provides comfort. It would give us a sense somehow of belonging to a species of machine-builders and thinkers, not moribund castaways on an uncharted island.

29

F REDERICK

IT'S NOT GETTING EASIER. THE OYSTER shells we have lined up in rows for catching rainwater are bone-dry. It rained three days ago. All this worrying makes me anxious, and I walk to the edge of the vegetation to pee. Just as I unbutton my pants I hear a shout from Amelia.

"Fred! What are you doing?"

I spin around. She is staring at me open-mouthed.

"I'm taking a piss. Do you mind?"

"I mind very much. That's my water you're wasting in the sand."

"Excuse me?"

She runs a hand through her rumpled hair. "We agreed we would drink our urine as a hedge against dying of thirst. Don't you remember?"

"Oh."

"You remember."

"You said you wouldn't drink mine."

"We agreed to each drink ours only. We said we would."

"Yeah. Right." I button back up. "Sure, get me a cup. I'll drink mine, and you drink yours."

She smiles. "That wasn't the arrangement, Fred. You said you'd gladly drink mine, and I don't remember myself saying anything about drinking yours."

"I don't remember saying anything like that."

"You wouldn't. You—your hand was under my—"

She chomped on her lower lip.

"Is that right?"

"That's right." She comes up close, thrusts her face up to mine. "What's the matter with my erstwhile navigator— changed your mind? You don't like the source where the water's coming from?" Her breath again is the baked spew of clam chowder, heavy on the razor clam. The freckles on her face seem to have doubled overnight.

"I retract that statement if I said it."

"No, you don't. Scout's honor. You wanted it, you get it."

Again, that smile. Despite everything, she is oddly appealing.

"And you'll drink mine?"

"Heaven forbid!"

"No deal," I say

"Deal."

"No deal. You drink yours and I'll drink mine."

"Here's the deal. You drink yours and mine. I drink some of mine and any water we get from the leaves on the shelter top. That arrangement holds until it rains again."

"Smart woman, aren't you?"

"I think so."

"You sure urine is safe to drink?"

"Very safe," Amelia says. She stares at me. "I remember it was you brought up the subject first time. Now you're asking."

"I did. It was a suggestion."

"Well, it's okay to drink. The kidneys filter and disinfect it. Many mystics in India drink only their urine."

"That's right. I forgot you were once a nurse and worked in a hospital."

"Yep."

"You go first. You pee into our container, drink from it, and I'll consider drinking from it. I'll pee into my container and drink from that too."

"We don't have a container."

"That big conch shell we found last week. That'll do."

"Right. I'll go find it, then I'll pee into it, and I'll bring it to you."

"No way. I'll stand there and watch you do it." My turn to smile. It feels like a wince. "I want to see how your pee comes out, and no tricks."

Her face darkens. "I don't know what you mean. You know what they say. It's hard to bring out anything when someone stares at you."

"Applies to men only."

"Says who?"

"I won't stare."

"No kidding," she sneers.

"Are you serious?"

"Very. Another woman watching, no-brainer. With you watching, I'd hold back."

I can only stare. "Fascinating."

 MELIA

I FEEL GUILTY. MAYBE WE OUGHTN'T TO start anything now until after one week. I don't know exactly what will show up in the cup or container when I pee into it. I open my mouth to tell him, then close it again.

Some things are better left unsaid.

He follows me to the side of the shelter where I retrieve the conch shell. I remove my underthings and squat down, placing the conch between my legs. Fred observes, trying to appear uninterested. I guess he wants to know if it's true that women can't pee into a bottle. Did he have sisters growing up? I want to shame him. I want to show him women could pee straight up, pee into a bottle, shatter all his beloved myths. The conch isn't a bottle; it's more of a small soup plate, and that's plenty for any woman. I look down to make sure my vagina aligns with the conch and nudge it against the external labia. I look up, lock eyes with Fred. Waiting for the urine stream to begin. Nothing comes out. I wait. This is weird. I am stiffened in the position of a hen about to lay a humongous egg, and nothing is happening. My sphincter muscles aren't bothered.

"Well?" Fred says.

"Give it a moment. It'll come."

I relax a bit and a thin spill of urine trickles, then shoots, out. Some miss the conch, some land on the sand, and I feel a few irritating drops on my inner thighs. Fred's eyes have shifted—he broke off contact first—and as the urine midstreams steady. He looks away. Maybe Afternoon Wood is playing on him. If he tries to grab me, I'll shove our precious urine down his parched throat. I finish in silence. Steal a glance into the conch shell—I don't see any signs of spotting—and hand the thing to Fred while I get decent again. The urine is yellow and there isn't much in volume, which means I'm dehydrated. No surprises there. That's why we're drinking our urine.

We lock eyes again. "Um, I guess I go first."

"That's right, Amy." He hands me the conch, bulbous end first. He has this pasty grin on his face. And I hate it when he calls me Amy. "The foam's the best part," he says.

"I just remembered something. We're supposed to let it sit for a while. Allow the sediment to settle."

"But you said it was sterile. What sediment?"

"There's uric acid in it. Detoxified, not sterile. Won't harm you."

"So you drink it."

"Give it five minutes."

We sit on the beach, watching the land crabs make their way to the vegetation. Fred and I observe without a word.

After five minutes I drink my urine. The taste is tangy,

sharp. Just taking a sip, I know there is no way I could ever drink Fred's pee. There would be too much of Fred Noonan in it, and I fear drinking anything coming from such an evil source! I put down my conch. How do I break the news to him?

Fred is watching me closely. "How was it?"

"Tell you what, how about I just drink mine and you drink yours? It's icky enough not to add the complicating factor of it coming from someone else."

"I like the way you put things, I do. You suggested drinking our urine, I suggested cross-drinking. I did because I thought it would strengthen our immunity, help our resistance to disease until we get rescued. You're the nurse, you tell me."

"Second thoughts."

"Great. Maybe your next genius thought will be for us to eat our goddamned shit to survive. No difference from the wild dogs roaming the cilantro fields in Mexico."

"You're gross, sailor."

"Tell you what I think: how about we squeeze some milk out of your breasts right now and use it to wash down our dinner?"

"Rude. You know I've never given birth."

His gaze drops to my chest. "That's true. You never really had buds to speak of."

He wanted those words to hurt. They do. Cruel, needless. I have no words. He glances at me, opens his mouth to speak, closes it again. Gets up and walks away.

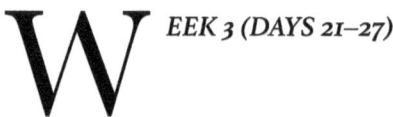

W EEK 3 (DAYS 21–27)

AMELIA

FRED LOOKS SO THIN, I'M WORRYING. He's thin in frame, so at first, it didn't show. Now, he's positively gaunt. His cheeks are sunken, the mouth sallow, ribs visible when he's not wearing his shirt. It occurs to me that he's suffering from malnutrition. Aren't we both? He reflects on me—on this accursed island, at least. If he's malnourished, so am I. We eat the same things, he more than I. I know from my nursing days the signs of wasting. Fred is wasting. Yet it's incredible even in his dissipated state he has such rock-solid morning woodsy. Maybe he thinks I'm wasting, too. I hope not. Hard to tell. The little compact in my handbag shows me only the upper part of my body. I have to hold it some distance away to get a half-body image of myself. At that distance, it distorts my body.

I should have seen rags by now. It hasn't come. Every woman differs, I suppose. Still, one should have a predictable regularity. I hate flying the USSR flag—what woman doesn't?—but here on this island, I have unique problems. I used up the last of my Tappies after our first week (or was it two weeks? Can't remember, can't keep track anymore.) I intended to stock up in Honolulu or the mainland long before this. Never figured we might miss our destination by over three weeks. Sure, I could do the Hollywood starlet bit and use nothing and bleed into the bed sheets or sand, whatever. Some idiots claim it enhances your femininity. Sheer nonsense. What could be more unromantic than a blood trail?

I think of George. Poor sod. I know he misses me. It'll be especially hard on him. I know he won't have spared any effort to have us found and evacuated from this island. Does he suspect us marooned on an island and still alive? Maybe everyone presumes we ran out of fuel, ditched in the ocean, and perished. Not an unreasonable supposition. The Pacific is unforgiving and vast. I left George enough mementos to keep him in suitable form. He doesn't even suspect I know. Oh, I do. Maybe most women do. Ever observe what men do furtively after they've copped a feel?

I think GP wanted a child from me, too. He already has two from his earlier marriage. I'm a stepmom to two lovely boys, David and George Jr. He kept mum about it, though, speaking only in roundabout ways about a third heir. Just as he had been heir to the Putnam fortune and business empire. He wanted nothing to crimp my style, my activities, my flying displays, and so he nixed having babies. There's pride in succession, assured lineage. I would not have made the best mother, but I would have tried. Sure, I would have resented the time away from airplanes and record-setting flights, but there it is. A female heir would have been a permanent testament to our union. GP would have been immensely unpleased!

 MELIA

AT LAST! THE RUSSIAN FLAG. THREE DAYS late. Better late than not at all. Funny thing: it comes scanty and bloodied and not the least vile, and I could have danced in joy. It stops again mysteriously by late afternoon. I've had sporadic flow in the past. People tell me I'm too skinny, athletic, etc., and sometimes that happens to us spaghetti-thin types. Yes, proper women do talk about it. And oh, if you're a woman reading this, you are not improper if you shiver in disgust.

Events seem unreal. Nothing seems perfect, idyllic, anymore. The sky is droll, looks threatening in alabaster, off-color sort of way. I think we are resigning ourselves to our circumstances. Just maybe we won't get rescued after all and we're here for keeps. Fred and I don't pretend to keep up a routine anymore for our sanity. Come to think of it, we never had a routine to begin with.

I catch Fred staring at me one time, lost in thought. It catches me off- guard, as it does him. He gives a guilty start. His look is so intense.

I stare right back. He looks away, lies back on the tarp, and pretends to nap.

I can relate. I know what he is thinking: hey, this is for real. We might end up dying on this island, forgotten by man and God.

The next day, during one of those self-illuminating moments, I suffer a panic attack. Overcome by the events of the past three weeks, I sink to my knees in a cry of despair, uttering prayers to a universe I cannot contain. For us, for our safety, asking the Great Cosmos to get us back to civilization. I plead with the earth's Deity promising I'll be a model lady and asking forgiveness for my sins (even though from the start GP and I had agreed on an open marriage) The tears roll freely down my cheeks as I cry, lifting my soul to the Great Power in the universe.

Fred, alarmed by my cries, runs out of the shelter. He stands there, gazing at me, comprehending. He nods several times as if he understands. Like me, he is not an overtly religious person, but under these circumstances what have we to lose? He goes inside after a while.

He doesn't mention the incident later, as we sift through a bird carcass looking for edible portions, free of feathers and what looks like cancerous lesions. The land crabs had been circling the carcass, and that got our attention.

Next day no Russian flag.

Or the next.

None.

Am I losing my mind? To have a period for just one day

and then not again in the following days? Has malnutrition made me crazy? Or is it our sorry state? Could heat apoplexy knock your body chemistry out of whack? I have never experienced such debilitating heat in daytime anywhere, and only the nearness of the ocean and the breezes, plus the ability to dip oneself now and again in it when the humidity becomes unbearable, eases the endless lethargy of each day. Yes, the ocean sprays from the waves that crash against the ancient volcanic rock help. We sit on the sand close to the water and let the ocean spray throw a fine mist on our faces. That's a definite pleasure. But we must take care not to sit too close. We've seen strange things in the water. A small fish that resembled some sea bass washed up on shore once. It floundered and twisted and turned in the sand, desperate for oxygen, for water. I expected the next wave or two would submerge it again. I reached for a stick to move it further inland, for our dinner. Something else beat me to it. I beheld a sight no one else would believe. I know I saw it. An octopus appeared from the water, apparently walking or dancing on its tentacles. I moved back instinctively, away from the fish, keeping my eyes on the octopus. It made unerringly for the hapless fish, engulfed it in the fatal folds of its slimy tentacles, and just as eerily danced back to the water and swam away like some floating parachute.

I had been holding my breath—or so I thought until Fred asked me why I gasped. I told him I saw an octopus, and he looked at me pityingly. "They eat fish, you know. Did you think they survive on steak and potatoes?"

I looked him squarely in the eye. "That isn't the point. This octopus—creature, whatever it was—walked, walked on the sand to collect a fish washed ashore. Really. I saw it."

I expected him to look at me patronizingly. But he

considered my statement, shrugged. "Yep. My days as a sailor—saw many strange things in the water. We haven't seen the half of what's out there yet, is what I say."

I know what I saw. Nobody can convince me otherwise, and I didn't need to pinch my arm to reassure myself or anything. Don't need that. Never did.

Now, I keep searching, looking for signs of my lost period. Nothing. From somewhere in my brief past as a nurse, I recall that women need the smell of men's urine to trigger timely and full periods. An ingredient in male urine, maybe androstenol, triggers something in the female limbic brain or some part of the brain important in regulating hormones, triggering normal flow in women. All this occurs on the sub-molecular, particulate level. We aren't even conscious of it. Little known fact, but true. Don't ask me how nuns in convents regulate their Russian flag indispositions with no men around. Holy Mary alone knows! Perhaps Count Romanov would know. I guess there must be priests hanging around who unwittingly fulfill that role. No familiar warmth coursing down south. I'm lubricating copiously as in ovulation mucus. Why is my system so out of whack? Must be the turtle blood we've been drinking. Believe me, when you're so thirsty that your life depends on it, you'll kill a turtle and drink its blood with no yuck factor. All bets are off when you're marooned on a strange island in one of the remotest parts of a vast ocean.

33

F RED (DREAMSCAPE)

I'VE NEVER GOTTEN SO MUCH PUSSY IN my life. I say this authoritatively, even married twice as I am. Theoretically, married men get it oftener than our single brothers. On this island, we have mostly boredom to contend with. First, we have little energy because of limited food and water, and it's like us against the universe. We have only each other to look at apart from the scenery. Abandoned, starved, and thirsty, we have to keep our sanity. Perhaps to reassure ourselves of our humanity, we've turned to each other for love and coupling. It is the true affirmation of being, of carnal love. We each have our legal spouses back in the States, to whom, if we're rescued, we shall surely return and perhaps not breathe a word of what we did here to pass the time—other than the activities of building rafts

and eating wild birds to survive, which everyone expects of
castaways.

I believe hunger sharpens both the mind and the flesh.
Moderate hunger, not extreme hunger. Your sinews are
bursting with vigor. Though you are weak from malnutrition, the flesh is lean; the loins inflamed. If the partner
you're marooned with on a remote ocean island is getting
shapelier by the day—the opposite of the common results of
nutritional deficiency—has a boyish ass, a smelly pussy, and
absolute sex appeal...well, there is nothing you can do
except succumb. I plundered what she offered me as though
it would go out of fashion, which it might if we ended up
dying on this island. I tired of the missionary position, and
we changed roles and she cowboy-rode me. I could see two
brown freckles on her nose and several others beneath her
cheekbones, near the chin. Her insubstantial breasts
jounced as she bucked me. She had the ass moves just right,
surprising me, not the ingenue I had imagined from the
Midwest. I mean, she was fierce and accurate, like she was
breaking in a wild bronco, with speed and unflinching need.
Seen nothing like it, her ass cheeks slapping my thighs
faster than I could count, the well-known face and wide
mouth puckered in feral ardor. I know I whimpered and
wondered what in hell was happening to me. It was unbearably poignant and insensate-causing—it would become
painful in the next thirty seconds... and I poured and
poured inside her and she absorbed it all, those gyrating
agile hips, and I had to lean up to seize her arms and body,
prevent her from moving again because the tip of my
member had become unbearably sensitive, electrically
charged.

In this embrace with her, I leaned back down again, she
on top, breathing hard, me strangely euphoric. Later, I fell

asleep as a warm, sticky mess oozed down my thighs and midsection. We lay thusly, ensconced, something Caravaggio might have painted in his century if he had painted cuddling couples. She was feathery light. The crook of her right underarm rested just above my face, my nose, in particular. I became interested in the character of that smooth, brown-furred underarm. I remembered that she is German by descent. The Germans have a very apt saying: where there is hair, there is joy. Occasionally in our position, her underarm rubbed my nose, my face. I detected pheromones, woman's essence, feral sweat, the blunt crudeness of coitus itself. She rubbed this texture all over my face, unaware of—or perhaps too aware of—its hallucinogenic powers. And I drank all of Amelia in, her musk, her ripeness. I could not help it. I felt myself engorging again without effort—no slyness, no holds barred, either. She let me suffer like this for a while, before reaching down to slip it inside her. She was wet as only an aroused woman could be. Is it possible that pleasure can be so enhanced it is beyond contemplation, surreal? I know so. We knew ourselves, Amelia and I, as never. Believe me, biological mother aside, only your serious lover knows you more than any other person, your true personality, and your musking signature (I wonder what I mean by that?).

We have only ourselves, no one else but us, in this desolate island in the middle of nowhere. It is as if we must copulate, do it with a vengeance. We must affirm our identity, carry on the species. Perhaps it is the destiny of men, that a man shall meet a woman, dive through a bushy culvert to propagate himself or for pleasure. The act of lovemaking gifts you a fundic aftermath. It's for the gene pool, I guess, an unmistakable gift from a woman's culvert.

It's all crock they have fed us about women being

modest and blasé about sex. How men are the violent aggressors and how women have a low sex drive, find sex uncomfortable or embarrassing, and have to be dragged, cajoled, into the sack. Hogwash. Did they make that up to control women? To contain a monstrous leviathan they fear if released, would shatter myths, explode shibboleths, and expose male sexuality for what it is: a tiny fraction of the woman's—inadequate and minuscule? We are at the woman's mercy, sexually, because we are in effect prisoners of sex. Perform or be cast aside. You need an erection, a sturdy one, to have access to a woman's breeding parts—or pleasure palace—and even then it's not a fait accompli. It is my ardent belief that women want sex more than men. I know. Try telling that to a hormone-fueled teenager aching for his first bonking. But we older men and married folk know the truth. Once they get going, women are the lustier sex. Women who seem prudish at the beginning are the ones who'll flatten you once they discover the joys of sex. Heck, I married my second wife, Mary Bea, just a few months before I joined Amelia for the trip, and I know how competitive women can be in bed. Now here's Amelia—the almighty Amelia, president of the Ninety-Nines, aviation's premier women's group, the toast of Madison Avenue and flying folk—here she is and she's trying to fuck my brains silly.

34

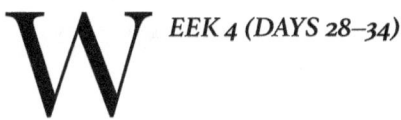

AMELIA

FRED DREAMS A LOT THESE DAYS. HE wakes up with raging loins, thick wood, eyes seeking me (hungrily I guess?). Can't help him. Won't even harbor the thought.

I don't care. I mean, I don't care. About anyone or anything. I've reached that point. I just want to take whatever comes by the moment—each moment, then the next, and the next. And so forth. Not even by the day. We can't even tell the days apart anymore. Time has merged into one continuous solstice of long, humid daylights and sweaty nights broken by pre-dawn coolness—the only time you can get blissful sleep. What's the point? The only motivation is to survive, to stay alive until... whatever. The only thing I care about is food. Yes, really. Food. I am constantly hungry. There's never enough food, and when you find something to eat, it's the same old mussels or turtle meat or oysters. The occasional bird enlivens our diet a bit and reminds me of the delicious taste of fried chicken back in Kansas. We can't even fry the bird: no oil. We barbecue it instead, with no sauces to enhance flavor. It takes half an hour, sometimes more, to get a fire going. We exhausted our matches days ago. So we use the magnifying glass we use for map reading, which we retrieved from the Electra before it washed away, to direct sunlight to the dried brush we've gathered. Depending on how dry the leaves are, it takes about ten minutes to get it smoking, and almost impossible to get a fire going. So we keep the embers hot or glowing for days on end, covering the ashes when rain threatens.

I spend hours just thinking about cheeseburgers and fries and delicious carrot cake and Baskin-Robbins ice cream sundaes.

It's good to have food. Awful if you don't. Water is even more precious. Here we are, surrounded by an ocean, gazillion trillions of gallons of water we cannot drink. To drink even a cupful of saltwater would spell illness, perhaps death.

Fred has come down with a bout of toxic fish poisoning. I made the diagnosis from observing his reactions. I hadn't eaten the same fish; I'm not big on raw fish despite my hunger, preferring instead more oysters. I've gotten sick so many times from the oysters that now I think I'm immune to any reaction they might cause. It's gotten so I can look at the jellied mess and decide this one or that one is a bit too cloudy for my liking and not eat it. So far, I've escaped serious food poisoning. Fred grips his stomach in both hands, his face knotted in pain, gritting his teeth.

"Bad?" I regret asking the obvious.

He nods, not caring, or else in too much pain to answer. I help him to a corner of the shelter and he kneels, then lies on his back, still kneading his stomach. I rack my brain thinking of what to give him from our vast island paradise. I do not know herbs—can't even distinguish a stalk of lemongrass from a garden weed. There are some aspirin tablets left in the first-aid box. I won't give him those. I know what aspirin does to the stomach linings.

He's trying to speak. I lean closer. "Fred?"

"Water...I need...water."

"Okay. You need water."

I look around the shelter, knowing even as I do so that there is no water. I consider giving him my urine, though I have little of that either since there's been brief intake these last couple of days. We are both dehydrated, Fred more so for his unremitting diet of oysters and fish. He even smells fishy, day and night, like the business end of a fisherman's mitten at Plymouth Harbor. I could feed him his urine. I rule that out. Whatever's bothering him, his urine would probably contain remnants of toxins from it.

"Find... turtle," he whispers.

I get it. That's not a problem.

You find turtles mostly at night when they come ashore for nesting. But after Fred and I constructed a makeshift alcove for trapping them, I find a turtle under the makeshift board we'd placed in a shallow cove and tied to two stakes. We constructed it from twine and tree branches laced together, allowing the rope twine some slack so the board would drift. Fred said he learned this trick from his sailor days. Sure enough, within two days one turtle found shelter beneath the board. The turtle was ours for the taking and with luck a sea urchin. I find two turtles beneath the board this time and capture one and bring it to Fred. It's a fairly large specimen; they don't have predators around here once they're grown. I imagine this should have enough blood for him as a substitute for water. I only dread the method Fred uses to get the blood. Now that he's incapacitated, I fear it may fall upon me to plunge the knife.

Fred has other ideas. He drags himself to a sitting position, still in pain. Grabs the knife, asks me to hold the turtle. The poor thing, about twice the size of a football, wriggles its legs as I hold it above ground, and turn my eyes away from the inevitable. The turtle keeps craning her neck, as if begging beheading—though I recognize the absurdity. But that's how it seems to me. I mean, no turtle worth its shell would show its head when it senses a threat. Not our luckless specimen. Fred pins it to the ground, and before I can figure out what he's up to, he plunges the knife tip inside the eye socket and excavates first one eye, then the other. The eyeballs fall onto the leafy bed of the shelter. Fred hurls the sightless turtle away and grabs the eyeballs, which he now squeezes one after the other into his open mouth. I'd expected some crude jelly to come out. Instead, a clear stream of liquid shoots into his mouth—about a quarter of a cup's worth. He offers me the other eyeball, doesn't wait for me to decline, before squeezing more vile jelly into his agape mouth.

I burst into tears.

We need water. But... this? Without sight, the turtle is as good as dead. I know Fred will keep it alive until he needs more water. He'll then slit the throat and pour out the blood to drink. If he kills the turtle now, the blood will congeal when he needs it.

What have we become?

35

A MELIA (NEXT DAY)

FRED ISN'T MAKING ENTIRES IN HIS journal anymore. I check on him. He's lying listlessly in the shelter, in some self-induced stupor. He hasn't updated his logs for days now. I shrug. I can relate. Even I find it difficult going. There's an indescribable ennui that attends the most mundane tasks. I welcome minor things which affirm humanity, even revel in them. You dwell on the mechanics of a burp or fart, milk it to the maximum, inhaling the sourness. This infantilism transports you to your childhood when you and your siblings and schoolmates contested who could cut the loudest wind and bad-cheese everyone out of the room.

Weird.

I find it weird. I examine myself constantly for another day of shedding. Nothing. My period appeared for just one day and never came back. I must suffer from malnutrition more than I realize. Maybe Fred's illness is symptomatic of both our states and in his illness, I should see a reflection of mine. Try as I might, I just can't. I would never admit I'm ill. Out of sorts, maybe, listless even. I have this feel-good uppity protectiveness toward Fred and anything and everything I lay eyes on. I feel I can conquer the world despite being a castaway, and I am confident that soon the Coast Guard will rescue us. I savor this bloated sense of superiority all day, not knowing where it comes from but content to let it ride.

I have to hunt for both of us. His stomach pain is not abating. I look for any leaf-based emetic to give him that would allow him to vomit up whatever toxins caused his upset. But I don't know if there are any plants or leaves available on the island that can do that. I prop him up and stick my middle finger down his throat and wiggle it. His violent retching seems to make things worse, not better, so I let him be. I dread having to get him another leatherback eyeball for water, so I hastily assemble the conch shells and containers and line them up to collect rainwater whenever it rains.

36

A MELIA (NEXT DAY)

I NEED TO FIND WATER FOR FRED. AND for me. I check under the makeshift board in our cove, but no turtles are lounging there since the last one. There's vegetation everywhere, and this appears to be a good bet. Leaves contain water, perhaps enough to stave off death. Avoid three-leaf clusters in the family of poison ivy. The trick is finding leaves safe to eat. The clusters decimated by transient birds and local insects probably mean they're good to eat. If they didn't harm the bird probably wouldn't kill me. As I ponder this, I spy a tree stump crowned by a strange assortment of leaves. At the foot of the bough is a rotten stump where several mushrooms are flourishing.

Hey!

Yep. Mushrooms. I know little about toadstools, but these appear to be the edible kind. White and capped beautifully with a ruffled stem. They look to be the exact type I used to pick with my auntie back in the Kansas meadows. God or someone has been looking out for Fred and me. I collect them all in the skirt of my dress and hug them back to the shelter. At least we'll have some nourishment for today and part of tomorrow.

Back at the camp, I scrape at a spot on my forearm with my index fingernail until I break the skin. A red dot appears, just a trace. I tear off a piece of the mushroom and rub it against the broken skin. Wait thirty minutes for a reaction. None. Repeat on the same spot with green juice squeezed from the leaves I collected. Again, nothing. Most probably safe to eat them, according to Fred's survival manual. I use the magnifying glass to focus sunlight on a prepared bed of dry, rotted boughs and build a fire to boil the toadstools. I make a rough salad of greens garnished by dried grasshoppers. Yes, the yuck factor no longer applies. That or starve to death. I feed it to Fred. At least I try to. He refuses. He hasn't been eating anything these days. Nothing I do can convince him to put food in his mouth. He seems to have lost interest in food. But he drinks any liquid put in his mouth, be it turtle plasma or his urine. I drag Fred by one arm into the shelter and sit down beside him to eat my mushrooms.

Less than one hour after eating the toadstools, I realize I've made a serious mistake. I become dizzy, nauseated, discombobulated, feverish. I have blurred vision, plus double vision. Soon I'm seeing things in triplicate. It's as if I am going through stages of an unfolding nightmare. Even Fred's ashen face grins ghoulishly from three separate Fred gargoyles. I hear rushing streams, feel myself falling backward into caverns I didn't know were there. A wide spiraling hole known as the Chasm beckons me. I know this because it communicated that information telepathically. I also have a distinct impression that I'm losing my mind, and knowing that, still cannot control my descent into madness and the Chasm. No, it is not madness. I have a heightened awareness, an overarching desire for deep knowledge, and psychic awakening. My head reels under the weight and speed of all that I know, all I can see, and what I shall see. For I am the Postulant One, am I not? The world's history, what I find pertinent, unfolds in clairvoyant detail. I see the march of armies across a scorched, decimated Europe, a dictator with a Charlie Chaplin mustache responsible for so much misery and death. Nicodemus called him Hister. It is a curious sight. Gypsies and Citizens Other being herded into gas chambers for no reason other than that they do not have Citizens Aryan bloodline. Such evil I have never seen and cannot comprehend, especially when carried out by people who look like me and my race. The doomed Citizens Other do not know (some may have guessed) what is to happen; they have been told they are getting showers to decontaminate them after the interminable train journey from Warsaw. They are herded into the steel enclaves, and outside the radial lock, looking like a ship's helm, spun anticlockwise until it clicks shut. No escape for the denizens. The only sound they hear is the sound of Zyklon pellets dropping into the acid pan. The "showers" that descend from the shower-heads is a deadly gas. The screams of men, women, and children. You could hear the panicked, desperate and futile banging of hands against the reinforced metal of their steel-domed coffin. It takes about fifteen minutes. The Citizens Other all draw their last breaths and are still. The gas spares no one. Afterwards the Citizens Aryan remove the gold teeth caps and crowns from mouths using strong pliers, and they dispatch the bodies to the cremation ovens. A thick, ominous smoke soon belches from special chimneys, an indescribable odor permeates the air despite the chemical filters used to disguise the result. It brings home to me the banality of evil as I view in the same camp as the crematoriums, the well-kept homes of the camp commandants, the beautiful landscaped lawns trimmed and maintained by Citizens Other inmates kept alive for that purpose. The children, the Schutzstaffel (SS) officers children, are playing in the gardens, pale faces flushed, blonde tresses flying in the summer wind. The heavens remain indifferent above the pallid skylines of Auschwitz-Birkenau and Bergen-Belsen. I see all these, yet it is years ahead, and I have no comprehension of the significance. I only recognize the dictator as the martinet from Austria, now a German Chancellor, friend to the Fascist Mussolini who had ogled me in Rome and whose countryman, a famed poet, had copped a feel right under the dinner table at a state function. In Germany itself, there's one noteworthy pilot, Hanna Reitsch, whose exploits I followed and still follow, as she looked to become a future competitor in women's record-setting flights.

I do not approve of what is going on in those death camps. I am saddened immeasurably by what I see. I see much destruction. The pounding of heavy guns from huge battleships, brave young men dropping on the beaches, many wading ashore to have their lives violently usurped by the unending deadly music of the Schmeissers. From all sides the boom of Gatlings, Thompsons, HMGs, the buzzing death of the MG-42s. The battlefields of Normandy, the Solomon Islands, Guadalcanal, Iwo Jima. I see every horror.

I see the Charlotte Four—black men accused and convicted of raping a white woman and whose trial is dividing the nation. Instinctively, I know they are innocent, even if I'm hard-pressed to say how I have concluded this. I see another blatant act of crass racism in Roosevelt's omission or failure to write a congratulatory note to Jesse Owens after he won four gold medals at last year's Olympics in Berlin. They say Hitler snubbed Jesse Owens, leaving immediately after shaking hands with the German victors only. But Hitler shook Owens's hand behind the honors stand, a fact acknowledged by Owens himself, and later he sent a commemorative photograph of himself to Owens. Upon Owens's return to the USA, President Roosevelt did not so much as invite Owens to a White House dinner or send a congratulatory message. Not even a telegram acknowledging his historic achievements. Our times are not good.

My dreamscape takes me to an oriental village, deep inside the Republic of China. The Kuomintang are fighting the Communists. I am teleported to rural areas, as pagodas, Buddhist temples flash by. I see peasants in sackcloths and wide straw hats outside their huts, in rice fields. They turn to look as I whiz by. The ones outside their huts grin at me —many teeth are missing, the smiles pitted holes in wrinkled masks. Back across Far Eastern lands, down again to Cambodia, down through the Malaysian Peninsula, across the vast, seemingly limitless expanse of the Indian Ocean, south until I am two thousand miles abeam Australia. This is one of the most remote spots on the planet. We swing again toward Papua New Guinea and the airport at Lae, where I took off on my flight into the history books. I watch my takeoff again and watch open-mouthed at how close we came to disaster. We were heavy beginning the takeoff roll, for this was the longest leg of our round-the-world flight at the equator. As we ran out of runway, we barely had flying speed. If I'd aborted the takeoff at that late stage, Fred and I would have entered the annals of history for a tragic reason: the runway ended abruptly before a sheer drop into the ocean. Glad I stuck it out. As I rotated, the runway ended, and we were over the water, dropping, not climbing. If it had been solid earth beneath us, we would have died right there and then. I watch the Electra stagger a few feet above the hungry waves, our prop-wash leaving a visible wake. It struggles like this, at the ragged edge of a stall for the next five minutes, which seems like an hour, then finally the rate-of-climb indicator shows a perceptible climb, and Fred and I are on our way. The plane passes one thousand feet, nearly five minutes after takeoff. By golly.

I see where were we went wrong. The long antenna wire for the radio that we cut off to save weight would have allowed the *Itasca* to detect the direction of our transmissions and vector us to Howland. That was our undoing. Despite the maps, we would have made it if the RDF had worked fine. Despite Fred having had only forty-five minutes of sleep the night before our departure, his initial calculations were fairly accurate. But when I see the Electra get to where we should have had visual contact with the *Itasca*, I realize that would never happen. Calculations based on the wrong map template will yield wrong position reports and estimates. The winds too were strong. Still, Fred with his sextant and star-shooting skills should have been able to meet the challenge and plot us a fresh course. But the heavy sky-obscuring clouds that dogged most of our trip denied him access to the very stars that would have helped him plot our correct position. We couldn't have flown high enough to clear the clouds, because the Electra is not pressurized and we didn't have oxygen—this was a mostly over-water flight with no high terrain anywhere.

For want of a hangnail.

I am taken back to our island, where, in my clairvoyance, I see that we have landed over three hundred miles southeast of Howland, our intended destination. This is an unfor-givable navigational error. But again, I see that the antenna we considered so unnecessary back in Lae would have allowed the *Itasca* to get a bearing on us, or myself to get a bearing on *Itasca*, had I understood how to use the equip-ment. I look for the ships supposedly circling in search of us —and I don't see any. The Navy has called off the search for us days ago. The closest vessel is near the Mariana Islands, a commercial steamer. And two rented boats in the Gilbert Islands hired by GP, my beloved and trustworthy husband, to continue the search. With a sickening heart, I realize we —Fred and I—are doomed. We will never leave this island alive. Our bones will inter here, scattered among other crab-eaten relics festooning the place. This is disheartening, that I shall never see GP again, or Eleanor Roosevelt, or Gene Vidal, my stepsons, my mother and sister, and many others. The shock is too much. I lift my eyes to the elements and cry. I shed loose tears at the utter hopelessness of it all. I'll never see GP again. Never see my beloved Rye countryside, the nearby Atlantic Ocean, my neighbors in Rye, and also in Burbank in California, my extended family in Kansas, my entire network of friends and family. Disheartening. What a waste.

I don't know exactly how long I remain in this state. I discern that I am seeing pagodas in the distance and a Chinese man of middle build with a Fu Manchu mustache is watching me without expression. I stop crying and return the man's gaze. His gaze is direct, unapologetic, yet without hate or remonstrance. He just looks at me, and somehow I understand that he is a shaman of some sort, or a monk from Tibet or wherever. There is great Wisdom in that expressionless, guileless round face. He leans forward and bows to me.

His voice is soft, modulated, and he talks in Uni-speak or
Universal Speak, which I understand as if it is English. He
tells me not to worry. In answer to my unasked question,
yes, I shall perish here and pass into the infinite mists of
history. They will find pieces of my disinterred bones years
from now. Again, not to worry. Our escapades, Fred and I,
will inspire future generations. The diary Fred and I have
been keeping is commendable. "Count about seven days
from today," said the Wise Shaman "then bind the exercise
books under three layers of tarp from the airplane, cover
them with the waterproof life jacket rescued from the
airplane, and place them in a location I shall direct you to."

He stretches out his hand. I follow as if by automation
and we float toward a spot I have never seen before. A
shallow part of the lagoon. I have to wade some twenty feet
to get to it. On one side, there is a dry oval, and when the
shaman points his finger, a hole about two feet deep miracu-
lously appears. He shows where I should bury the bound
logs and exercise books there. It is a safe part of the island
and will survive through periods of submersion and will
remain dry and unscathed for over seven decades, after
which a group of men from my country will arrive on an
expedition, trying to find me. They will find artifacts that
will prove to them that Fred and I were castaways on this
island.

"The final story of your sojourn on this island will be
revealed to a Postulant One, an aviator from the Dark Continent, who by the stars, will be born on a date exactly eighteen years from the day you landed on Gardner Island—for
that is the name of the island you landed on. The name will
later change to Nikumaroro, but that is by the by. The Postulant One will write your tale—your stars align. You may be
linked with him in a previous life, details of which I need

not go into. He will write your story, how you and your companion spent your last days on the island.

"You have taken in with a child," the shaman goes on, much to my shock. "I do not know the sex of the embryo yet. It is too early, and by the signs, it will not come to pass that the child will be born. It is a consequence of your being marooned on the island. Please accept my sympathy.

"Your vision is real, my dear friend," the shaman says, "and it will come to pass as I have detailed. Please do not go back to eat the fungus that gives the Great Vision. It may prove toxic to you, and the diviner you see may be the wrong one, an evil one. I bid you farewell, my wonderful friend, and I thank you for seeking me out."

With that, the great shaman bows solemnly, and fades out, his Fu Manchu mustache drooping, deep sadness in those beautiful and deep almond eyes.

I remember shaking in palsied excitement and dread, shouting, "My baby! My baby! Oh, my baby!" I wake up thinking I am drenched in sweat, but when I pass a hand across my forehead, it is cool. A mid-morning breeze blows and somehow I am at peace, and I can't figure out exactly why. The news of my future is nothing to dance about. I don't how long I stay in this position, while Fred lies passive in the background. He didn't partake of the hallucinogenic mushroom and does not understand what I've been through. He sleeps and sleeps day in and out, far longer than he is ever awake. He mumbles to himself a lot. I fear for his future, but I've got my worries.

It rains outside. I rise and go out to catch some rainwater. But as soon as it starts, the rain stops. Five minutes at most. Flash rain. Typical tropical rain. Not even two cupfuls. But from the different eaves we positioned for catching rain, I get about three and a half cups total, which I share with

Fred. I give him more since he hardly eats now. He sits up, and I hold his head to my breast as he sips. I don't know. If he had toxic fish poisoning, shouldn't he have recovered by now? Instead, he is slipping away from me daily.

What to make of the meeting with the shaman? A hallucinatory parley or a true mystic vision?

The shaman says that I'm pregnant. I should have suspected from the beginning after the one-off rag day. It's an unfamiliar sensation for me. Should I believe him when I know I'm just a tad over forty years of age and miracle baby isn't the thing I daydream about? Fred is in no position to be a father, nor am I to be a mother. I suppose I could fulfill my maternal duties if I may be allowed to live. The entire thing is unreal, yet so...real. I can't tell if I'm in a dream or fully awake. I saw and heard what I did after consuming those mushrooms. It's all woven into a beguiling tapestry of truth and biology—truth, because the prophecy is too vivid and devoid of the foggy ambiguity of dream fare, and biology because I am too young yet to be having senior moments where an elaborate prophecy is unveiled to me in a trance.

37

A MELIA (NEXT DAY)

FRED HAS SHRUNK, REALLY SHRUNK TO an unreasonable facsimile of himself. His gaunt frame has withered to near-scarecrow proportions. His eyes bulge, his cheeks have hollowed, and he perpetually reaches out, trying to tell me something. Yet when I cradle his head on my lap and stroke him and urge him to tell me whatever it is he wants, he just stares into space and sometimes mutters, "Goddamn!" or, "Where are those stupid gofers?" At other times he will, without warning, shout, "Avast there! Heave to starboard thirty!" or something like that. Then he cuts loose a long string of invective, hurled at unseen foes, castigating erring deckhands. His life at sea overshadows his flying career. At such times, I can only cringe and wait for the verbal torrent to subside, wondering if I acted wisely in sharing my DNA with this man.

Once done with spewing instructions at some hapless seamen, his mien softens, his body relaxes. His eyes close, a thin smile plays on his lips. Satisfied they have carried out his orders out to the letter, he drifts into an untroubled sleep.

Since Fred eats little or nothing, the little food I scrounge up is mostly for myself. Still not a simple task. It's amazing how, on a verdant island with so much fish and land crabs and other creatures, you could starve to death. That is slowly happening. I can't see myself eating raw fish indefinitely; a considerable number of them are toxic, laden with harmful parasites, or just inedible. The brighter the color of the fish, I've learned, the more likely it will not be stomach-friendly. There is also a toxic variety of land crab, a red-colored monster I've seen marching sideways across the grove more than once. Even the other crabs, the drab-colored ones, avoid them. I find some dropped coconuts from the coconut palms scattered on the island, and this is always welcome. But peeling off the off the husks, then smashing the hard shell on a stone to get to the water and the edible flesh takes a toll on our single bone-handled knife. The knife is just about done, despite being sharpened every other day.

I venture again to the lagoon grove where I picked the hallucinogenic mushrooms. The rotted stump and the crevice where the errant fungi flourished is still there. I see three specimens, brown, stately, delicate, an umbrella of inviting ruffles crowning the stalk. It looks edible. I mull over the shaman's words. Here in front of me is a path to another reality, a unique perspective—escape from my present troubles. Green leaves of the tiny mangrove sway to the ocean breezes, and from the skies, jackdaws and rooks caw in dull excitement. Everything looks normal, sane. Yet within an hour, at the least, it could transport me to China or Tibet, wherever the shaman materialized from. Despite my hunger, both for physical food and spiritual experience, it is a simple decision to make. The shaman warned me about coming back here to eat the fungus again, spelling unfavorable consequences. I'm in enough trouble already—marooned on a strange island in the middle of the Pacific and given up for dead by the rest of humanity, my fellow castaway sick and incoherent, and feeling huge hunger pangs. The shaman's statements were uncannily accurate. His words had the unmistakable ring of truth, and there is no doubt in my mind this was not merely my mind wandering.

I walk away, resolving that if ever it comes to where I could no longer carry on, I would come back here and consume a fatal dose of the mushrooms. And that will be that.

I try not to look back. A deadly hue, a whisper of the grave, suffuses that lagoon with its tiny mangrove. The pristine sights Fred and I have seen, and continue to see, make it clear that we are the first humans on the island in perhaps half a century.

Or are we?

That mangrove thicket seems to suggest otherwise. Something's there. For sure. A Being, an Unseen Presence, a Brooding Evil. That we might not be alone on the island, or that the island has ghosts, unsettles me. Yet I still believe we are not unwelcome here. How do you explain that the crabs and lizards and other creatures have no predators and know no fear, coming within inches of our shelter or where we lie on the sand, even scurrying to our feet until shooed off? There is no malaria or other parasitic illness on the island unless Fred and I have inadvertently brought it with us from

Lae. The parasites could have entered our bloodstream anywhere in South America or Africa, or through the Asian continent. I blame the fish.

Blame the fish. Always!

I still cannot convince Fred to continue making entries in his journal. He's too sick. Best to wait until he recovers.

38

MELIA *(NEXT DAY)*

FRED'S CONDITION HAS IMPROVED A bit. He sits up, asks for water. I give him from the rainwater I have stored. He takes about four gulps. Stops. Stares at me.

"Amy...Doolittle," he says.

My turn to stare. "Doolittle?"

"Where you been, Amy?" he asks.

Okay, humor him. He's on the mend. "Right here beside you. Are you feeling better any?"

He nods. "Right."

Minutes pass. He says again, "Right."

I give thanks silently. Afraid that if he's on recovery mode, any untoward word or gesture might send him reeling back.

"Yes, Fred."

"What do you think? I mean...."

"Mean what?. Go on."

"Food...poisoning. Maybe?"

"Probably."

"Fish? Oysters?"

"Could be. One of the other."

"Your own sweet poon?" he says.

From nowhere. Just like that. I feel the blood rush to my face.

"Not nice, Fred."

"Is not?" He ponders. 'Okay. Sorry."

"Accepted."

"I mean it, though. Your—yours is damn good."

"I don't know what you're talking about." I know exactly what he's saying.

"And fishy." He darts me a glance.

I stare him down. "Maybe you have FISH poisoning."

Prolonged silence.

"Yeah," he says.

I say nothing.

"Went off for a bit there, didn' I?" he says.

Dare I tell him it's been four days exactly?

He rambles on, "Had a dream there. Headlines, you know. New York Times...St. Louis Post-Dispatch."

Pause.

"LA Times...Chicago Tribune. Something about...Amy Earhart and Fred Noonan missing for weeks now. Lost in the...Pacific."

"That's us. That's us."

"General Doolittle ain't pleased...his darling daughter is missing."

"It's Earhart, honey. Amelia Earhart Putnam."

"What?"

"I'm not Doolittle's daughter. My father's name is

Edward Stanton Earhart. My married name is Amelia Putnam. There's never been a Doolittle in my name. I'm not sure I've ever met any Doolittles."

"Oh." Total confusion in his face.

I confuse him more.

"My maternal name is Otis. Like the elevator. Not Doolittle."

"Oh," he says again.

"I don't know if General Doolittle even has a daughter. We're the ones missing on a trans-Pacific flight."

He considers this. "Well, General Earhart's daughter is missing with Brad Newman, her navigator," he insists.

"Noonan," I say. "Fred Noonan."

His eyes are a dull red and he's a bit off, but it's good to have him back. The fuzzy memory will fix itself in a few days. I wonder if his "dream" coincided with the period of my hallucinogenic trip. I smile at him.

"Would you like something to eat?"

"What you got?"

"How about some insect protein?"

That's what we're down to: eating bugs to survive. I hear insects are all protein. No details there. I can't even relive it in my diaries. Just know that if collected in a bunch, offending parts delicately removed (depends on which parts you find offensive—eyeballs, tentacles, ovipositor?), and then slipping them into the mouth and chomping down— the taste isn't bad, though it is distinctly crunchy. It helps if you close your eyes. I avoid picking up insects with stingers since that means there's venom inside. Without a doubt, the bugs are keeping us alive, supplemented by the fish we can catch and some edible shrubbery.

That's what I said. Shrubbery.

Hunger is a terrible thing. You think of food all the time.

You spend inordinate amounts of time imagining recipes and variations on recipes and how you would prepare them if given the chance again. You have all the time in the world to plan your recipe. Like a prisoner serving a lengthy sentence, imagining food becomes gastronomic masturbation. Even food I loathed before now seems like heavenly manna if only I could get it. Thus, I concoct elaborate recipes involving cabbage, iceberg lettuce, broccoli, spinach, coriander. I know exactly how I would mix the salad or soup stock, how it would taste, how I would let my taste buds soak in the essence of each ingredient. A good, medium-rare Salisbury steak simmering in succulent gravy would be just the thing to follow the salad appetizer and spritz, and a tart-topped chocolate mousse to nail it all down. Or grilled wild Alaskan salmon served with rice pilaf and scalloped potatoes. The leftovers I had routinely thrown to our dogs or stuffed into garbage bins back in Noank or Los Angeles now seem a horrendous waste. Never again would I take food on the table for granted. I mean, we're still in the Great Depression and I lived through the worst days of it. I remember eating a slice of bread and a single potato spud for an entire day. There were weeks I couldn't find meat—sausage, beef, ham, anything—to eat. A dime in those days went a long way in feeding you—if you could only lay hands on a nickel. We took in the lessons. Many Americans still save money compulsively, don't trust the banks, and never throw away unspoiled food. As FDR's policies made the economy better, some (myself included) drift back to the old ways.

Never again. Lord, please give me another chance. I need food. Not just me, Fred too. Whatever I eat is nourishment for two adults. Yes, reader, something in there all right. If I am wont to feel greater hunger pangs than Fred, let it be. My friends back in Long Beach, California, or Westchester, New

York, could attest that I hardly do more than pick at a celery stalk or half a plate of tossed salad and two glasses of buttermilk for dinner. My favorite beverage is buttermilk. We won't find it on Gardner Island. Who am I kidding, really?

Fred nods. I sense he's disappointed. Big grasshoppers sun-roasted a few hours are nutritious. He looks at me for a moment. His blue eyes are lusterless, and they still bulge, as if searching for something just around the corner. Those eyes bother me. I've seen them in hospitals. Either Fred has dementia or a desperate underlying disease. The eyes seem to push out the orbs, searching, clinging to an elusive reality.

I massage his chest with my palm. His skin is rubbery, bony, the ribcage visible. Malnutrition will do that to you. Perhaps mine looks the same way. His abdomen is light, concave. It's like kneading a sack of bones. My palm caresses his lower abdomen, skates over the shriveled hump of his groin to the thighs. Back again to the hump. More pressure, light massage, alternating a feathery touch. The hump comes alive. He has lost so much weight the trousers flop around his waist. My hand slithers inside, finds him flaccid. I help it along, and after some effort, it rises. He enjoys what my fingers are doing, but he doesn't have the energy to indulge it further. Yeah, right? Meeley's luck. Amelia's box! When Fred's member has wilted and won't get up again despite much persuasion, I tuck it back in. I sigh and get up. Time to go look for those grasshoppers.

The trick to snaring them is to anticipate the leap. They are quick, smart things with long proboscis and huge eyeballs on each side of their tiny heads. They can see in all directions. As their long, cutting proboscis exfoliate the grass centimeter by centimeter, they watch your approach without appearing to do so. When you lunge for them with your palms cupped, they launch themselves with their long, thin legs to another location. They seem to sense when you begin the dive and they split a nanosecond before you do so. You end up grabbing a fistful of grass and brown earth. Sod the buggers. They're probably laughing at your clumsy efforts to catch them. The trick is to leap ahead of or behind their launch trajectory and pin the bugger to the ground as they leave the ground. Yes, they can leap backward or side-ways. Snagging one is always one success out of four or five attempts. The green-colored insects match the surrounding fauna and are difficult to see unless they've just leaped. I was stalking a greenback once and was getting ready to make my grab when I noticed another gruesomely silent monstrosity just inches from my face, sitting still.

A praying mantis.

I shrieked and leaped backward, scattering everything from land crabs to sundry lizards. I could never eat a praying mantis. Something about their sentinel stance speaks of pure evil or piety—I can't tell which—can't be bothered either. They're probably harmless to humans, I don't know. Other brown-colored grasshoppers are hard to see when they're on the sandbar; you spot them when perched on the foliage. They are delicious if you can get them. Some are big as crickets and might be cicadas for all I know, though I hear little chirruping in the night.

39

MELIA *(NEXT DAY)*

FRED DIED TODAY.

I didn't know for some time after it happened. We talked in the morning about nothing in particular, about what we would do when they rescue us. He ate three dried insects and drank about half a cup of water saved from the previous rain. He seemed well along on his recovery, and I thought maybe later on in the afternoon, if the mood was right, I might press my luck again. He slept in the afternoon, and so did I under the relative coolness of the shelter. The tropical heat outside was like an enemy. Nothing stirred and the slap, dance, and froth of the waves crashing on nearby rocks, and the sandbar lulled one into religious somnolence. There is music to that wave dance if you listen, and it works best if it soaks into your subconscious, and you become one with the rhythm of the Great Ocean and the spheres.

I nodded off.

When I awoke, Fred was still asleep or appeared to be, and I imagined I saw the rise and fall of his shirt marking his breathing. I stretched and went down to the water's edge to take a quick dip. By now, I'd found the courage to do this without fear of jellyfish stings and Fred not watching out for sharks or whatever. Afterward, I lay on the cool sand, and as was typical, was sun-dried in minutes. I went back inside again a half-hour later and lay down on the tarpaulin. Fred still slept, and I was reluctant to wake him. I drifted off again, waking up barely an hour later. I lay still, like a statue, the music of the waves in the background lulling me. I stared at the shelter top and it occurred to me that I had to find food for the evening. I didn't relish another plate of sun-roasted grasshoppers, crickets, palm weevils, and turtle blood. If Fred was up to it, perhaps we could experiment on the menu: sun-sautéed cricket on sushi garnished with a leaf salad. No idea the name of the leaves. They passed the edibility test. As for crickets, Fred knew just which tiny rocks to upend to find those pesky chirrupy insects. When we couldn't find birds and fish or crabs, that is.

"Fred?"

No answer. He had slept too long. I watched for the usual rise and fall of the chest. It was there, barely perceptible. I relaxed. Then stared. No, it wasn't. He was too still. I bent closer. He appeared to be sleeping, but something was off. Before I went out to bathe in the ocean, he'd been sleeping facing the ceiling. He hadn't changed his position in nearly two hours. Was that normal?

I touched him. "Fred?"

His skin was cold, his body unresponsive. I shook him several times. Searched for a pulse on the neck, the wrist. None.

"Fred!"

If Fred had... no! I pounded on his chest, knelt beside him, and administered vigorous CPR, tasting the dried, basement-mold character of his mouth, blowing air down his windpipe. I do this perhaps ten, twenty minutes.

Nothing.

I give up when I could no longer continue. I was dizzy with all the blowing. Nothing. He never stirred. He appeared to be sleeping peacefully.

Fred was gone. And that is that.

I AM ALONE ON THIS ISLAND.

A great foreboding engulfs me.

The sole human being on this planet within a planet. Even flying across the Atlantic at night in the Lockheed Vega, even the few times I have descended in a powerless airplane to a dead-stick forced landing—never have I felt so alone.

Fred's there, yet he's not. I feel twice betrayed. Thrice, in fact. First, by getting marooned on this island. Second, by the failure of the Coast Guard or the Navy to find us. Third, by Fred's death.

I sit there, staring at Fred's corpse. I want to cry. I want to break down and weep and throw myself on the floor at the mercy of God or whoever is in charge of the universe, whichever deity controls life and death. I cry.

He is Fred; you remember. We started this adventure together. Now he has left me. I can forgive him for his sins. They are legion. Getting us off course, his sins against me, against nature, our complicit betrayal of GP. Somehow I cannot forgive him for dying on me. Dead he is.

I don't know how many hours I sit there waiting, watching. Waiting for him to jerk awake and jeer at me, telling me he'd played a colossal joke on me. Not a stir.

He moved once. It was the rigor setting in, reflexive, no conduit to his brain. I didn't even start.

The thought of being alone on this island terrifies me. Whatever else he did, regardless of how ill he was, Fred had provided company, a bulwark against the island's unseen ghosts.

I tell myself to get off my duff and take charge.

Mount Rushmore weighing down my body.

More staring at Fred's body. More staring into space.

I have to do something, move before nightfall. It requires superhuman effort.

Lead ingots in my muscles.

I tell myself that this is not the time, nor is it convenient to play the helpless female. Just as the skies can be remorseless, cruel as the sea, so could nature. I have to be strong for three of us—Fred, myself, and the baby—so I'm not consumed by the same forces that ghosted Fred. Yet the whole situation seems insurmountable. For a moment, I consider just running out of the shelter and wading into the ocean and not looking back until I'm too far from shore and Mother Ocean swallows me up. At that moment, I even imagine I hear the ocean itself calling. It's a soothing lullaby, mesmerizing, the rhythmic crash of the waves.

"A. E., A. E.," the waves seem to chant. "A. E., A. E., come to us, A. E."

It would be quick. No mess.

I couldn't lift one foot.

It comes back gradually. I become myself. I force myself up. It becomes easier after that.

I go outside. The sun-bleached heavens, scattered cloud

wisps, lapping wavelets. Tiny ocean spray touching the face. The world couldn't be more normal. Yet, inside the shelter, Fred Noonan is dead, and I am alone in the world. Over seven thousand miles away from my home in Rye, New York. Stupid and idle thoughts at such a poignant moment. Yet here I am. Time loses meaning when there are no telephone calls to make or answer, no grocery shopping lists, no housekeeping tasks, no preparing dinner in a proper kitchen. No sound of traffic outside as in downtown Manhattan. No friends to connect with.

Have to be strong. Amelia against the world. GP, I know you didn't abandon me. Eleanor Roosevelt, I know you want me back on US soil. Residents of Atchison, Kansas, I'm certain you want your daughter back home in the flat farmlands of the Midwest. So why am I the loneliest woman on earth, on an unnamed, uninhabited island, surrounded by a hostile ocean and thousands of land crabs? I feel the crushing weight of the obstacles facing me, the futility of it all. I hear a sound, like a whimper, and realize it's coming from me, and I dash inside the shelter again, throwing myself down on the tarpaulin, shutting my eyes tight against all enemies within and otherwise. The sudden panic seizes me. I refuse to open my eyes, to behold the unending Pacific Ocean. The skies seem vast beyond comprehension, daring me. I have surfed the heavens on my wooden and aluminum wings and my trustworthy engines and known the absolute, indescribable joy of flight. I rode the skies to where I am stranded. Now, the firmament seems indifferent, hostile, faintly mocking.

I have nothing to relieve an anxiety attack. I can only lie there with eyes shut, alongside Fred's body, and wait for the chaos to abate. I hyperventilate, find it difficult to breathe or think, and have this crazy idea I am dying. I grab something from the corner which turns out to be one of Fred's nylon shirts, and I drape it over my face and tie it in a useless bowknot behind my neck. I breathe into the shirt, noting Fred's strong, masculine scent, elements of him I remember.

I get better after some time. I rise and take stock. Fred's legacy from the shirt stays on me. I look at his body. It occurs to me that he will soon have a different legacy if I leave here his body to decompose.

His eyes are half-open. Perhaps his body sensed the onset of death and he struggled to wake up, but the Reaper froze his eyes midway to opening. I close them gently. I consider staying the night with Fred's body in the shelter, and decide what to do tomorrow. My instincts tell me this is an awful idea. Death attracts so many other universes to itself; even carrion birds over the Pacific Island will know something has passed. A million microbes from Fred's gut will at this moment be feasting on his innards, invading his bloodstream where it has pooled at the places in contact with the ground. The lividity. Soon, land crabs will crawl into the shelter, pulled by some unseen cosmic signal. I know all this, yet I cover Fred's body with his old shirt—most of his face, at least, and his body so that only his legs protrude. We've all heard of people certified dead waking up in the morgue days later. I have a half-hearted hope that Fred will wake up and say, "Ta-la!" and grin at me. He would say, "Scared you, didn' I? You thought I was dead, I know you were. Ha! You should know better, Meeley. Death has no business with Old Freddie. Not without my permission."

I'm repeating myself. I know. Can't help it.

No movement. As recumbent as a corpse.

I have to dispose of the body, no matter what comfort I derive from seeing it beside me. Who knows what else death's invisible halo might attract? I steel myself. Lift him by both arms. The arms are wooden, the body heavy. I drag him from the shelter, pulling both arms, looking sideways to see where I'm going, not looking at the body. I can't hurt him at this stage, so if I'm rough and scrape his right leg as it catches a boulder, it won't bother him. I don't stop until I reach the water's edge. He was a sailor once, so a committal at sea is appropriate—given his longstanding fondness for the ocean. I suppose it is appropriate to say a few words to my old friend, wishing him Godspeed on his journey across the Styx. I haven't been to church in a long time and can't for the life of me remember even one word from The Litany for the Burial of the Dead. All that comes to mind is the phrase, "Ashes to ashes, dust to dust." I'm sending Fred to the Greek god of the Seas, Poseidon. I look at his face again. He is merely sleeping. I draw strength from his immobility, knowing somehow that wherever he is, he would want me to do this for him. Death confers responsibility on the living. The responsibility to claim the deceased, to accord the remains proper respect and decent burial, or cremation. One recognizes that here is someone much like ourselves now gone to the place we must all go when our time comes. There is no victory or comeuppance in being alive and seeing another human, younger, or the same age, die before you. To gloat over another's remains would be indescribably evil.

Tears run freely down my cheeks. I say a few words, to the effect of, "Fred, I shall miss you dearly. I forgive you for everything. For my benefit and ability to move on, I must forgive everything. Go in peace. Please, please watch over me, protect me from the land crabs or other creatures I haven't even seen. Get into the minds of the searchers and the government, tell them I'm still alive, and guide them to this place. Talk to a medium, a psychic, or somebody—let them give information to the authorities on where to find me. Bye, Fred. I miss you already. And here's something you don't know, and I never told you: your baby's on the way."

I choke out those last words. In truth, I am wondering what kind of life the baby will have.

I drag the body into the water, up to my knees, thighs. Wait for the next wave to come in, and as it recedes, I let go of Fred. His body submerges in the frothy breakwater and swiftly disappears.

I must not look back, heading to the shelter.

I am alone in this world.

A deep calm settles over me.

I am at peace with the inevitable. Where there should be chaos and anxiety, great unease—there is nothing. Nothing. A void. I am ready for the demons, whatever they may be, wherever they hide.

 MELIA *(NEXT DAY)*

FRED'S PERSONAL EFFECTS LITTER THE cabin. I should get rid of them all. I just couldn't. Sometimes I sniff his faded shirt, and Fred is there. The tall, dark, blue-eyed sailor with a drinking habit and adventurous hands. He is there all right, the gruff, dark, stale effluvium of an alpha male, worlds traversed, human interactions experienced and unknown. I shall miss him. I need his raw serum, his mustiness enervated by the tropical heat, and clinging to his shirts—to stimulate my endocrines. Biology would tell us we women need male spoor to function optimally. Perhaps in convents, with no priests around, nuns unconsciously flock around the androgynous ones amongst them. I don't know. Don't care. I just want to live.

I rub my tummy. It feels good to be alive. Does it?

~

DREAM SEQUENCE:

LIFE DOESN'T MATTER. YES, IT DOES. FOR the baby's sake. Must remember that. The baby is everything. Which baby? Are you dreaming again, Meeley? You started this round-the-world flight four months ago, before which you performed your marital duties with GP some weeks before. Could it be possible? How would GP know he'll be a father yet again? It's a novel experience for me, and I love it, would love it, but the uneasiness is there. This is not Manhattan. This is a remote island where I am my antenatal clinic, my doctor, my midwife. Trust Amelia to always toe the alternative path by hook or by providence. I am malnourished enough to be in touch with my body rhythms. A passenger is there all right, in the embryonic stage. A beloved passenger, not a stranger, and we shall get acquainted as the months pass by. I picture how she will look—it has to be a girl! Will she have my blond looks and freckles or GP's cynical side to her beauty? I picture how I might handle the delivery myself. Back in the States, on Indian reservations, tribal women have good midwives, yet further out in the boondocks, many women deliver their babies unattended. I will have to sterilize the bone-handled knife that served Fred and me so well in the past, and would if I'm not rescued by then, crown our stay on the island when I use it to cut the umbilical cord. I smile at the thought of myself, legs splayed, sitting on a pool of *lochia serosa,* undergoing the ritual of childbirth. I shall eat the placenta after searing it in a fire.

To get through the night, I leave some coconut shells

and stuff from the Electra outside the shelter entrance, to alert me if an intruder tries to get in. Still, sleep eludes me. I am alone—the thought ravages my mind throughout that first night without Fred. I am alone in the world. The bone-handled knife lies within reach, inches away. I figure if sleep won't come during the night, it will come in the day when I shall, perhaps, be safer. I don't know. With Fred, nothing ever came to bother us at night, except perhaps the occasional errant land crab. But who knows? Animals might sense vulnerable prey and seize the night.

I must have slept, for when I awoke, shafts of sunlight illuminated the shelter and full daylight blazed.

41

A MELIA (NEXT DAY)

I HAVE CRAMPS. SERIOUS GUT-CRUSHING cramps, like a wrench tightening a nut in my appendix. I hope I haven't come down with food poisoning like Fred. I haven't eaten fish or fish products in the past twenty-four hours, so I can't quite figure out why I'm having cramps. I look around and wonder if in a few days I'll be dead, too. No! I own this island. This is my home. Barring a telepathic communication with the coast guard and navy ships, I have this heavy feeling I am condemned to die here, on this pristine island in the middle of an endless ocean.

I limp around my island clutching my abdomen. I admire the iridescent rainbow of ocean spray shimmering in the volcanic breakwater. The hiss and slap of the wave slipstream. The damp salt and mussels tang of the ocean. This would be paradise if I wasn't so apprehensive, so unsure of what comes next, cramped in pain, awed by nature's power. Perhaps I should just surrender to nature, let her take care of me her way. Perhaps then I'll be safe. The cumulative tension of the past few weeks is getting to me. It would be easier to lie down and die, like Fred. To be one with nature and God. Ah, God. Are you there, God? This is Amelia Earhart Putnam calling. Do you hear me? Help me. Help. I don't want to die. You don't want your daughter to die, do you?

The heavens are silent. The silence of the universe is the solemn breath of God. When there's thunder and lightning, it's nature's fury.

Why these random thoughts?

I am a hopeless philosopher, yet I end up philosophizing.

I find a few sea urchins and after some hesitation eat them raw. I am hungry, there's the baby to think of, (Amelia, are you hallucinating?) and hey, this isn't exactly a buffet table out here. Well, if I'm suffering from toxic fish poisoning, this wouldn't help. I harbor this crazy notion that any toxin from the urchins might overpower the one already nested in my stomach, perhaps neutralize it.

Pooh!

I miss flying. There's something about racing down a runway, heaving back on the stick, and unfurling yourself from the sultry bonds of earth. It's a feeling understood by all airmen. You are of the earth, yet in another dimension, jockeying an aluminum tube through the skies, obeying recent laws, the laws of aerodynamics, viewing the earth as other mortals never will, not even frequent flyers. I long to hold the controls of an airplane again, rack stick and rudder into an aileron roll, dive toward the earth and arc gracefully into a loop, snapping into a vertical roll, a Cuban eight, all the delightful dances in the sky. I can see sun-dappled clouds above an October landscape, glorious, fiery, burnt colors effusing the charm and rhododendron scent of mid-autumn. I see a layer of snow beneath a cloudless blue Kansas sky in December, not a ripple in sight, the smell of oil and radial engines and flight tunics, goggles and helmet, the throbbing of nine-cylinder Pratts. There's that special feel of hand-propping a Hispano-Suiza on a spring morning and hearing the beautiful purr when it comes to life. Possibilities seem endless and you're glad to be alive and glad to be flying airplanes for a living. The bark of a Wright Whirlwind belching blue smoke as it sputters to life... for a moment I am overcome by the memories. Tears come to my eyes, and I find myself on my knees, worshiping the heavens, blessing the moment, wishing again for those fond times.

42

A MELIA (NEXT DAY)

DREAM SEQUENCE

I WAKE UP CRAMPED AGAIN. I'M sitting in a pool of blood.

My baby.

Just like that. Gone. I cry out in anguish, scoop up the blood, wail to the skies at the injustice and cruelty. There's betrayal here—I'm not sure from whom, flushing out my embryo without apology, removing my dear little forming baby from her warm cocoon. I watch the dark red splotches course down my thighs in disbelief. Circumstance or nature, what a cruel joke.

My baby.

My baby.

Give me back my baby. I'm so sorry, love. So sorry, honey. Mommy could not save you. I did all I could. The times we could have had, had I got out of this island prison. I hardly knew ye.

I scrape as much blood as I can onto a piece of the tarp I have torn off. I know I'll bleed for some time, but I don't care. I dig a small hole in the shelter using the bone-handled knife. My baby deserves a decent resting place. A proper burial.

God, what a betrayal. First Fred. Now my baby. I never had it so bad.

Gazing down at the blood rivulet pooling where I sit, I seethe in fury and desperation. I plead with the powers that govern the universe. The tides, the moon, sunspot activity, God, whoever. I don't care who—just give me back my baby. To be so untimely ripped. My fingers run through the clotted blood, seeking communion with what was mine. Tiny strips of gray tissue, the intense and earthy smelting-iron hue of a delivery room. Or a slaughter slab.

I'm so sorry.

I am consumed by fits of weeping and agony.

Oh, life.

So cruel.

43

MELIA (AFTERWARD)

I KNOW I'M DEPRESSED. THEY SAY having insight into your problem helps. I cannot stop the dour moods. I don't know how many hours, days, perhaps weeks pass by. I am an automaton. A walking dead woman. I scrounge and eat.

I know I have gone mad when I poke through a recent bowel movement with a stick. I tell myself I am searching for clues my life has taken the last corner in the march toward certain death. Let the heavens observe. Either I'm crazy or I'm a scientist. A mad scientist.

When the cramps have dissipated, and am mourning silently, I watch the land crabs and the turtles meander past the tent. What do they think observing this lady from the American Midwest splayed out on the sand, hand in her crotch, talking to herself? They would understand. They are creatures of the earth. I enjoy being immersed in my own fetid, damp, ripeness. I wish to claim my right as an earthly being since humans have abandoned me. More than once thus ensconced, I jump to my feet, convinced a rescue ship is on the horizon, and some unbelieving deckhand on forward watch has just sighted me through his binoculars. I see the mad rush to stern by his mates as he announces his sighting.

Time stands still for interminable periods on this island. Periods of absolute inertia where the hypnotic song of the ocean can be broken by the sudden searing pain of a chigger bite. That moment when you think your back is on fire, you don't know exactly what you're dealing with. Then you flail and throw off your shirt, find and squish the little critter that crawled up your back from the sand to deliver its painful gift.

I try again communicating by telepathy with Eleanor Roosevelt, with GP, with Gene Vidal, telling them I'm still alive, that they shouldn't give up on me—trying to send them the coordinates of my position from the one Fred had plotted. Fred's in the water, the Electra's in the water, and sometimes it seems appropriate that I join them to make a perfect finish to the job we started together. From Miami, Florida, to San Juan, Puerto Rico, to Caripito, Venezuela, to Paramaribo, Suriname, to Fortaleza, Brazil, to Natal, Brazil to Saint-Louis, Senegal... around the world at the equator, to end up here on effectively the last leg but two of the flight. Had we made Howland Island, the next leg, Howland to Honolulu, would have been a routine crossing.

I consider going back to the lagoon grove and partaking once more of the hallucinogenic mushrooms. But the shaman had warned me against it. When Fred died, and I had that spontaneous evacuation of my cyesis, any doubts I had about the truth of his prophecy vanished. I shall prepare my journals and Fred's writings, bind them in waterproof material, and deposit them at the designated place. One day, people will read them and know about our ordeal and our last days here.

Yet I cannot resign myself to the shaman's declaration that I shall never leave this island alive. I wish to have my bones interred in the land of my birth, the land of the brave and the free, of purple mountain majesties, amber waves of grain, on a Kansas alfalfa or wheat field, if not in a proper cemetery in Atchison. I'll even take a mausoleum in Kansas City.

If I'm to die, I don't want to die knowing my end is near. I shall be insensate when my body rots after the land crabs are finished with it. They will surely make a meal of me when the time comes. I've seen the crabs disassemble an unfortunate bull shark carcass washed up on the island. I had approached the carcass myself, hoping to get some meat off it. The putrefaction drove me back. The crabs are like piranhas, only much slower. By nightfall, the carcass was a barely distinguishable skeleton. Well, land crustaceans, I hope all of you rot in a special and inaccessible part of Malebolge.

44

MELIA (AFTERWARD)

I DON'T KNOW HOW MUCH LONGER I can keep up this diary. I've run dry two ink-pots and am using Fred's last one right now. Perhaps I will dilute the ink to make it last longer.

I have a mind to end it all now.

Di-di-dit-dah-dah-dah.

It makes no sense. What do I know about Morse Code? A male flight instructor once tried to teach me the Morse Code. "Nothing to it. In a few weeks you should be able to tap out 'I LOVE YOU' in Morse," he said, looking me straight me in the eye.

I find my way to the lagoon grove, to the old tree, and its rotting trunk with the mushroom bed. The wasted hole in the trunk is there. No sign of any fungus. Wrong tree? No. Only one grove in the lagoon with a sizable tree. I look again, search everywhere. No mushrooms. Fiddlesticks. What now? I only meant to harvest the mushrooms and keep them in the shelter, and then, if life became unbearable, leave with some dignity.

I have my own opinions about suicide. You leave on your terms, at a time of your choosing. To me, there's no dignity in doing so in the absence of a terminal illness or unbearable mental demons. I think my demons are manageable. Unless the land crabs crawl all over me while I still draw breath, and I can't remove them, there is no desperate reason to end my life. It would be the irony of the century if I took my life, and then, a day later, perhaps days, a coast guard cutter shows up to rescue me.

Mellie.

Strange I should think of myself that way now. A family nickname. But why do I bring up the name now? I know from my time working at the Denison House in Boston that childhood regression is a common feature in the terminally ill.

My epitaph might read: Here lies Amelia Earhart, of Atchison, Kansas, USA. She loved aviation and lived life on her terms.

45

MELIA (SEVERAL DAYS THEREAFTER)

HARDER AND HARDER TO KEEP GOING. With everything, not just the journal. I don't have the energy I once had. This is my island. Whenever you find me, dear wonderful people of America, remember that. I bought this lovely island with my bones. Fred was here too, but he's gone. Washed away into the ocean's cavernous depths. I have only his clothes. Even his aura has receded. Now he's a memory, the man who inhabited this island with me and gave me a pregnancy I never saw coming. What a world. What an island.

I wake up in the night. Slap at my forearm. Something bit me. I scratch furiously, and it takes some time before I drift off again. By morning, I have three spots, two on the same arm, and one on the thigh. Two blood specks on the tarpaulin. I search and pick what looks like a brown bedbug or dust mite from the floor. Ticks? In this region?

It's a harbinger of death.

I've seen them on hospice beds, nursing home hammocks days, perhaps weeks before an elderly patient passes on. Tick marks spot the bedspread, and if you looked carefully, you could identify blood specks. They sense the onset of death. Or, as I had wondered then, was the patient already decaying internally, death so close that the ticks picked up on it?

Are the ticks giving me a message?

Are you out there, God? This is Amelia. You know which Amelia.

Is anyone out there?

The Ninety-Nines won't care at all about me, their president. The ones with clout in the organization hate me, anyway. Professional jealousy? I don't know. I suspect that anyway.

GP, I feel for you. You don't deserve this at all. You stood rock-solid for me. The sweat from Gene's underarm could turn me on. Your stuffy, rigid, conservative persona, draped on you like a cloak, couldn't. You went to bat for me. Life is unfair. The same way I found it is the way I'll leave it. We'll resolve it, I bet, in the next world. I'll be a better companion then, if we're still enmeshed.

Forgive me for now, George Palmer Putnam. I can feel your love for me. I just know you are still out there, spending money looking for me, organizing expeditions, searches. God bless your simple soul. You could read financial ledgers, you understood profit-and-loss charts, balance sheets, stock market bull, and bearish spikes—but you know nothing, zilch about women.

Land crabs. I keep thinking of them. They are the most abundant creatures on this island. I shall become their meal once I no longer draw breath.

46

MELIA *(Time Frame Uncertain)*

I'M SEEING MORE AND MORE CHIGGERS, mites, on the tarpaulin in the mornings after I wake up. Spots of blood appear in various places on the mat. Bite marks on my body. These mites are not bedbugs. I don't know exactly what they are. I consider sleeping on the sand, but many invisible creatures live inside the sand. Only the squiggling on the surface tells you something is active underneath.

47

A*MELIA (Time Frame Uncertain)*

I FEEL A DISCONNECTION WITH LIFE. IT'S coming soon. That, I am sure of. I am still lucid, but I feel the stanchions crumbling. Perhaps time to will myself for the last time, get the diaries inside that parchment, where the shaman showed me.

If you get to read this, my beloved America, please remember that I love my country above all else. I love GP Putnam above any man and love my family as much as it is possible to love them. I didn't desire this type of happenstance to my adventure, but I would have it no other way. I could only have lived my way.

This is Amelia Earhart signing off.

THE END.

48

ABOUT THE AUTHOR

Frank Okolo is a retired airline captain with over 21,700 hours. *Journal of the late Amelia Earhart* is his third book.

Dear Reader,

Thank You for Reading!

I hope you enjoyed reading *Journal of the late Amelia Earhart* as much as I enjoyed writing it. If you did, consider leaving a quick review on Amazon. Your feedback helps other readers discover the book — and it means the world to me as an author.

Thank you so much for your support.

 instagram.com/frankchikeokolo
facebook.com/frankokoloOfficial
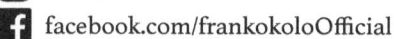 tiktok.com/@commandantejika

www.ingramcontent.com/pod-product-compliance
Lightning Source LLC
Chambersburg PA
CBHW020401110726
47899CB00006B/1805